"The opening gambit of the forces of chaos on the planet Camelot would be met and checked. The problem remained, however, that the Galactic Foundation, even now, had only the smallest knowledge of the nature of the power of Om. That it existed, yes! That its overt manifestations were as yet simply bloody war between opposing feudal factions, yes! But this war could well decide the control of the planet's land surface. And since we knew of Camelot's magic, we knew that if King Caronne and others like him were destroyed, all of Camelot would likewise go down—and with them all of civilization as it was now known.

"What would then ensue we could only guess.

"There were those of the Foundation who suggested ominously that since the nature of the forces in opposition were at best obscure, then the threat might extend beyond Camelot —to the very g

A WORLD CALLED CAMELOT

Arthur H. Landis

DAW Books, Inc.
Donald A. Wollheim, Publisher
1633 Broadway, New York, N.Y. 10019

FIRST PRINTING, JULY 1976

5 6 7 8 9

DAW TRADEMARK REGISTERED
U.S. PAT. OFF. MARCA
REGISTRADA, HECHO EN U.S.A.

PRINTED IN U.S.A.

"There are two fundamental principles of magic. The first is that like produces like and effect resembles cause. The second is that things that have once been in contact ever afterward act on each other. Number One is the law of similarity, Number Two is the law of contagion. Practices based upon the law of similarity may be termed Homeopathic magic; those on the law of contagion, Contagious magic."* Both derive, in the final analysis, from a false conception of natural law. The primitive magician, however, never examines the assumptions upon which his performance is based—never reflects upon the abstract principles involved. With him, as with the vast majority of sentient life, logic is *implicit*, not *explicit*; he knows magic only as a practical thing. And to him it is always an *art*, never a *science*. The very idea of science is quite alien to his thinking.

The road was a simple, well-traveled cart path, undulating gracefully through the forested hills and deep valleys that led to the distant river. Birds sang in the afternoon sunlight, their voices blending with the sound of bees and insects, completing a picture of summer quietude in a countryside that seemed both wild and virgin.

It was something like Vermont-land, I mused, thinking of Earth and the Foundation Center. Or better yet, England-Isle. They were both like this. I shifted my weight from one heel to the other while I crouched lower on the flat rock of the promontory that overlooked the road some hundred yards below. Yes, they *were* like this: England-Isle naturally so, and Vermont-land deliberately, artificially. In fact, I recalled,

*Sir James Frazer, *The New Golden Bough* (*Anno*: circa 2000) Introduction, p. 35.

there were great keeps and castles of runic and eld taste all over Vermont-land today, and they were owned by the most obviously "opportuned" people. I sighed inwardly.

But, hey! Wouldn't those same yokels be purple with envy at the wondrous rockpile which I estimated to be but a short twenty miles distant? My eyelids focused purple contact lenses to six magnitudes while I admired the crenelated ramparts, great turrets, dour aeries, and brave pennons fluttering against a background of mountain crag and heavy, blue-black forest. Then I took a deep breath and returned regretfully to the cleft in the hill through which the road came.

Just as the sun was sinking on the far horizon of late afternoon, so clouds were beginning to appear now, especially in the direction of the forested hills and the castle.

Anyone looking in my direction from the road below would see a somewhat tall, rangy-looking Earth male (disguised), sporting a heavily tanned face and an air of smug complaisance. I was dressed—from the point of view of my adopted milieu—loudly and romantically. I wore green ski pants tucked into soft leather boots with golden spurs to show that I was a full *heggle*—or knight; a heavy green shirt opened to the waist in the purported style of the country, and a green jacket and green cap with a contrasting bright red feather. Over my left shoulder and around my waist, respectively, was a six-foot bow with a quiver of arrows, a broadsword, a dagger, and a leather pouch. It had been suggested aboard the *Deneb-3* a few short hours ago that I could easily be from the mythical Sherwood Forest, or from fabulous Gabtsville on Procyon-4. Kriloy and Ragan, the Adjusters, and Foundation crewmates of the starship *Deneb-3*, had most enviously concurred. But just as the forest ensemble that elicited envy was not the natural state of affairs, neither were a lot of other things which just might put a damper to both their envy and my pleasure.

The blue-purple contact lenses covered a pair of worried brown eyes—mine. The bow and the sword—except for neural preconditioning—were strangers to my hands. The ground I trod was alien to my feet. And, in just a few minutes perhaps, I would be witness to something which all the science of the Galaxy would deem impossible. The "something" was a part of a bigger thing that I was either to prevent or to control. I was to play it by ear, actually, for in terms of alternatives we of the Foundation were at a loss. The facts were that we did not know where failure would lead. We could only surmise, and our conclusions were anything but pleasant.

The planet, in Galactic listings, was Camelot; to the natives it was Fregis. The situation, as stated, was a mixed-up mess. I was Kyrie Fern, thirty Earth years old, Foundation graduate *cum-spectacular*, and expert in the lore, customs, mores, and idiosyncrasies of feudal societies. I had been chosen as the Adjuster.

We had known of Camelot for some time. Over a period of two Galactic centuries, ten pairs of Watchers had spent an equal number of months there. Unlike Adjusters, Watchers worked in opposite-sexed pairs of high compatibility potential. Their work was what their name implied—to observe, to avoid boredom and frustration (thus the pair), and to report accordingly.

This they had done. And to read a Camelot report was a joy indeed; that is except the last one. The fun and games, it seemed, were over. Bloody war, though seemingly the usual state of affairs, was now of a scope to involve the entire planet. The circumstances were such that all we had watched, all that had evolved, in a positive sense, might well be destroyed.

And how did we know all this?

Well, that's an introductory point, you see. For our last pair of Watchers—living in the guise of wealthy tavernkeepers in the seacoast village of Klimpinge in the land of Marack— had witnessed the unfolding of a predicted, most perilous series of events in which Camelot's forces for progress were ruined, driven back upon their heartland by dark hordes, so that extinction threatened. . . . *And all this in the crystal ball of a wandering soothsayer.*

But since the planet *was* Camelot-Fregis, second of the sunstar Fomalhaut, *they believed it.*

And, since all the zaniness of the preceding nine reports, across two centuries of Camelot time, inclusive of prophesies, had proved true—*we believed it, too.*

Even to the final point—that sorcery would pluck the princess Murie Nigaard, daughter of King Caronne of Marack, from the king's highway on this very day. It would somehow be the opening gambit of the dark forces of Om for the dis-

7

ruption of the land of Marack, as a part of the total plan for planetary conquest. . . . I was here to prevent this—or at least to come up with an explanation as to how it was done.

All things considered—the black arts were never a part of my curriculum as fact—I felt abysmally inadequate. I awaited my fate with most ambivalent feelings. The musical tinkle of bells preceded the fact. Then, within a space of seconds, there came over the hill a dappled, low-slung, and ponderous six-legged steed, trotting dog fashion and followed by another, then by three more in single file.

I got to my feet and quickly pressed one of a series of brightly colored stones that adorned my belt. It glowed warmly pink. "Contact," I said softly. "Contact, dear hearts. The sacrifice—to wit, me—is about to offer his throat to the fal-dirk. I'm going in now. The princess has arrived—with entourage."

"Why, the Adjuster's palpitating," a voice sang blithely in my brain. "His nerves are shot already."

The voice, coming like a webbed aura from the metal node imbedded at the base of my skull, was Ragan's. "In the archaic," he continued, "the princess is a woolly little dolly, and you are an ungrateful, cowardly flimpl."

"Bless you," I said. Then I ignored him. "The lifeboat's been damped," I reported. "If you wish to recover, in case I can't, the grid numbers are three-seven, two-nine, four-one."

Kriloy asked, "Any butterflies? Any regrets?"

"Lots of both," I said. "But, sirs and gentlemen, the moment is one of action." I was heading down the steep bank to the road below as I talked. "And I'm going to have to cut out. I'll check back as arranged. Keep me open on the sixth hour, Greenwich. That's it. Bless you again."

"Bless you."

Ragan and Kriloy echoed my farewell just as the stone went cold and the realities of a predicted peril closed around me. I paused to gaze for a fleeting second at the blue sky, trying to penetrate its depths to the primal dark beyond, where a great ship became translucent, then disappeared from the environs of the second planet, Camelot, of the sun-star Fomalhaut.

The last thirty feet was a seemingly solid wall of vines and brush. When I came out on the road, I was breathless. I halted to wipe the bits of dirt and leaves from the fur of my throat and chest. I had made it just in time. The first animal, all white, was rounding the bend. On its lacquered, wooden saddle sat a petite, well-rounded, pouting young female in resplendent traveling attire. She had golden hair, golden fur, languid purple eyes that were almost blue, an elfish face, and an imperious demanding tilt to her chin.

Behind her rode a somewhat dumpy, middle-aged female in austere gray; behind her a young girl, black-eyed and frowning. Two armored heggles, or knights, completed the company. At sight of me they shouted, snatched swords from their scabbards, and instantly pushed their mounts to the fore. Right then and there I learned what I had already been taught: that fighting on Camelot was akin to eating and sleeping. If you didn't swing at somebody at least once a day, you weren't completely alive.

I breathed deeply to still the pounding of my heart and moved arrogantly to the center of the road. "Stay your weapons, sirs," I called loudly. "I am a friend and I mean you no harm." My accent, syntax, and degree of sincerity were perfect. But if I had thought to halt them with mere words, I was dead wrong.

Their advance was swift, silent, and purposeful. I barely had time to draw my own sword, throw the bow to the ground, whirl the sword once around my head and shout the equivalent of "Slow down, damn it!" when they were upon me.

Though the broadsword was strange to my hand, a month of preconditioning with every known weapon of the planet had actually put me in the category of "expert." I was expert, too, with the longbow and the fal-dirk, with the heavy lance in full suit armor, with mace, cudgel, sling—with everything, even the throwing sticks. And all of this expertise without once handling a single weapon . . . patterned, imposed neural conditioning, infused during the hours of sleep. It worked . . . and it worked well.

I crouched low as if to avoid the sweep of the first blade. My opponent, as signified by the heraldry of his shield and embossed armor, was a lord of some stature. He was also huge, bearded, and grinning. At the moment he was leaning far out of the saddle, sword held for a flat vicious sweep. He was confident that I could not escape. One small thing he was totally unaware of, however, was that my muscular superiority was as much as one hundred percent of even his great bulk, since I came from a planet with more than twice the mass of Camelot.

When his blow came, I arose to meet it, tossing my blade to my left hand and slashing up and out. The force of my sword's swing almost broke the man's arm. And while he bellowed and tried to hold to his weapon with fast numbing fingers, I sprang to the back of his clumsy saddle, holding my dagger to his throat while I simultaneously brought his mount to a halt with my knees and spun it around to face the second adversary.

I now used the bearded bellower as a shield. "You will sheathe your weapon," I said sternly to my new opponent, "else I will sheathe mine in the throat of this idiot—and in yours, too, I promise you."

The second knight was young, dark, slender, and possessed of a spring-steel tautness. The flash of untarnished spurs at his heels proclaimed him to have been but newly heggled, or knighted. And he did not lack for courage.

He maneuvered his mount to circle me. "Oh, think you so, sir?" he said calmly. "You have bested but one man. Now let him go, as would befit your honor. Then we shall see whose throat will sheathe a fal-dirk."

I pushed my man to the ground, placed my foot at the back of his neck, and shoved. Then I pivoted my mount to face the young stranger.

"It would be better," said a sweetly imperious voice, "that you stay your arms—both of you. And that is a command."

I remained poised but calm, watching the eyes of my would-be opponent, which he finally lowered while he backed away. I pulled my own mount up sharply and also backed away from their circle.

I had known that she would be lovely.

I had actually been quite close to her for an entire week. In between treetop-level scanning of the land area of Camelot —and that took some doing—I had also watched her assiduously. The rather interesting result was that despite my programmed objective conditioning to the matter at hand, I had become intrigued with everything about her. In effect, I had never met anyone quite like the princess.

10

And here she was, alive and vibrantly real. My breath came hard again, and for seconds I foolishly stared and lost a decided measure of control. I shrugged, breathed deeply, and then began strongly: "You," I said, "are the princess Murie Nigaard. And I am Harl Lenti, son of Kerl Lenti, onus [earl], but of the least of your nobles. I meant no harm, my lady, and I truly beg your pardon and your grace." I made a most artful bow from the clumsy saddle, and simultaneously whirled my feathered cap from my head in the intricate pattern of greeting and homage. "It was my intention," I finished, "to be of some service to you."

I smiled boldly then as I straightened. I focused a twinkle in the contact lenses, calculated to put her at ease so that the beginnings of Adjuster control could be initiated. The young knight had reined in with the others and they had placed themselves in a semicircle around me—the old lady, the maid, the two men in suit armor (one afoot now and glaring), and the princess in the center.

She stared haughtily back at me.

My mention of the name "Lenti" should have connected me instantly in their minds with the fabled "Collin," a folk hero slated to show up in Marack's time of need. By their expressions, however, they hadn't made the connection—either that or they were ignorant of the facts.

But there was a Harl Lenti, and he did have a father, an earl or onus, so the role I played was real enough. He was but one peg up the ladder of nobility, however. His domain, if one could call it that, consisted of a few barns, a stone "big house," and a peasant village of but fifty inhabitants. Its sole claim to fame was that in ancient times it had been the birthplace of the Collin. I had had a personal peek at it as well as its inhabitants. It was a bleak place, located far to the north of the heartland of King Caronne's far-flung kingdom. I wore my "father's" insignia at my shirt tab, a sprig of violets on a field of gold. . . .

"I know naught of you, sir," the princess announced, "nor of your father. Nor why you stand here in mid-road when the bans of travel have been proclaimed throughout the land of Marack. You are without steed, sir. And you carry neither the insignia of my father, *your lord,* nor do you wear his livery as those upon the highway during the ban must do. What means your presence here?" The purple-blue eyes held mine in a steady gaze. They were guileless, naïve—but insistently questioning.

The bearded one stepped forward. His eyes continued hot, angry. He surveyed me with open hatred while he held his injured arm with his good hand. "You should have a care, m'lady," he grumbled. "My blows are not to be turned aside so lightly. I'll warrant there's the strength of magic in his arm."

"He's right," I said quickly. "There is magic here. But not of my making."

The faces of the three women blanched. The scowls of the two men grew darker still. . . . "And," I persisted, "I repeat, my lady, I am not here by accident."

"Then you will perhaps explain, sir?"

I let my gaze rest solidly upon each of them in turn before beginning. I sought to calm them, to dominate whatever might ensue. "When I told you of my person," I said quietly, "I explained that my father was of the least of your nobles; so much so that I, his son and only heir, have never appeared at Glagmaron castle and your father's court. We are land-poor, my lady, and cannot afford the luxuries of court dalliance. This is why you do not know me, and why I do not wear your livery, nor the sign of your father, my lord's grace. Nevertheless, as to my story: My mother, who is fey and with second sight, received a vision nine nights ago in which it seemed a great bird perched upon the lattice of her window and spoke of storms, red-war, men and blood, and an enjoining of enemies against your father, King Caronne. Within this alignment was the lady Elioseen, witch and sorceress. The bird of evil said that within nine days—this day my lady—you would be seized upon the road while journeying to your sister, the lady Percille's manor. I have no mount now, my lady, because it lies dead of a burst heart, the result of a most wearisome ride. I have only my sword now. And I pray you accept it and that we turn back to your father's castle without further delay."

The story, too, of the wicked bird and his predilection to prophesy was straight from the crystal ball. Not a word had been changed; nor any added.

The princess's eyes were wide now with puzzled anger. She

12

said, "What say you to this?" directing her query to the older woman, who drew close to answer.

It seemed that as of that very moment the swift-formed clouds changed to a whirling vortex of lowering mists, smacking also of magic. They touched the forested hilltops . . . black, purple; roiling with a pent-up fury that spoke of tempests, and a coming night in which all should seek shelter. Lightning flashed toward the setting sun, followed by great thunder. The two knights made the circular sign of their god, Ormon, upon their chests, then touched their lips. The old lady did likewise, as did the maid. The princess sat quietly, holding tight to the reins of her mount, regarding them all with a frown of indecision.

I, too, made the sign of Ormon upon my chest.

They accepted the idea of abduction by magic as a very real possibility. They would question my role in that which would or would not happen—but the intervention of magic? Certainly not! That was commonplace. And the damnable part of it was that they were right in thinking that way. Because it *was* real. According to ten pairs of Watchers across two centuries, it was a part of their very lives. In a matter of minutes, in fact, I was to be a witness, if not a participant, to the actuality of a sorcery to confound all scientific law, as advanced by Galactic Control. . . .

The old lady's eyes remained closed while she talked. Her voice was soft, a monotone; it seemed a telling of runes. She said, "I would ask you, m'lady, to heed the words of this young man. There is something of this that I cannot scan. The auras are thick, m'lady. And the mists are such as I have never seen them. This I know. The young lord means you no harm, thought he seems as a wraith—not of magic—but also, not of this world."

Her concluding sentence startled me. The jolt was further enhanced when I saw, for the first time, that a small and most peculiar animal had been peering at me from behind the delectable figure of the princess. Its shape was round, symmetrical, hardly two feet in height. It had short sturdy legs and arms. Two fur-tufted ears graced a puff-ball head punctured with curious, friendly, shoebutton eyes. It reminded me, I thought whimsically, of a cuddly toy I had owned long ago in the dreams or the play of my childhood. . . . Then I remembered what it was—a Pug-Boo. I smiled. I had been briefed on them, too—like the dottles, the six-legged steeds, and a half hundred other lower-order species—but I hadn't expected to meet with one so quickly. For the moment it clung to the princess's small waist, watching intently, almost as if it knew what were taking place and must needs be informed of all pertinent particulars.

The thunder came again and the five mounts shied wildly. Their front legs lifted and forced their sleek, thick-furred bodies back upon the remaining four, while their great blue eyes rolled to catch the attention of their riders, and to thus indicate their fear and their desire to be elsewhere.

And they had reason to be afraid.

"My lord," the princess said, and in oddly submissive tones, "if my Watcher, the sweet dame Malion, sees truth in the things you say and virtue and goodwill in your person, then we have naught but to follow your advice—if—"

That was as far as she got. . . .

Though expected, I mused later, it came so suddenly that my own reaction was almost one of amusement. Not so the others. . . .

It was like a page from the book of the mythical Earth Sorcerer Merlin. The first sensation was all-encompassing. The prick of a needle accompanied by the smell of fire, the roar of thunder, and an instantaneous inundation of rain. I instinctively knew what to do. I literally flung myself at the princess, pulled her from the saddle, and encircled her small body with the strength of my arms. . . . Wherever the princess was going, I would go, too. There was an immediate physical numbness and disorientation. It was as if we were at the bottom of a deep lake, held in place, as it were, by countless tons of water. The great forms of the dottles, the dame Malion, the two knights, and the maid assumed a vague but noticeable transfiguration. They then became amorphous, transparent, receded before my rapidly dulling vision. As my brain whirled before this first onslaught of the magic of the planet Camelot, only one thing continued real to me; that was the soft flesh and the heady, perfumed warmth of the Princess Nigaard. I had wondered how real fur would feel (mine was artificial, naturally). I can only say it was wonderful. I was pleasantly aware, too, as I sank into oblivion, that it was not just a question of my arms around her waist—she held me, too. Pressed tightly against me, in fact, with her small head buried deep in the protection of the hollow of my shoulder. *Hola!* I thought. *The stimulus of fear has its redeeming features.*

That was the last I remembered.

"Where did you come from, baby dear?"

The Pug-Boo's voice came softly, insidiously from the edge of darkness. His fat little body reclined in midair, or so it appeared in the gray mist of my semiconsciousness.

"Great Flimpls!" I managed to groan in reply. I made an effort to shut my eyes, only to find that they were already shut. This, when you think about it, suggests a frightening situation indeed. I relaxed then, into the dream. Who's afraid of Pug-Boos?

"You're the only flimpl here," the Pug-Boo informed me. "And besides, I asked you a question." One shoebutton eye was about an inch from my own. But, as I said, mine were closed. So I was safe.

"I'm an Adjuster," I confessed to the little black nose and the fuzzy ears—thereby breaking the first law of the Foundation: never to reveal one's presence, or the nature of one's business. . . . "I'm a bona fide graduate of the Galactic Foundation. I hold four degrees and sundries. I've got an I.Q. that can be equaled but never surpassed. You have to be chosen from five thousand of the best even to be considered for the Foundation. An Adjuster is a troubleshooter, a man with a thousand skills. Like the Earth's chameleon, he can *adjust* to any level of a developing civilization, merge completely with the fauna. And our purpose is not idle games, sirrah. . . . We intervene only after carefully considering the following. One: Is there a crisis sufficient to demand our aid? Two: Can it be 'intervened' safely? Three: Will the intervention be beneficial, and if not, will it at least prevent a potential disaster and preserve the status quo? You see, my fuzzy-headed friend, our real purpose, other than crisis control, is to judge the level of development of a society, find an area where influence can be exerted—and then go to work. With a little sweat, blood, and luck, we can sometimes advance a specific civilization as much as a thousand years with no awareness on their part of any untoward influence."

All the time I was running off at the mouth I was thinking, *Great Galaxies! What am I doing?* But I couldn't stop. It was as if I had been turned on; that I had become some sort of uncontrollable wind-up doll. The only factor to reassure me that I hadn't actually flipped was that, after all, I was asleep; I definitely *was* asleep.

"That's all very well," the Pug-Boo said. "But you've not answered my question—where did you come from, baby dear?"

"I told you, Butterball."

"No you didn't. And you've not told me why you came here, to Fregis, either."

"And I never will, Button-Nose," I said. "What do you think of that?"

"Don't you love Pug-Boos?"

"Should I?"

"Should you? *Should you?* Great Flimpls, *everybody* loves a Pug-Boo."

I tried to snap my eyes open, and I did—but I didn't. The Pug-Boo was there, anyway. This time he wore glasses and a mortar-board on his head. He said, "If you don't tell me why you came to visit me today, you won't go to the head of the class. As a matter of fact I'll drum you out of the regiment. I'll strip you of your red feather. And what's more, I'll see to it that you never get a crack at the princess."

"Hold it!" I yelled silently, trying desperately to open my wide-opened eyes. "Leave the princess out of this. Or better, leave her in it and *you* get out."

Forcing my somnolent thoughts to dwell upon the princess, the image of the Pug-Boo began to fade. But not without a struggle. Just before I completely hallucinated—kissing the princess's softly furred tummy and straining her to me—the Pug-Boo managed an archaic nose-to-thumb at me. Then it got gray again, gray and black. . . .

This time it lasted longer. So long that when I came out of it, I felt as if I had been encapsulated for a myriad of parsecs of space-time.

The gray remained gray. But it wasn't in my head. I could see clearly that I was in some sort of stall, a part of a stable. There was the equivalent of straw beneath me. I could feel it, wet. And I could smell it. I felt itchy-dirty. My rather fine pelt of quarter-inch black fur that laid so flat I looked like a mink didn't help. *I must smell,* I thought, *like some Farkelian peasant.* So be it. My hands were bound loosely, my feet not at all. I moved to the edge of the stall and peered out.

In one direction it was all black, night, with pouring rain. I tried infrared with the contacts. It was worse than normal. I switched back to twenty-twenty. There were no doors to the place, just a large opening, free to the wind and rain. There was a clump-clumping on either side of me and I surmised that dottles occupied those stalls. There were additional stalls across the way, but it was much too dark to see anything. To my left, away from the rain-swept entrance, was the gargantuan guts of the place. It seemed, actually, that I was in a great cave, hollowed from the base of a mountain; which, in effect, told me exactly where I was. . . . In my week-long treetop scanning of Camelot, I had not only checked its two great continents thoroughly—Camelot was largely a water world—I had also checked the towns and villages, castles and keeps; the ice-world; the great swamps and deserts; and the far "terror-land" of Om—called that, according to Watcher data, because from it sprang all evil, death, and horror. Therein were the hordes of the dead-alives and the mutated spawn of the Yorns who served Om's rulers; therein, and again according to the Watchers' soothsayer, was the very vortex of the gathering storm that threatened all Camelot. Oddly enough, I had seen none of this through the scanners. Only volcanoes; dank, mist-shrouded valleys; sea towns with plodding, gray people living in squat, salt-encrusted buildings; and great lonesome moors.

I had scanned other areas pertinent to the supposed data of the princess's abduction, however; especially in the great aerie, the Castle-Gortfin of the witch and sorceress, the lady Elioseen. . . . Therefore, I knew where we were. But, strange thought—we had been but twenty miles from King Caronne's Glagmaron when we were seized. Aerie-Gortfin was some two hundred miles to the east of Glagmaron.

Wall to wall, near the entrance of the cavern, it was at least one hundred and fifty feet. Inside, toward the great room's farthest depths, I would have sworn it was carved from the solid rock had I not seen the great and shadowy arches reaching aloft to a distant roof, the floor of Gortfin itself. Two fires burned in the hall's depths. One of them outlined a singing, sprawling, drunken group of men-at-arms and some others who seemed only vaguely human. These last cast weird shadows, bestial, deformed, against a far wall. Some of them sat around a massive table, hulking, brutal. Others lay about on the cold stone floor. It was difficult to tell if they were drunk, asleep—or just plain dead.

The second fire, the one nearest us (because the entrance to this huge tomb was to one side and not in the center), outlined a smaller tableau. A heavily muscled man—or thing— sat cross-legged upon the stone. His forehead sleepily touched a naked sword which he had placed across his knees. Directly beyond him was a small table with food and a low couch covered with furs. On this couch was the reclining figure of the princess Nigaard. She seemed still asleep. Her maid, the young girl with the frowning face, was nowhere to be seen; neither was the Pug-Boo. The good dame Malion, however, was there and awake. She sat on the couch's edge, stared at the fire, and swiped halfheartedly at the princess's heavy tresses with a brush.

One last "scene" from the soothsayer's ball had been forwarded to us by the Watchers. It was one which showed me as fleeing through a night-darkened forest valley, and into a redgray dawn of today, tomorrow, or next year—crystal balls seldom give dates. There would be Harl Lenti (me), the princess's cocky young knight, Dame Malion, and the princess. So said the picture. For the moment, however, there was no picture, only a reality, and a developing chess game that had a momentum and a purpose all its own.

Keeping close to the wood of the stalls, and always in the direction of the princess, I explored each one of them. In the last one I found her young knight. Again the soothsayer had been correct. His hands were as tightly bound as mine had been, and he was still out. This time, with my hands free, I used a detachable part of the belt. I ran a cardiovascular check on him to determine what condition he was in. He checked out reasonably healthy, so that I gave him a shot in the arm to bring him out of it that would have brought his great-grandfather to full salute.

His blue eyes opened, startled and wide. "Sirrah!" he shouted before I could get my hand over his mouth.

Fortunately his yell coincided with a great peal of thunder. And, as there seemed no reaction beyond the stalls, I cautioned him to silence and took my hand away.

"Heed me," I said fiercely. "I do not know where your loudmouthed companion is, nor the maid of the princess Nigaard. But the princess and her dame are just yonder, in the great room beyond the wall of this manger. . . . Voices have told me," I improvised, "that this hall is guardroom, cellar, storehouse, and stable to a great castle—possibly of a sorceress, the lady Elioseen. What lies without, I do not know. But whether it be wall or moat, you, me, and the princess will soon know; for I propose to leave this place. So up, and to your feet, sir! And I will unbind you."

He stared coolly back at me, and there was something of pleasure in his eyes. There was also, and for the first time, something of fear.

He said curiously, softly, "You would go into the night, Sir Harl? You would risk your immortal soul?"

I had forgotten their aversion, if not terror, of the night's darkness; predicated, so Watcher data said, upon the belief that they would be killed by sorcery, and their bodies taken across the thousands of miles of unknown lands to Om—there to become a slave, a dead-alive. Considering their conditioning in this matter, I marveled that the young knight had concealed his fear to the extent that he did.

"I am not afraid, sir," I told him bluntly. "I would do much for the princess, my lady, and for the brave land of Marack."

"Well say you so, then, Sir Harl. And if it is for the Princess, my sweet cousin, I would share the danger with you. My name, sir, since we have not been introduced, is Rawl Fergis, of the fief of Rawl. My father, the onus, is brother to the Princess's queen and mother, and the lady Tyndil. . . . But one last thing—how do you know so much, strange lord? And since when do you give *me* orders?"

At that point he peered around the stall's side to the fires and the guards beyond. His eyes narrowed. His jaws clenched. "Yorns," he said. "Devil's spawn."

He started to stumble forward, being off balance; but I grabbed him, lifted him bodily, as a feather, back into the stall where I tackled the fibers of his bonds.

"By Ormon," he said when I had freed him. "You seem possessed of the strength of a Yorn yourself. Whence comes it, sir? Is it more of your cursed magic?"

"Wrong on both counts," I said tersely. "I simply live according to Ormon's grace. . . . Now if you are with me in this, you may follow after until such fortune as I may have provides you with a broadsword."

He tried once more with the "who is subordinate to who" business. But I ignored him, saying simply, "Prepare four dottles—then follow or not, as your courage pleases you." At that he blanched angrily, but thought better of it and ran to the stalls behind us, returning almost instantly to tell me that four stood ready.

How would I do this so as to leave no questions of a kind that would betray my presence? A few guards *would* be slain. The forces of King Caronne *would* be forewarned of the terrible dangers of the gathering storm. That I would achieve this was beyond question. Fool's Mate would be blocked. And King's Pawn—in this case, the princess Murie Nigaard—would be rescued. This, so that the opening gambit of the forces of chaos on the planet Camelot would be met and checked. The problem remained, however, that the Galactic Foundation, even now, had only the smallest knowledge of the nature of the power of Om. That it existed, yes! That its overt manifestations were as yet simply bloody war between opposing feudal factions, yes! But this war could well decide the control of the planet's land surface. And since we knew of Camelot's magic, and that the forces of King Caronne depended not so much upon this power as upon the few existing feudal universities with their rudimentary offerings in the arts and "sciences," we knew, too, that if he and others like him were destroyed, all of Camelot would likewise go down—and with them all of civilization as it was now known.

What would then ensue we could only guess.

There were those of the Foundation who suggested ominously that since the nature of the forces in opposition were at best obscure, then the threat might extend beyond Camelot —to the very Galaxy itself.

During the interim of Rawl's preparing the four dottles for flight, a guard had detached himself from the main group and stalked across the great hall in the direction of the princess. The situation, thereby, grew slightly more difficult.

One would suggest, perhaps, that I simply switch the ion-laser at my belt to full power and destroy them all. That would have been the easy way. But it was taboo. It was also impossible. I could neither do it, use others to do it, nor even suggest that it be done. This, too, was a part of the preconditioning process—built-in limitations to the use of any and all equipment I carried. The final limitation, to keep me completely in line, was blackout. Before my hand ever could touch a stone for death or sentient destruction, I myself would be made instantly immobile; protection for the natural development of Camelot and, indeed, the evolutionary process of life on any *intervened* planet. Needless to say, I was both aware of these limitations, and in complete agreement as to the need for them. In effect, the Foundation would spawn no proconsuls. . . .

Rawl had moved close to me; he stood peering into the double fireglow and breathing hard on my cheek.

"Take care," I cautioned. "We'll make our move *now*. You will follow at a distance of thirty paces. What must be done, I will do. If I fail, you will proceed on your own. If I succeed, but am wounded unto death, you will do me the kindness of killing me. You will then flee with the princess Nigaard. Do you understand?" I looked him squarely in the eye.

My bravado was overwhelming. Despite his warrior's background, I was willing to bet he had never heard anything as unequivocal and as carefree as that. He gulped, stared in awe, and just nodded dumbly. I knew then by his acquiescence and the light in his eyes that if I succeeded I would have a follower and a friend for life.

I smiled boldly and held up a casual hand. "Good," I said. "Remember! Thirty paces."

Then I strolled out over the earthen floor as if I were the very owner of Castle-Gortfin. I walked with such absolute assurance that even when I was but twenty feet from the two guards, their gaze was simply curious, without concern. I came on quickly, noting from a corner of my eye that the princess, too, was awake. She stared at me, I might add, with a curiosity to equal that of the guards. Then she recognized me, and her interest turned to heart-warming concern.

The guards were huge and heavily muscled. One of them, the man seated on the floor, looked Neanderthal—to borrow an adjective from Earth. He had a great prognathous jaw and beetle brows. His features were grotesque. I assumed he was one of the Yorns of which Rawl spoke. I was seeing one for the first time, since I had spotted none through my scanning of the lands of Om.

They continued, curious, absolutely unaware that I brought them their death.

It was quite simple. My reflexes and my superior strength were more than adequate. The newly arrived guard had time only to ask, "Who are you?" before I chopped him a lightning blow to the throat which crushed his larynx. I simultaneously dropped to one knee, snatched the naked sword from the hulking Yorn, and plunged it through his body so that it stuck out a forearm's length beyond the muscles of his shoulders. Then, without pause, I withdrew the blade, stood up, and whirled it once to catch the first man. His face was already blue, though he still fought for air and fumbled desperately for his sword. He needn't have bothered. I did him a service, actually. I brought the steel solidly down upon his helmet, cleaving both head and helmet to the shoulders—and this with one hand. . . .

Rawl had kept his thirty paces to my rear, though at the instant of action he had increased his speed. By the time he had reached my side I had stripped the guard's quivering carcass of his gear. I tossed it to my young companion. "Your sword, sir, as I promised," I shouted, simultaneously reaching for the Xear of the Yorn—the belt, the fal-dirk, and the sheath of the sword that I already held. . . . "See quickly to the dame Malion now," I said. I moved toward the princess. "We will carry them both." He was looking at me in awe. But this was no time to bask in the aura of hero-worship. "Quick, man," I shouted, "or our luck will have availed us naught."

Across the hall at a distance of some three hundred feet, the singing and the brawling had stopped. Silence filled the vacuum. Those standing, sitting, even those on the floor still capable of movement were looking in our direction. There were at least a hundred men-at-arms, with half again as many house-servants and handlers of the castle. But there were no liveried knights.

I looked to the princess. Her blue-purple eyes stared boldly back at me. I said, "Come, my princess, yon group of oafs will not stand idle long. We're for the night and away from here, the four of us."

As she arose, I noted her size for the first time. By Earth standards she was about five feet two. She weighed, perhaps, a hundred and five pounds. She was without her furred cloak, though she hastily snatched it up. She wore a sort of velvet ski suit—shimmering purple-gold—with soft leather fur-topped boots that reached to just below her knees. Dark fur trimmed the neck of the suit so that her own, quite golden fur stood out in bright contrast.

Rawl had tossed the aged dame Malion to his shoulder. He was already moving, running with giant steps toward the stalls. I thought to do likewise. I bowed to the princess. "My lady," I said. "I offer you my arm and my shoulder. In that way we will move much faster." My right hand still clutched the naked, bloodied sword.

She barely had time to ask, "What manner of man are you, Harl Lenti?" before I scooped her up and over my left shoulder with my free arm.

"Not just a man, my lady," I said, moving quickly toward Rawl and the stalls. "Consider me your knight."

"It may be that you presume too much, sir. And it may be, too, that you are not a man at all." Her voice came jerkily from over my shoulder, edged, I thought, with a slight note of anger at her helpless and rather undignified position.

I ignored her remark. There was no time to talk. Besides, though dire peril threatened—since behind us a hue and cry and the first sounds of pursuit were clearly audible—I was most content with the perfumed warmth of her slight body so close to my cheek . . . so warmly clasped against my chest.

The dottles were out of their stalls and ready.

The dame Malion was perched upon the wooden saddle of one, looking slightly dazed. Rawl Fergis straddled the great bulk of a second, holding the reins of two more. He controlled his dottle with his knees.

The ensuing action encompassed only seconds. I placed my

disheveled princess in one of the saddles and gave a mighty slap to the rumps of the princess's and Dame Malion's steeds. Then I leaped aboard the fourth dottle. Rawl, who had ridden back perhaps ten paces to face the oncoming horde, was whirling his broadsword above his head in a shimmering, challenging arc, and yelling the equivalent of "Go! Go! Go!" Then he turned sharply, came up behind me, and gave my dottle the same thumping whack I had given the others, so that the four of us streamed out into the rain and darkness in one seemingly liquid current of dottles and riders.

A final surprise was that Rawl had thought to free most of the remaining dottles so that they followed after. There were some eighteen of them in one large pounding herd.

Looking back through the herd and beyond Rawl to the great entrance, I saw a screaming horde of mixed Yorns and humans. They brandished swords, axes, pikes, and whatever weapons had come to hand. I wondered if, since they were on the side of dark magic, they, too, would be afraid of the night's darkness. They were. For with or without dottles, none ventured forth beyond the great hall's entrance. . . . A small voice told me, however, that this observation need not be wholly true.

Exactly how Camelot's magic worked, I didn't know. I therefore wished to put as much distance between ourselves and the sorcery of Elioseen's Castle-Gortfin as I possibly could. After all, if she had managed to transfer the four of us the two hundred miles from Glagmaron by "witchcraft," what was to prevent her from doing it again?

On we went. The road was a facsimile of the cart path of the day before—as were all roads in Camelot. Great crags of dripping black stone loomed beyond the expanse of bowered trees on either side, all visible in the myriad flashes of blue lightning. The path led downward, a slow descent from Gortfin. We rode on, pressing silently through the rain and the lightning. A keening wind began to blow, and to howl then like all the banshees of Earth's Hell.

After many hours the road began to rise again. Wearily we followed it until, in the faint pearling of what seemed the coming dawn, we arrived at the apex of a great crest or pass.

We halted then to survey each other and to look back across the thirty miles we had ridden to the shadowy bulk of far Gortfin. It was as I had seen it in the scanners, huge, darkly beautiful—and darkly ominous: no pun intended.

The herd of dottles gathered around as would the dogs of a pack as indeed, other than the fact that they were herbivorous, they actually were. We sat our mounts in the herd's center and looked at each other.

The princess, observing me, laughed aloud and said, "You are now a most sorry-looking knight, my lord. I would that I had comb and brush to take to you. And you, my sweet cousin"—she turned to Rawl—"look hardly the better."

Rawl grinned. He, too, had the flashing blue-purple eyes, though his fur was a saffron orange. "No better at all, my lady. But," he admonished us all, "we are in full view here. So let us away, at least beyond the height of this pass."

"My lady," I said, "I agree with your good cousin. Let us leave this place where all can see us." I forged ahead in the act of talking, leading the others at a slower pace down the far slope. "We must rest, too," I continued. The princess and Rawl rode on either side of me now. "Full daylight is soon here and they could be upon us by midmorning."

"Rest our steeds, sirrah? You certainly are no rider, for we now have all of these to choose from." The princess smiled at me curiously and indicated our pack of dottles who, by their friendly blue eyes and constant gentle pushing for attention, seemed forever fresh. "Even our good dame Malion has not complained, sir."

She was right. The fact that I was tired and they were not reminded me that strength and stamina are two widely separate things. The dame Malion had come through the ordeal undaunted. I saw her now as something of steel and leather—as were they all.

"Good," I said. "But after we move some small distance, *I* shall rest. For if the dottles are tireless, madam, I am not."

Murie Nigaard lowered her pretty head. "Well then, indeed," she murmured as we rode on, "you are human after all."

A bilious sun tried hard. It peeked through various shifting holes in the low, scudding cloud mass; to no avail. The total effect was nondescript gray. Despite the missing sun—since it was summer on Camelot—it was still quite warm.

We presented a most peaceful tableau. The four of us half

reclined on great flat stones some two hundred yards off the road. It was the only dry spot in the whole area of dripping flora and rain-soaked soil. It was also somewhat hidden from the highway. Our dottles peacefully browsed, glancing at us from time to time to see that we had not gone off without them. . . . they had a security problem.

All wooden saddles on Camelot, so I found, are kept stocked with important sundries such as flint and steel, needle and thread, honing stone, salt, fishhooks, arrowheads, and a jerked meat that tastes like sun-dried leather. At the moment, to all of us, it tasted like anything we chose to imagine. We chewed it with gusto.

Seated unassumingly close to the princess while we ate, I engaged her in small talk about the toughness of the meat, the duration and intensity of the rain, the whereabouts of the missing maid, the bettle-browed knight, and the fat-fannied Pug-Boo. From time to time, Rawl glanced angrily at the road as if spoiling for a fight.

I said finally, "My limited knowledge tells me, my princess, that we still have far to go. We are as many as three days from your father's castle."

"That is true," she said. "I have been on this road in pleasanter days. But with our many dottles, we should make it in two. Now tell me more of yourself, sir. For I would fain have knowledge of you when we inform my lord of your protection."

I rolled to my belly. I had taken off my wet shirt, as had Rawl and the princess, and even now they were spread to dry on the body heat of the first three mounts. Only the dame Malion had chosen not to do this, though the princess's delectable upper half gave no indication of a general coyness in the displaying of parts.

"My lady," I said, and I let a gentle ripple run up my back muscles to fix her attention, "I am who I said I am; which is indeed not much in one way, but could be much in others since there are things about myself of which even I am unaware."

This last was a deliberate ploy designed to titillate their imaginations in case I needed an explanation for a lack of memory regarding things I knew nothing about, or to explain, perhaps, any other unorthodox potentials I might have to display. "I confess to both you, my lady, and to you, my lord Rawl," I continued, "that I have been much out of the world. So rather than discuss my dull self, I would much prefer a telling to me of all that happens now in our great land of Marack. I have heard, for instance, of much war on our borders, and of war beyond that; and on the high seas, too, from the marauders of Kerch and Seligal. Why, my princess, if there is so much unrest in the world, inclusive of the land of Marack, do you feel so free to travel upon the highway?"

"My journey was for but a few miles only, sirrah! And though it was already afternoon, we had but five more to go. Other than the witch and sorceress, the lady Elioseen, ruler of Dunging in Marack—about which the lord, my father, will soon have something to say—no part of our kingdom is invaded or taken. Nor actually are we at war. Therefore, my lord, we felt it not strange at all to travel upon our personal highway."

"If we are not invaded," I asked, "how account then for the presence of Yorns? Are those beast-men not of the forces of distant Om and her vassals?"

"They are indeed," Rawl muttered. "I have fought them in the far lands where I served my apprenticeship but one year ago . . . but never have I seen one across the river-sea, let alone in our sweet land."

"Yet there have been rumors," Murie Nigaard said.

"All too many," Rawl agreed. "And a country grows not strong on rumors."

"What are these rumors?" I asked softly, and with the proper tone of harmless curiosity.

"That Om masses its forces; that many of the kingdoms to the south and west are, in fear, making peace with the hordes of Om and its ruler, the dark one, the Kaleen; that those who even now fight among themselves, as is our tradition, do so at the hidden instigation of Om; and that black sorcery moves upon us and all that is good in the world of Fregis. . . . I would say, Sir Harl," he finished bluntly, "that this last be not rumor, since we ourselves have been its victims."

"They are not rumors, great sir," came the high voice of Dame Malion. "We of Marack, greatest of the countries to the north of the river-sea, are too prone to make light of danger, as is our wont. This time, however, the clouds gather quickly.

And it may be that our world will not survive. We belittle that which is true. And we deny, even to ourselves, that which is fact."

"But what is other than cloud and rumor?" I asked. "What is *fact?*"

"Kelb and Great Ortmund have already made their peace," Rawl said bitterly. "And it was in those lands, guarding the roads from the river-sea, in which I earned my spurs last year. Now they are at peace with Om, which accounts, perhaps, for the Yorns and other dark soldiery who may, even now, be garrisoning the fair ports of those great lands."

"As for other things that have not been before, the lands of Ferlach and Gheese are in bloody war with each other—as is traditional—but while fighting simultaneously with the first columns of Om upon their borders. One rumor has it that sorcery caused blindness to knights and men-at-arms alike who guarded a pass from the river-sea in Gheese, so that now Om sits astride that pass and gazes down into the fairest valleys in Gheese—and bides its time."

"A question, good Lenti! As behooves our knightly prerogatives: from whence were your own spurs won?"

I knew, so I told him. "From the sea battles off Reen in Ferlach," I said. "That was three years ago, and we fought off the raiders of the Seligs, from the isles of the river-sea. I have since"—I smiled wryly—"been bloody bored with distaff and gog-pen."

"Distaff, you say, sir?" the princess interjected hotly. "Are you married, then?"

"Nay, my lady." I laughed. "I but speak of my mother and the rigors of the household she runs. She has forced me, betimes, to milk nine gogs in a row as a help to the serving wenches."

The princess smiled and blushed—and it is possible to know this because though the fur of the body, short, soft, and lying flat upon the skin, is fairly consistent, it fades somewhat at breast and throat and face so that there is but a fine down to note its continuance.

Rawl laughed, too, and I made note of his alertness. Then he said, "I have heard of your sea battle, my lord, and that it was hard, with more than one engagement. I have heard something, too, of your insignia, which I cannot quite remember."

"Dubot!" the princess exclaimed. She referred to a small, rather silly animal. "It is the heraldry of the Collin, the greatest of chieftains. Four families claim his blood and his blazonry in one form or another—but I recall not yours, Sir Lenti," she said to me.

She said this last sharply, and turned to me with bold questions in her blue eyes. As an Adjuster, however, I knew the fine points of her history better than she.

"There are *six* families, my lady," I explained. "We regard our claim as of the first . . . since he of whom we speak, the Great Collin, was born in the manor of our village some five hundred years ago. I might add that he was born where I, too, was born."

They looked at me strangely then, and with good reason. For the Collin was legend, as was Earth's El Cid, Arthur Pendragon, Quetzalcoatl, and Kim Il Sung. . . . All had been of great service to their people, and all were to return in the hour of the indigenous nation's greatest peril. . . .

The princess said finally, against a background of noise from four quarreling dottles, "Would you then choose his actual name, sirrah?"

"I have no such illusions, my lady."

"Perhaps we *could* use a Collin now," Rawl put in, as I had hoped he would.

Then Dame Malion's voice came as if from far away. "Hey!" she said. "He is not the Collin. But this I seem to know. *He is more of the Collin now than any other may ever be.* This is so that you *use* him thusly." She stared hard at the princess, then turned away.

The fighting dottles were roaring at this point, and the princess arose and pointed a finger and shouted at the most belligerent one so that it ceased its brawling and sneaked off, ashamed, to hide itself in the herd.

"I repeat," Rawl said strongly, "Marack could use the Collin now! How say you, Sir Lenti? Let us present you as his potential. Great Ormon, man! We need but tell your story straight."

"Sir Fergis," I said with feigned severity, "to even *think* thusly makes mock of the Collin."

"Not so." The princess spoke up. "If we present you, and

29

you take his name in good faith—and for no evil or self-gain—there is then no lack of honor."

"But for *my* small deeds?" I asked. "My lady, please!"

But there was no stopping her, the young knight, or the semi-ethereal dame Malion. A few more minutes of conversation and the idea of presenting me to the court of King Caronne as someone possibly imbued with the powers of their legendary hero, the Collin, became quite real.

" 'Tis a sacrilege," I said, baiting them more.

"What does it matter?" Rawl insisted firmly. "If you fall in the first battle, Marack at least will have had a hero around which to rally."

"I do not like it," I said stubbornly.

"What matter *your* likes," the princess exclaimed. "There is much at stake, and if my father accepts the idea, so be it, sirrah!" Her voice had turned haughty so that I smiled at her in such a way that she soon smiled back. And then I agreed . . . especially since the idea was mine in the first place.

Historically the situation then and now was similar—except that now, what with the magic of the Kaleen, it was worse. The original Collin had been instrumental in defeating the invading forces of Selig who, at that time, had conquered all the lands to the north of the river-sea so that only a section of Marack itself continued free. His personal feats of arms had become like the greatest thing since the invention of Flegian sviss. . . . I agreed again and we mounted our dottles with the intention of developing the details as to just how we would do this thing on the still long voyage home. Barring, of course, any new attempt by Om and the sorcery of Elioseen to prevent us.

As we approached the highway, or cart path, the princess exclaimed sharply and dashed to the fore, her small heels beating against the ribs of her dottle. For brief seconds I was unable to see the reason for her excitement. But when she halted within a few feet of the cart path, all became clear. For there, sitting upon an upright stone marker, grimy and smudged and with a variety of leaves and whatever stuck to his fur, was the Pug-Boo. He had a most happy smile on his little round face. And as the princess dismounted to gather him up into her arms with sundry croonings of "Hooli, you naughty-naughty . . . where have you been, you wicked Hooli?" he winked at me over her shoulder. He *actually* winked at me.

Then we were off—the princess, Dame Malion, myself and Rawl, who looked defiantly over his shoulder from time to time, and our eighteen happy, cavorting dottles. I played with the stones of my belt and wondered whatever happened to the sixth hour, Greenwich time and whether the town and castle of Glagmaron, the land of Marack, and the whole damn planet, for that matter, was worth the proverbial candle. . . . Looking beyond Dame Malion to the petite figure of Murie Nigaard, I knew indubitably that it was.

The great sun Fomalhaut blazed away.

Camelot-Fregis had a rotation period of twenty-six hours. The extra sunlight contributed greatly to the accumulated heat of the day, though this was offset by the extra hours of night. The extremes of noon and midnight were more pronounced, however. This held true for the entire year in that since Camelot's orbit was some 283 million miles from nuclear center, the four seasons encompassed 490 days.

All this provided, actually, for a generally temperate climate in the northern and southern hemispheres. Marack was to the north, Om to the south. The tropical zone covered only a part of Om, its extreme southern section and the Dark Lands beyond being temperate, too. Frigid zones existed to the north and south, directly below the two ice caps which resembled those of Terra as, indeed, did Fregis-Camelot itself in size and density.

Kriloy, Ragan, and I had remarked upon this similarity aboard the *Deneb-3*, when the starship had warped into the total aegis of the Fomalhaut system.

There were sixteen planets in all, two with multicolored rings. Camelot was a blue-green—white with clouds—water world. Its earth was distinct from its seas, spiraling around the body of the planet from pole to pole. It had gleamed like an opaline jewel against the background of star cluster and yawning void. But Fomalhaut was a binary; at a distance of two degrees, but within the same parallax, a companion star, Fomalhaut II, shone as a great blue flame, brighter than all the planets of the system. Fomalhaut II possessed but three planets, one of which a cursory scanning had long ago shown as having been ravaged by some nuclear holocaust. Whatever the life-form in past millennia, it was long since dead—obliterated, to be precise.

The heat mounted. Sweat ran through the black mink hairs of my chest and waist. We rode on in silence until finally I asked what had happened to the bearded one I had flattened at our first meeting—who was he, who was the maid, and where did they think the both of them had gone? I also questioned them as to the stated "ban of travel" about which the princess had cautioned me, and why the Pug-Boo had not been with us at Castle-Gortfin. . . .

My first adversary, Rawl explained, was Fon Tweel, Kolb (lord) of Bist, a province of Marack. He had been with the princess simply because he had court seniority. Fancying himself a suitor, he had demanded the right to act as protector of the princess for the short distance of her journey.

Murie then let me know by certain gestures, frowns, and moues that she considered Lord Fon Tweel a bore and a dubot. As for the maid . . . well, she was daughter to the onus Felm of Krabash, another of Marack's provinces. She was lady-in-waiting to Murie's mother, Queen Tyndil. Where the maid and knight had gone, as far as they were concerned, was anybody's guess. And further, I gathered by Murie's disinterest that she cared not a Terran fig. The ban on travel was simply explained. This was late spring, a time of a gathering of young knights from across the land—all to meet in Glagmaron, and all to go off to the wars. They would "blood" themselves, as it were, in Gheese, Ferlach, Great Ortmund, Kelb—wherever, in fact, there was blood to be shed. The ban on travel merely protected a knowledge of their numbers from wandering spies of the above-mentioned countries. As to the Pug-Boo's reappearance, they were at a loss there, too. So I let it pass for the moment.

Silence reigned again, and we continued on beneath a sheltering bower of enormous deciduous trees, with here and there a clump of conifers alive with birds of varied size and hue. Dainty antelope-type ruminants and sundry small animals preened, gawked, and peered at us from their particular bit of turf, each indicating a most beautiful and balanced ecology.

The sixth hour, Greenwich. My Galactic chronometer, imbedded in one of the jewels of my left wrist-band, told me that
it was now the twelfth hour. The question I asked myself was
"How many sixth hours had passed me by while I lay in the
dungeons of Gortfin?"

At times I rode side by side with the princess and Rawl,
and at times by myself. I had become quite aware of her
physically, which, as was my wont, I made no effort to conceal. Her reaction to this was a smug satisfaction, together
with a series of purple-eyed side-glances to make sure she had
conclusively "hooked" me. That she so readily assumed me to
be the potential, sweating facsimile of an enamored swain—a
slave to her softly furred tummy and her round little bottom—
was something of a letdown. I could only conclude that suitors
at Glagmaron had accustomed her to think in this way so that
what I sensed was simply conditioned reflex.

I was keenly conscious of the Pug-Boo, too. The reason
being that whenever he saw that I alone was watching, he
would deliberately wriggle his fat little ears, roll his eyes
counterclockwise, or wrinkle his nose in a series of rabbit
twitches. Once he slitted his eyes and stared at me—just
stared. Almost instantly I had the spine-chilling sensation of
having been weighed, judged, and filed in some strange Pug-
Boo cabinet of the mind.

Another rather outlandish phenomenon was that the dottles,
thought they seemed to love all of us to distraction (I
wondered at the time if they were also as friendly to Yorns
and such), they loved the Pug-Boo most of all. This was
made evident when from time to time one of those closest
to the Boo would give him a big kiss with a sloppy, blubbery,
wet muzzle, and promptly prance off in a veritable frenzy
of animal ecstasy.

Murie and Rawl were right. The dottles could seemingly
sustain a fast gallop forever. The mud and wet sand from their
great paws on the cart path was a constant rain around us.
The heat continued to rise. The clouds still hung low. And,
though I knew this last was but a tentative state of affairs, I
was thankful for its illusion of protection.

There was no pursuit, however. Indeed, by late afternoon
I was ready to assume that there would be none.

At times we passed from deep forest to broad meadow, with

33

here and there a cluster of bright-eyed peasants to view us as we thundered by on the "great road." There were even a few rough-hewn bridges to cross, where I thought of trolls and sundry goblins which Camelot might just be capable of producing.

Just before dusk, while we looked for a woodgirt meadow in which to spend the night, we came to another small bridge. Beyond it was the very meadow we sought; the idea being, according to Rawl, that in a meadow we could ring ourselves with dottles as protection against the night. The dottles would simultaneously be able to rest and to browse.

This meadow, however, was already occupied.

Two tents were up, topped with heraldic pennons that fluttered in the late afternoon breeze. A dozen dottles were grazing and at least four men-at-arms could be seen lolling before the tents. At our approach they sprang to their feet, called to us to halt, then yelled to someone inside the tents.

Almost instantly two figures came out to confront us, both in light body armor. Two dottles, saddled and waiting, were brought to them. They mounted and rode briskly toward us.

One of them was slender and small, the other huge to the point of being gigantic. We remained on our side of the bridge and in line—myself, the princess and Rawl, and the good dame Malion to the rear.

They pulled to a halt just opposite us, and with a great flourish of hardware. The giant's booming voice sounded over the meadow: "Oh kerls," he shouted. "Oh, oafs or sorry swordhands that you be—and you must needs be *something* since you dare ride noble dottles—we do now and hereby bar your path. We are of a mind to play flats, ere the sun sets. And I confess that 'tis my intention to gog-tie you for the future amusement of my good host-to-be, his majesty, King Caronne." At this point the big man ceased his shouting and made several circles upon his chest as obeisance to Ormon and explained this by yelling further: "We, of course, do seek the favor of Great Ormon in our venture, as no doubt do you. Therefore, oh kerls, it is meet that you join us in prayer—which I, of course, will lead."

With this last statement the man genuflected by bowing from the saddle, and began some chanting monotone in which he truly expected us to join.

We didn't. But he kept at it anyway, filling the meadow with an interminable list of Camelot's saints and aves. It seemed after a while, since he was intent upon his worship, that he had forgotten our existence altogether.

At one point, while he shouted paeans to the sky, the female dottle supporting the smaller of the two riders pranced daintily, showing off, as it were, to our quietly watching herd. Its rider was hard put to hold it in check.

I was secretly amused, and I remained silent through it all. But the princess Murie Nigaard was of a different breed. She had watched me through most of the praying and prancing. And since I made no move, she herself took up the cudgel. She yelled angrily above the booming aves, "Oh, stay your prayers for but one single second, pious oaf—" her tone was one of pure sarcasm—"and you will know and instantly that those you bar from the king's road, and make reference to as kerls, are none other than the king's daughter and her knight protectors."

At this outburst the huge one stopped, cut off in mid-ave-Wimbily. (Wimbily being she who sits at Ormon's right hand and is the mother of Harris of the Trinity.) He sputtered and advanced to the bridge peering and shading his eyes against the orb of fast-setting Fomalhaut. It was at that point that he made his second and most foolish blunder. He concluded, after looking us over, that the cloaked figure of Dame Malion was the princess, while Murie was simply a part of the escort.

"Ho!" he yelled. "My greetings then to the most demure and ladylike daughter of the king, for she seems of royal demeanor indeed, while you, young sir," he was directing his words to Murie, "are an impious loudmouth. Great Ormon is not unaware," he cautioned, "of how you slight him, and the Gods, generally, to whom we all—*and this is written*—for each and every second of the day and night do owe our lives, our goods, our families' health—our—"

"Cease, idiot!" Murie fairly screamed. "I am the princess!" She outshouted the giant in her anger, which was a thing to see and hear. "I am the princess, Sir Knight. And more for your dull-witted arrogance than for your impertinence, we shall deign to play the flats with you. . . . Would you gogtie others? Indeed! Sirrah! Well, we shall see."

With that she gestured most imperiously and I, her champion, rode forward on cue, for there seemed not the slightest doubt in the princess's mind that I would do that. And I would not let her down.

The game of flats was but another form of dueling, designed as a "sport" to limit death wounds. Remembered research told me, however, that this "sport"—used when no jousting spears or suit armor was available—had contributed to many a broken head, spine, or limb. For flats meant simply the flat of the sword instead of the edge.

The four men-at-arms had mounted, too. They were now sitting their dottles behind the giant and his lithe companion.

At the bridge's center I halted. And, as if to confound the princess and show her just who, actually, was head man, I did *not* draw my sword. Instead I addressed the big man deliberately. "Since it is quite obvious, sirrah," I said, "that you have achieved great error by a lack of knowledge, it may be that a simple apology from you to our princess will suffice. This tactic will also save your bones for future battles. For I would not needlessly harm a liege of our lord in these times when all men are needed."

"Apology? *Apology!*"

The big man ran true to form. He ignored all else but that single word. His tone had become instantly that of one who has suffered a most sudden and unbearable offense. "Oh, m'lady," he said contritely to Murie, "though I now acknowledge *you*, it is easily seen that what I first said is true—that you are accompanied by oafs and kerls. . . . Know you, silly bumpkin"—he switched his attention to me—"that I am the lord Breen Hoggle-Fitz, driven from Great Ortmund by my own false king, and bound to present my sword and fortune to King Caronne, and to ally myself with him. That I should now be put upon by an impious snotnose such as yourself is beyond endurance! *Have at you, sirrah!*"

I drew my sword, let it dangle, hung my head, and said softly—but not so softly that he shouldn't hear—"It is again, that I do not wish to hurt you, Sir Loudmouth. . . ."

"Great Ormon!" He literally roared. "Did you hear him, m'lady? I cannot now in all truth forgive him. With your permission I shall flat him to the turf and beyond, as is my prowess—and I shall do that *now!*"

With that, and with no more ado, he came charging mightily toward the bridge.

My dottle of the moment was a young female, both graceful and capricious. She weighed at least three hundred pounds less than the great beast who bore the bulk of Breen Hoggle-Fitz. And, since Hoggle-Fitz was half again my weight, we were, suetwise, "heavily" outnumbered. All in all, however, my needling had worked and Fitz was now a mindless bull to my potential as matador.

We met at the bridge's end. Hoggle-Fitz, moving forward at express-train speed, stood tall in his stirrups, whirled a gigantic sword, and roared again. I, too, stood high from the saddle. I held my sword loosely until that very tenth of a second when he swung. Then I was instantly down and over, to cling to the side of my sweet-smelling dottle's belly, while overhead Hoggle-Fitz's metal broke the sound barrier. Rawl swore later that there was actually a "boom" where his steel had passed.

The very momentum of this mighty sweep turned him halfway around in his saddle. My dottle, under pressure from my legs, simultaneously threw on the brakes so that the two animals were halted rump to rump. It was then that I rose up and almost casually gave the big man a whacking thump on the back of his head with the flat of my sword, so that he fell forward across his dottle's neck. And then, because his dottle chose to move ahead with this new transgression, he tumbled to the grass directly before the marveling figure of the princess Nigaard.

The collage of whirlwind action then expanded to include the man's slender companion who, thinking that Fitz was gravely injured, dashed by me and across the bridge to his aid. At which point, in this completely mad charade, Rawl placed himself before the princess and whacked the giant's companion across the belly, tumbling the slender figure from the saddle.

All action took place in a space of seconds. But the last scene was, by far, the wildest. Upon sailing through space the woven metal hood of the companion fell back, releasing a veritable wealth of bright red hair, plus accompanying female features to match a most feminine scream of outrage.

I was instantly back across the bridge to seize her, which

I did, and this beneath the sudden glare of Murie Nigaard. But I couldn't hold on to her. For despite Rawl's tummy-whack, her wind was good and her squirming abilities beyond belief. And, too, with Murie watching, I dared not cling too tight. Within seconds she was away and after Rawl, who had dismounted and started to approach us. He, however, seeing the absolute rage in the girl's eyes, and not wanting to whack such a dainty creature again, took to his heels.

It was that, I think, that saved us further nonsense: Rawl running in circles and yelling for mercy, though laughingly; the girl in hot pursuit shouting blasphemies which were later most diplomatically overlooked by her fanatic father. She finally managed to clip his left heel with her toe, sending him sprawling; upon which she straddled his back and began to pummel him. . . . Hoggle-Fitz, now awake and sitting up, Murie Nigaard, the four men-at-arms, the dame Malion, and myself roared with laughter.

It was Dame Malion who finally saw fit to rescue Rawl, and to bring the young lady to her senses so that we all, with-out further ado, crossed the bridge, dismounted before the tents, and flung ourselves down upon the meadow grass before the largest.

The three women, sitting side by side, made their mutual adjustments to the situation. The redhead had been introduced to us by Hoggle-Fitz—after he had been lifted to his feet, brushed, and smiled at—as the lady Caroween, last of his ten children, who, he pronounced sagely, was somewhat of a warrior, too. This boast caused the maid to blush, Rawl to stutter an introduction of himself, and the princess and I to button our lips as was appropriate. The four men-at-arms simply smiled and said nothing.

The odd thing was that the previous claim to insult, or to any of the events leading to the altercation, was simply *not* mentioned again. The habits of Camelot being what they were, the culture had of necessity to produce this most peculiar form of safety valve, else the whole population would have long since slaughtered each other.

Over bowls of lukewarm sviss (the local mead), which Hoggle-Fitz had served, along with food, he made proper obeisance to the princess. And we were told of his reason for being in Marack.

He had not, nor would he ever, he explained, accept the peace with Om that King Feglyn had proclaimed. He had rejected it, in fact, to the point of open rebellion. Four of his sons had been killed, as had many hundreds of his household. Four other sons and one daughter, together with her husband and children, were now in hiding. And he, Breen Hoggle-Fitz, kolb of Durst in Great Ortmund, had been forced to flee. . . .

"How so," I asked, "in this matter of Om? Are there forces of Om's soldiery even now in Great Ortmund? We have heard that they garrison Ortmund's port cities."

"No so, young sir," Hoggle-Fitz said. "At least not to my knowledge. Our peace was simply that we would not war with Om, or Kelb, or Kerch, in return for Om's support in certain claims against Marack which have long existed."

The princess's eyes slitted at this, but she said never a word. Then we told them of our abduction to Gortfin; of the presence there of Yorns; and finally of the pattern that seemed to be developing against Ferlach and Gheese. At this point the princess did ask about—as she put it—"these so-called claims against Marack," and how Lord Hoggle-Fitz stood in the matter.

He flushed, but answered boldly, "Our king Feglyn is not of his father's blood. Of the 'claims,' m'lady, I would gladly have gone to war against you to settle them, but *not* with the support of Om. I am somewhat dull-witted at times, m'lady, but not so much that I would sacrifice all Fregis to Om and to the Kaleen of the Dark Lands—and *that* is where such an alliance would lead."

I watched Murie and Rawl as they pondered this. And for the first time I was actually pleased with the bumbling, pious, boasting—but oh-so-brave-and-honest—Hoggle-Fitz.

We continued in this vein, sparring with words and exchanging views and *bons mots* until darkness surrounded us along with a swift and penetrating cold.

We drew closer to the fires, wrapped in our various fine-woven saddle blankets.

It was then I noticed that they all seemed to be waiting for something, a thing wherein my research had apparently failed me. . . . I moved to Murie's side in a gesture of intimacy and asked her when she would sleep. She said simply, frowning, as if I should have known, "Well, after, m'lord—after Hooli plays."

I said nothing more so as not to disclose my ignorance. I withdrew instead to the half-circle of men, facing the women on the other side of the fire.

The Pug-Boo made his appearance. He simply wandered into the circle of firelight, seated his little fat body upon a flat stone, and placed a tiny metallic object to his lips. Then he began to play a tune.

I watched and listened, fascinated. The Pug-Boo was actually *playing* a musical instrument. *I couldn't believe it!*

The Pug-Boo was an animal, a little fat furry facsimile of a Terran honey-bear with raccoon hands; yet there he sat, playing music such as I had never heard—nor ever would again, except by Pug-Boos—on any tape, disk or crystal gauge. And I finally knew, too, as I listened to the introductory bars, why "Everybody loves a Pug-Boo." Pug-Boos were the planet's minstrels, the only ones, perhaps, that Camelot had ever known.

The fire-pit gleamed in dancing, hypnotic yellows and reds. The night clouds parted and one of Camelot's two moons shone all silvery bright through the limbs of the great trees. Light splashed on the placid wash of water of the small river, and on the sheen of the grassy meadow. The dottles, too, stopped their browsing to listen. And they sat around us— thirty now—on haunches and at full length, like gigantic dogs at rest. And all was silent.

The music was symphonic: a medley of every reed or brass or string or pipe that had ever played in any part of the Galaxy. There was no explaining it or its source, or how it was done. I learned later that the Pug-Boo's instrument was a simple hollow tube of some unknown metal upon which no one else could produce a single note.

And so I listened—*we* listened, rather. And my mind was invaded with sound and color and mood and imagery, each facet a variation of a thousand themes, melding, growing, expanding to explode finally into great bursts of light that was not light, in a blackness of space that was not space. And through it all a thread emerged. A story of worlds and suns shattered and ruined in seas of cosmic fission, of a Holocaust beyond all understanding. There was a repetitive image, too—of a humanoid planet resembling Terra, Camelot-Fregis, and ten thousand kindred worlds. The planet was of an indescribable beauty. The events depicted were of its death in the great cataclysm, and a hint of total evil beyond the very limits of time. The suggested horror was so enormous, so all-pervasive, as to blast the mind that sought to understand it.

Yet still another thread ran through this montage of imagery and sound. It was one of beauty, peace, and above all, *hope*. And I thought as I listened that those around me, even the dottles, could quite likely find a measure of themselves here—as it was no doubt planned that they should do. It would be a tapestry, perhaps, dim viewed, of a fairy world which once was theirs, though they knew it not. For them it would simply be a personal contact, a gossamer thread of liaison between themselves and the essence of their god. There was no precedent for this in the Galactic history of humankind, no counterpart in the patterns of evolution. The thought was frightening. For it spoke of the manipulation of the lifeforms of a planet, of a system—and perhaps of an entire galaxy.

The Pug-Boo was more than a bridge to their past, more than their race memory. Somehow I knew that he would play his song until that new time when they would understand its meaning; and when that time came they would be ready for a destiny worthy of any gods who had ever possessed the minds of humans. And thinking in this way I realized, too, that what I now knew—that they were of an elder race—I, like the Pug-Boo, could not tell them. Indeed, this small scene in which I was to play a minor role was but a page of a play so gigantic as to numb the very processes of reason. Knowing this, the music became suddenly filled with unbearable pain; with a rushing, all-pervasive sadness; a harbinger of a world death that had either been—*or was still to be:* a frightening thought. I pushed the concept, in its future tense, from my mind. After all, had I not seen the Pug-Boo's version of the Holocaust? And surely that was *then* and not *now*—and certainly not *tomorrow*.

The others sat gazing hypnotically into the flames. In all their faces was a sublime peace, an ecstatic reverie—*because they did not know*. But I, Kyrie Fern, *Harl Lenti,* the Adjuster, "the Collin," dared not listen longer. I blanked out the music with its beauty and its horror and waited numb and corpselike until the Pug-Boo finished, until the others laid down upon their respective beds and the fire died and only the second moon shone to define our lonely position in the meadow. Then I, too, slept. . . .

I was awakened in the small hours by the soft wet muzzle of my last "charger" of the afternoon, the young female dottle. She *wheeed* softly and then *whooooed*, too, in my ear, so that I sat up to see all the dottles quiet, though alert and watching. They stared in the direction of the road and over the bridge to far Gortfin.

And then I heard the sound—the oncoming noise of a myriad of dottles, of the Erl-King of my childhood—all thundering through the night. I awakened Rawl, who slept at my side. He in turn awakened Hoggle-Fitz and the men-at-arms. Then we secured our weapons, remained prone, and silently watched the bridge.

At one point Rawl moved to alert the princess, but I cautioned him and he returned to our group. . . . Then they were on us.

It was my first experience, my first sight of organized Camelot cavalry. Even though it was night, it was still a beauteous thing to see. On they came, two abreast, short spears at the stirrup, shields slung, swords and other weapons across the shoulders according to their tastes—and their armor all twinkling and jingling in the moonlight. . . . Rawl and the men-at-arms had collapsed our tents, and since they thundered on we had only to assume that they saw us not. Our shadowy dottles, yes! But a herd of dottles, though certainly uncommon, was, at least in this case, not a thing to delay them.

"Now, by Great Ormon!" Hoggle-Fitz was saying in choked tones. "Look there! Yorns! Yorns and men! Yorns in Marack!" There was such hatred in his voice that I moved to restrain him, but he held himself in check.

Rawl's expression mirrored that of Hoggle-Fitz, and this was true, too, of the men-at-arms.

We counted one hundred riders and three hundred dottles. And at the end of their cavalcade there seemed to be a flying thing, something that passed overhead with great wings, and that left such a stench that all the meadow was filled with it for several minutes.

I looked to Hoggle-Fitz. His eyes were bulging, red now with an absolute insanity. "By all the Gods," he breathed in guttural tones, "Om is *here*, young sir! *Om is in Marack!*"

"Aye," Rawl echoed him, and his tone was equally fierce. "And never in the history of man has a Vuun been north of the river-sea."

They seemed almost to ignore me then, sensing that I was aloof and not a part of their anger. "*They* are resurrected," Hoggle said. "*They* have come again." He began to pray. He rose to his knees, bowed his head, and made the triple circle of obeisance a number of times. I unobtrusively joined them, alert, watching from the corners of my eyes. I tapped my programmed memory and found that a *Vuun* was a creature long thought to be extinct on Camelot-Fregis. It was a mammalian, winged, of a fifty-foot span and akin to the Terran bat, though with a great beak and rending talons. History had it that in the ancient wars Vuuns had been used by some forces as allies and cohorts, for they, too, were possessed of intelligence on the order of mankind.

"They ride at night," I stated bluntly, when the praying was over. "Their fears are not those of true men."

"Nor should they be," Hoggle-Fitz answered, looking at me strangely. "For they are a part of Om's dominion and need not fear the dead-alives."

"I fear not the night, Sir Lenti," Rawl said with a burst of courage. "And I would follow to see where they lead."

"No," I admonished. "It is not meet. We will know soon enough, so let us go to sleep again. Whatever the morrow brings, and I truly think that all our morrows will now be like none that have ever gone before, we must be ready."

Surprisingly, they did as I suggested. And I had the premonition that, for whatever reason, individually or collectively, they would continue to grant me leadership. Hoggle-Fitz was my senior in station and in age, but he, too, deferred to me. Possibly, I thought, before I, too, returned to sleep, for the simple reason that I had bested him.

Dawn broke with mists shrouding the great trees and the small river so that the road was not visible from our camp.

The one thing all species of humankind on Camelot had in common, other than fighting, was an inordinate compulsion to cleanliness. This fact found us all at the river's edge to plunge and revel in its stingingly icy water. After that came a mutual rubdown and sundry pats of fragrant oil in the appropriate places. Then we were off again.

Since the events of the night were still clear in our minds, and since we knew not where the one hundred riders had gone, I sent Rawl ahead for a distance of many paces. He would be our advance guard. He was to have four dottles in front of him and four in back as protection against sudden attack. We—myself and Hoggle-Fitz—were to ride with the women. The four men-at-arms were to ride to the front of us. They would be preceded by a half dozen dottles, while the remainder of the herd brought up our rear. Thus did we proceed at a brisk gallop toward the castle and city of far Glagmaron—with one exception: the lithe and airy lady Caroween, still in mesh armor and with small sword sheathed across her back, rode to the front to join Rawl Fergis. She said, with a straight face and twinkling auburn eyes, that since she had bested him the day before, it was now most seemly that she act as his protector.

Murie Nigaard smiled at this. And watching her closely, I had the odd impression that though she seemed softer and less prone to a flexing of feminine muscles, she could no doubt hold her own with any fledgling warrior. . . .

I gazed, too, at the Pug-Boo, and with new respect. He stared calmly back at me as if he knew that I had psyched a part of him, and glimpsed a purpose in his being, a small part of the iceberg. It bothered him not a whit. After holding my gaze for a time he clutched Murie's waist, leaned his fat round head against the small of her back, and went to sleep.

The mists lifted. Fomalhaut shone brightly; all around us were the scenes and smells and rustlings of yesterday. On a promontory, at one point, we were calmly observed by a huge, six-legged striped creature which caused the dottles to roll their big blue eyes and feign indifference in their fear. At another point a great creature browsed in cane thicket and long grass. It resembled a dottle, but seemed half again its size and strength. It had a massive double horn protruding from the front of its heavy head.

"Have you ever ridden a gerd, Sir Lenti?" Hoggle-Fritz asked, as we passed the creature by.

"I have not," I said.

"I *have*, good sir, and all that you may know of them is true. They are absolute devils of Ghast. At this, since he had mentioned the name of Ghast, Ormon's competitor for the souls of men, he made the triple circle and mumbled a few words.

"They are verily Vuuns from Best [Camelot's Hell]. But once conquered, they are loyal to the death." he finished.

"Was it so with the one you rode?"

"Aye. And I rode *him* unto death, and that but recently. We fought, my supporters and I, on the fields outside fair Durst, which was my fief in Great Ortmund. We fought all one day and into another. And in the end the thousand-man guard of the false king Feglyn, fresh and unused until that moment, did drive us from the field. And they did slaughter my brave gerd, using two squadrons of spearmen to do it. But even so I escaped."

Hoggle-Fitz fell silent then, no doubt reviewing, in his mind's eye, that bloody battle. . . . I looked back at the great gerd, who, from his far distance, seemed staring calmly back at me. It was indeed a noble beast.

We passed through our first village an hour after dawn, then another and another, spaced but one half hour apart. In each were those who told of a great thudding of dottle paws in the night, and of the muffled calls of men. We knew then that Om had passed this way. Almost at high noon we thundered over the lip of a great valley in which, at some ten miles distance, we saw a fair-sized city. It was Gleglyn, according to the princess. It was the last town before Great Glagmaron, though many villages still lay between. Halfway across the plain the north-south branches of a crossroad paralleled a fast-running river. We gathered then with Rawl and the lady Caroween at its apex and sought for signs of where the men and Yorns of Om had gone.

Though the tracks of a dewy morning had dried with the sun of noon, the path was easily evident. They had gone south. In the direction, Rawl said, of the borders of Gheese. . . . And we wondered why.

We dined in Gleglyn, being ushered through the great walls and into the town by the king's garrison captain, who had been called to the gate. We ate at the town's fairest inn, but we did not linger long. I had suggested, and the princess agreed, that we make all haste to Glagmaron. Since she had told me while riding of the powers of her father's sorcerers, and since the sixth hour, Greenwich, had passed again twice with never a burn of the transmitter, I wished immediately for a place of some safety. I had no doubt that this, too, would be an illusion like the safety of mists and clouds. But at least we could take stock and plot what moves were available.

There had been much movement through the town. Young knights and squires, student warriors from the local Collegium, as well as others who were passing through for the spring gathering, thronged the streets. Many were headed for Glagmaron castle and the great, equinoctial tournament of the morrow. Little had been said of this by Rawl or Murie. And I, therefore, assumed that perhaps it did not touch upon the court. But during lunch Rawl suggested casually that we enter the lists. I was noncommittal, but Hoggle-Fitz was instantly for some sort of murderous "Onset of Fifties," as he called it, with himself leading the charge.

Some twenty students most happily attached themselves to our entourage—honored to be so privileged. The troop was assigned to the command of Lord Hoggle-Fitz, who spaced them appropriately in front and rear, dividing them with Rawl. For the first time I was truly alone with Murie Nigaard —this with the exception of the dozing dame Malion and the sound-asleep Pug-Boo. I used the time to good advantage.

We rode side by side, each dottle matching perfectly the gait of the other. I could tell that Murie was as pleased as I. Her feminine arrogance of the previous day had waned somewhat. Her glances now seemed quite intimate and her countenance most warm and friendly. I sensed, knew actually, that with but the slightest pressure a conquest could be made here.

And this, together with the memory of her soft-furred figure in my arms in the race for the entrance to Castle-Gortfin, was heady mead indeed.

I told her more of Harl Lenti—all that I knew, in fact. And I hinted at other things. I told her truthfully of the imminence of great danger to all Marack; that somehow I knew this, and that she and Rawl and I, and others, were destined to share an adventure such as had been given to few men in all time. She listened, wide-eyed, thrilled. I spoke of memories that were not mine, but which *were* mine: of a knowledge of destiny and fate likened only to that of the old gods before the Trinity of Ormon, Wimbily, and Harris. . . . She believed it all. I half did myself. Then, as our shadows lengthened to the rear, the forests parted again to disclose in the distance the great walls and myriad faceted windows of the city of Glagmaron.

We rode so close, Murie and I, that my lips as I talked were at times within inches of either her ear or the nape of her neck. That she was aware of this was evident, for at such moments she would stare straight ahead, afraid to turn and look at me and risk the chance of further contact. At each instance she heard me laugh softly so that once I caught her smiling, too, and knew thereby that we had much indeed in common.

The lady Caroween and Rawl came up once, drew near, and laughed together. Murie Nigaard blushed a bright red against the gold, and they then withdrew with discretion.

Other than the hundreds of stone houses and market-stalls clustered at the base of the mighty, hundred-foot walls, Glagmaron was a fairy city to rival Glagmaron castle, high on its great hill to the south. I recalled that it was from that same south road that I had first seen it while awaiting the entourage of the princess. The pennons of the castle were now equaled by those of the city in display, variety, and color. Only those of the king's household were at half-mast. This, we concluded quickly, was because of Murie's disappearance.

I signaled Lord Hoggle-Fitz, my arm held high. He galloped to my side and we broke together from the center of the train and thundered to the fore to join Rawl and the lady Caroween. Then we rode across the plain to a distance of three hundred paces from Glagmaron's mighty gates. We were followed by our men-at-arms, our twenty young student knights, and our dottles. At that point we hoisted the princess's colors, made with silk sundries found in Hoggle-Fitz's baggage. And these, together with those of Lord Hoggle-Fitz and Rawl, caused somewhat of a stir among the rapidly assembling squadrons of the great garrison, plus whole coveys of excited citizenry, peering from the walls.

Our dottles *wheed* and *whooed,* greeting the dottles of the garrison. And it was not long before a young knight in resplendent attire rode forth. He leaped from the saddle before the princess, made a sweeping bow with cap and outstretched hand, offering her, as was the custom, her father's city.

As if on cue, heralds appeared. Silver horns blew a medley of pomp and acclaim. And all of us, to the very last dottle, made our weary but proud way into the sprawling, beauteous feudal sanctuary of Glagmaron city. . . .

I glanced to my wrist as we passed beneath the great arch of the gate, noting with some interest that once again it was the sixth hour, Greenwich.

We rode through the teeming city and beyond to the winding, stone-hewn highway that led to the castle. For one long length of a half-mile or more, it was cut from the very granite cliffs upon which the castle rested, with the awesome sight of the rushing river named the Cyr some hundreds of feet below. The river had not been visible on our approach to the city, being on its opposite side beneath a bluff that fell off toward the south and west.

The city itself, I noted, was like every museum print, sketch, or woodcut that I had ever seen of medieval architecture. There were cobbled streets and stone, wood and slate-roofed houses and buildings. Some were as high as five stories. Here and there was a great square with a fountain, statuary, and a market; and all of it ringed by the city homes of noblemen and merchants. One great building had carved above its almost gothic entrance, in Glaedic, the root language of all Camelot: *Marack Collegium. Home of Scholars, Students, Poets, Minstrels, and Those Who Teach.* Below this was a list of courses offered. I had little time to study them since we went by so quickly. But my previous scanning had told me that they encompassed minstrelism, the playing of instruments; the telling of tales, the recital of poetry and singing;

simple medicine; philosophy, as expounded by certain Camelot sages; the law. And, since this was Camelot-Fregis, "Introductory Steps to Magick, Sorcery, and Astrology."

Across the great square was another institute devoted to the study of theology and the Trinity. Despite their parallel existence there seemed to be no competition here.

The Collegium was coeducational. The square was literally filled with groups of young men and girls, all in light dress, though with some mesh armor. They were socializing, eating and drinking, or were being addressed in groups by a lecturer or an individual reading from a vellum textbook. Each student carried a slateboard and a small packet of waxed vellum sheets with stylus and chalk.

I thought as they cheered us with a youthful exuberance that here, indeed, was evidence of Camelot's real worth. But I remembered, too, that though a contradiction existed in terms of the feudal society in which the Collegium functioned, still it presented no threat to the hierarchy, for it was but a mote in the total scheme of things.

As we passed through each great square that punctuated the maze of streets, all hailed the return of the princess, the students, seemingly, most of all. And *all* hailed the presence of Hooli the Pug-Boo. Hooli sat apart now as he rode with Murie Nigaard. His fat little legs bounced far back on the round rump of the dottle, while his furry round face was wreathed with a dimpled, half-moon smile. His eyes seemed to emote, to twinkle, to exude an aura of benign if not smug benevolence. And I sensed as I watched him and the crowds around us that the role he played far transcended what the Watchers had told us. I was determined, at the earliest, to find out why. . . .

I asked Rawl what *he* had majored in, in his Collegium. For I was aware that all the sons and daughters of aristocrats attended collegiums for from one to two years. The "trades"—such as those of the ironmongers, armorers, weavers, fletchers, tailors, masons, and carpenters—were left to the sons of burghers, guildsmen, and peasants. The alternative to these diverse schools, *for everyone,* were the parochial or theological seminaries of Ormon and the priesthood of the Trinity.

Rawl looked at me, his blue eyes twinkling. "The lute," he

confessed blithely. "Certain roundelays. A few poems—and a bit of magic. . . . And yourself, Sir Harl?"

I grinned. "The same—except we had no single sorcerer in far Timlake, the nearest city to my village. So I have no magic. But what of yours? What can you *do?*"

"A spell. A spell for love which lasts two weeks, and can be used three times—and one other."

I stared, one eyebrow cocked quizzically, until he grinned and sheepishly said, "I can turn gog-milk into sviss. . . ."

"Great Ormon," I said. "Always?"

"Almost always."

"For a warrior," I said, "in this matter of the sviss, you have a value beyond that of the weight of your sword. How do you do it?"

"The *words*, Sir Harl. The *words*, pronounced properly."

"Aye," I said. Then I was silent, hoping to hide my so foolishly displayed ignorance of the power of the *words*. The problem was that I had treated the idea of words, a normal concomitant of forensic magic, disparagingly—in my own mind that is. I shouldn't have. For, as stated, on Camelot they worked.

Rawl looked at me strangely and was about to say something, but his dottle chose that very moment to look at him fondly over her left shoulder, and thus distracted him. Murie was staring likewise in my direction. No doubt she wondered how I was making out in this great metropolis of some hundred thousand souls.

I smiled boldly back at her and we continued on.

The granite-hewn ledge above the Cyr was also a lengthy site for meditation and soul-searching, since the roar from the river below precluded all conversation.

But it was soon passed. Indeed, before I knew it there was suddenly nothing before us but a great field fronting the castle gates. In size it seemed a square mile or more, covered with a velvet carpet of grass upon which many hundreds of dottles grazed. Here and there were pleasant stands of broad-leaved trees, surrounded by carpets of wildflowers at their roots. To our right, as we progressed, was the field in which the tournament and sundry other battles would take place on the morrow. Silken tents with banners, flags, and pennons of heraldry were already spotted here and there around its periphery. On the side of the field nearest the castle a series of interlocking tiers of seats had been erected. And all was covered by a great canvased canopy. From moment to moment our ears were deafened by trumpet blasts. This was explained by Hoggle-Fitz, who said the custom was such that when one great lord signaled his trumpeters to blast, for some imagined reason or other, each of his neighbors replied in kind; their reason being that they would not be outdone in any way. Already certain knights, would-be heroes, and student warriors were to be seen going over the ground to check it for the morrow. We rode on and through them to the castle gate. These, though there was no moat, were beyond a sudden deep ravine fronted by a portcullis and drawbridge in classical style. Across this now-lowered bridge there thundered a half hundred knights and men-at-arms to join our already unwieldy entourage.

We were escorted across the bridge and through the gates to find that, once inside, the first great wall was paralleled by a second of equal size. We swung to the right for a full three hundred meters before reaching the second gate. Seeing the lay of this I wondered at what would happen within that narrow alley to a horde of invaders who had pierced the outer defense only.

In the ensuing melee of some two hundred *wheeing* dottles and shouting riders in the great castle courtyard, we were sorted for bed and station. The circumstances were recognized as such that there would simply have been no chance for a greeting by the king and queen. We were taken in hand, our dottles that is, and thereafter went straight to the chambers assigned to us.

Rawl claimed me as his personal guest.

After a labyrinth of great stone halls and stairs, we found ourselves in the apartment assigned to him, befitting his rank as nephew to the queen. It was large and airy, overlooking a section of the winding Cyr some three hundred feet below. And because it occupied one of the many jutting cornices, we were also given a view of the great flagstoned courtyard. The rooms possessed wall tapestries, and enormous beds with sleeping furs, a fireplace of immense proportions, and sundry closets and skin rugs. It was, indeed, quite livable.

Glagmaron castle, like all other castles, buildings, and keeps throughout Camelot-Fregis claimed ownership, too, to a thing few feudal societies in all the Galaxy would deem important—*plumbing!* The aforestated inordinate compulsion to cleanliness was such that long ago a crude pumping device had been invented. This, together with the use of sunlight and rooftop reservoirs, plus a veritable web of hollow cane-pole conduits, gave Glagmaron castle a plentitude of differently temperatured water.

Adventures over for the moment, we showered and soaped in an atmosphere akin to euphoria. We were like a couple of student-warriors, fresh from the Collegium. All this, despite the fact that a part of my mind was apart from the scene and into the mesh of the job I had to do. There had still been no glow of stud upon my belt or wrist-band, nor voice of caution or advice from the metal node within my skull.

We slept then, taking advantage of the last hours of late afternoon. The bed was large enough for ten. Indeed, the citizenry oftentimes slept in just that way.

But again, desired sleep did not come. And when it did, it was forthwith interrupted by the image of the Pug-Boo which intruded along with sunlit patterns of laced stonework against the slate slabs of the floor, and the faint *whoooing* of dottles from the meadows beyond the walls. . . .

We were in a small star-taxi, the Pug-Boo and me, released (I supposed) from some great mother-ship. We were self-strapped into cushioned contour seats while we gazed through viewports and gyrated within the gravitational influence of a great ringed world with a covey of satellites, each with an atmospheric film.

"You can have that one there," the Pug-Boo said seriously. "The one just tacking around the night-side. It's listed as Miocene, lower primates only. It's all yours, you and the princess."

"Most magnanimous," I grunted, accepting the scene as reality.

"You could say that."

"What will I do with it?"

"Live there, idiot—away from 'the madding crowd.' "

"Thomas Hardy," I mused reflectively. "It's as if I were talking to myself, Master Boo."

"You are! You are! I'm only the intermediary—the 'marriage counselor,' as it were."

"Great Gods!" I said.

And we were no longer in the star-taxi. Now the scene was that of a Camelot-Fregis field of grass and trees. We were picnicking. . . .

"Would you like some wine?" the Pug-Boo asked.

"Room temperature?"

"But of course."

"Look!" I informed him, sipping a tepid Riesling. "I'm suddenly aware that this dream, as one might call it, is not exactly of my choosing."

"And that's indicative, right?"

"Of what?"

"Of the fact that you're something else, baby."

"What do you want with me?" I asked bluntly.

"To know who you are."

"Why?"

The Pug-Boo leaned forward above the white linen and the lunch basket, across which there now marched a file of ants. His little spine was rigid, his round button eyes snappingly sharp. "Because you are not of Fregis, Great Collin. And because in the things which will soon happen, you will most certainly die if you do not have my help."

Of a sudden my flippant, raised-eyebrow, tongue-in-cheek attitude (it was real in part) came an absolute cropper. For something happened. It was as if an icy, soul-destroying breeze swept softly over the dream meadow so that the nonexistent sound of insects became truly nonexistent. A monstrous tension grew within me. My features turned hard, stone cold. My pulse beat heavy, fast. It seemed, in what was left of my mind's eye, that I would shortly witness my own death. . . .

"Oh, say you so," I said slowly, in the vernacular and above the keening of that odd death wind. "How would I know then—if my demise is near—that it did not come from you?"

The non-wind in the non-meadow died as swiftly as it had

been born. In its place came a great wave, a fog of horror, a mind-eating fear of an unfathomable something, intruding, reaching out to me, into me, so that the grass and the scene itself began to fade. My dream seemed now a three-way thing. And the Pug-Boo's eyes became wide, strange, and wavering. A voice other than his—which was still mine—came on with a low humming: a moon-gibbering hysteria, faint but all-pervasive. And there were words. But they seemed of a language such as banshees might have used between shrieks, had they a language, withal. I felt dread sickness seize my body. A nausea encompassed my very mind. It was such that I had never felt in all my life before. Then the Pug-Boo's features, which had faded, became suddenly solid again. And he was staring, listening, too. Apparently to something I could not hear. He spoke strangely again, *with my voice,* forced himself into my new dream. "Awaken, Harl Lenti," he demanded. "For your life's sake, awaken!"

And, imbued with his quite obvious concern and my own fear, I tried to do just that. But it was too late. The soul sickness persisted so that the greater part of me wished only to die, to allow whatever was plaguing me to prevail. Then, before I succumbed entirely to this death-wish, a strobe-flashing crept into the sickness's outer rim. It was a sun-laced, 3-D still of Murie Nigaard. It became animated and the scene was a section of our trip to Glagmaron, and she was peeping back at me over her shoulder as her dottle forged ahead. Her smile was elfish, and oh, so intimate; her blue-purple eyes and bouncing page-boy bob, an absolute of warmth and beauty. Each strobe-flash lasted but seconds longer. And the nausea and the sickness waned and the scene began to hold. I helped by concentrating on the face and thought of Murie, for I knew this was the Pug-Boo's doing.

Then I awoke.

Though naked beneath the breeze from the window, I was bathed in sweat; trembling, too. I lay still for seconds, breathing hard. I walked to the opened windows, paused en route to pour myself a glass of water from an earthen jug.

I leaned on the balustrade, drank, breathed deeply again, and scanned with unseeing eyes the view below. I had seen, I was sure—albeit, it was a small enough peek indeed—the very Hell of the Terran world, plus that of all the Gods who had ever evoked an "opposite" of their particular heaven. I thought, too, that for this very reason, what I had experienced, *had seen*, was not a product of Camelot alone. And if that was true, what then of the origins of Om? For the Kaleen and the Yorns of the Dark Lands were still—or were they—humanoid, indigenous to the planet. A thought came again, and it was almost an alien intrusion: I wondered suddenly just what the "opposite" of Pug-Boos would be. . . .

Then, below in the courtyard, there was a great shouting of men, a *wheeing* of dottles, and the blast from a score of trumpets. A most important personage had evidently arrived. The fact failed to stir me, however. I was determined to know more of the other—and *now!*

I crossed the room to the saffron-colored, lustily snoring heap that was Rawl Fergis. I shook him roughly so that he came wide awake, almost as I had done.

"Ha, la!" he exclaimed, rubbing his eyes furiously, and then, "Great Ormon, Sir Lenti. Is it time already? Have the hours so soon fled?"

"Indeed they have," I replied. "But not in the way that you mean. I am sorely troubled, Sir Fergis. I have dreamed strange dreams of sickness and evil. And it seems that all that has happened since my mother received her bird of ill omen will be as naught to that which will happen now. Tell me of the Pug-Boos, Sir Fergis; all that you know of them. For they will play a most important role in that which will come to pass."

As I had done previously, Rawl stretched to the breeze, breathed deeply. He then went to the earthen jugs on the table, for there was more than one. He chose the mild, cool wine of Fregis, made from the filka fruit. It had a faintly maple taste and bubbled like champagne.

He drank and then said sharply, "It would appear, Sir Lenti, that after knowing you for four days we still know you not. *All* know of Pug-Boos. Why not yourself?"

"In sooth, I do not know," I said. And I answered just as sharply: "But let be! If there are areas in which my memory fails me, this fact decrees no harm to you or Marack. If this memory is not refreshed, however, then, perchance, great harm *can* come. Trust me, Sir Fergis. Trust me, Rawl! For I am indeed a true friend of Marack and of Fregis."

"You are not of Fregis then? Are you from our moons?" Rawl's grin was impish.

"Let be," I said again.

And so he told me. And we sat in great fur-draped chairs before a middling fire and drank jointly from the jug of filka wine, passing it back and forth between us.

"Pug-Boos," Rawl explained, "as your memory would tell you, had you a memory to speak, are sacred in every way throughout all the lands to the north of the river-sea—though, and this must be understood, they are not of Ormon and the Trinity. To harm a Pug-Boo is to court instant death—and this *to* all and *from* all citizenry. There are but three Boos in Marack; two each in the lands of Ferlach, Gheese, et al. The Boos in Marack are Hooli, who is with the princess; Jindil, who stays solely with the king; and Pawbi, who resides with the great sorcerer in the snow-lands to the north. In Gheese, Great Ortmund, and the like, the Pug-Boos were with the king and the court wizard, always. Hooli, I would point out to you, Sir Lenti, came to us with the birth of the Princess."

"From where?"

He looked at me long and steadily and said, "And now I truly believe that what I said in jest was true. You are not of Fregis, Sir Lenti. It remains to be seen if you are of Best itself . . . though somehow, I do not think so. No one *knows*, sirrah, where a Pug-Boo comes from. And he who seeks to know will most certainly find his death."

"And they are always with our king and sorcerer?"

"Indeed."

"Why, always?"

"Because that is the way it has been."

I mulled that over and then said slowly, "There is a question, Sir Rawl, which we—you and I—must ask the noble Hoggle-Fitz tonight."

"Which is?"

"If the Pug-Boos of Feglyn, king of Great Ortmund, and of his court wizard have been seen at any time since the pact with the Kaleen of Om and the Dark Lands."

Rawl's eyes glittered briefly, but he said simply, "Pug-Boos, as your memory would have told you, do not campaign to the wars."

"Aye," I said. "This I know. But since there is no Boo

56

above the river-sea, would one remain when the river-sea came north to Marack?"

There was a knocking then upon the door. Two pages, resplendent in house livery, appeared bearing new raiment for the both of us—though Rawl's wardrobes seemed already bursting with cloaks and hose and pantaloons and such.

One of these young men informed us that we were to be received by the king and queen prior to the great feast, which now honored both the princess Murie Nigaard's safe return, and the advent of tomorrow's tournament.

I had thought that we—Rawl, Hoggle-Fitz, and myself—were to be presented during the meal itself. The princess had so told us.

We were informed by the same page that the hubbub and bustle which I had heard in the courtyard below had been nothing less than the arrival of the heir to the throne of Kelb, Prince Keilweir. He had come with an entourage of a hundred men-at-arms and sundry knights. Rumors already swept the castle, our page informed us, that this fair prince, in accordance with all custom, would seek the princess Murie Nigaard's hand in marriage. He meant to bring her home with him.

At this last Rawl glanced quickly at me, but managed to hold his tongue. To hide my own discomfiture—a sudden odd dissatisfaction that I had never thought to feel—I bent quickly to the page's ear and whispered some instructions. At this he looked at me and grinned and then withdrew with his companion.

We dropped the subject of the Pug-Boos and dressed, while outside dusk fell swiftly. Rawl had been given a suit of rich dark brown trimmed in heather blue. It went well with his saffron pelt. I, for my mink black, was given an outfit in ebony and silver; linen undergarments, hose, full shirt with pleated ruffles, boots of a soft and silken leather, and a thickly silvered jacket, hussarlike in its fit. The final item was a court saber. This weapon, to me, could very easily have been the deadliest blade on all Camelot; but to those who knew only the great broadsword, it was but a weapon of dalliance. I attached it to my many-stoned, silvered belt.

Rawl chose to say, while running a comb and oil through my matted but cleanly washed hair (we exchanged this grooming favor), that he doubted that the princess would favor this bold prince of Kelb. To which I smiled and said that I thought not, either.

From our aerie windows, we could see a true river of torches and lanterns accompanying what seemed to be the wealth of Glagmaron city, plus the knights and lords from all the tents around. There was a *wheeing* of dottles such as to cause the very air to thrum like a cloud of locusts. This feast night promised to be a most gala affair.

Then we were ready. The crude water clock gave us the proper time—something on the order of the fourth hour, Greenwich, or 7:00 P.M., sidereal. Just prior to this moment the page to whom I had given instructions returned. He carried a platter upon which was a cup covered with a linen napkin.

I flipped the napkin off and nodded to Rawl. "Gog-milk," I informed him, and I grinned from ear to ear. "I would see your skill, Sir Sorcerer."

He shook his head, saying, "If I had doubted you, sir, and thought you a thing of Best, I take it back, for you have a certain childlike humor untainted by Om's blackness. . . ."

I laughed and took the tray and held it out to him. He placed his hands upon the cup, screwed up his eyes, and intoned what seemed a funeral dirge of words, impossible to duplicate. Then he bent to the cup and sniffed.

He looked up smugly.

I raised it to my mouth and sipped. It *was* sviss. He had done it! I smacked my lips. "Not bad," I said.

Then we shared it and left.

Though Rawl knew well the way to the king's reception chambers, protocol demanded that we be preceded by the page. It seemed a full fifteen-minute walk, through halls, courtyards, and great, tapestried rooms; all well-guarded by stalwart men-at-arms of the household troops. These saluted us smartly, while throngs of citizens and such promenaded and eyed us in bold speculation.

The atmosphere of the king's reception room reflected a royal informality of the king and queen. Splendor was their costume and splendor became them. . . . From there, all together, we would move to the great banquet room.

The lord Breen Hoggle-Fitz was already present and he

gave us a loud hello of greeting and seized my hand and pumped it vigorously. He looked as a great beribboned parakeet, so resplendent was his attire. Lady Caroween was present, too, an auburn-furred dainty wisp of peacock. I knew now who had chosen Rawl's brown and heather clothes, for they matched the lady Caroween's attire. She seized upon his arm possessively while he gazed back at me in feigned helplessness.

But Hoggle-Fitz, the lady Caroween, the king and queen—*all* faded before the utterly ethereal iridescence of the gold, milk, and purple apparition that was Murie Nigaard. The one thing that the Galactic Foundation had *not* prepared me for was that I should be so smitten. At that very instant, had the Princess but crooked her finger in command, I would have taken on the prince of Kelb and all his entourage.

I dropped to one knee instead, shook my head of silvered cobwebs, and sought composure. I brushed her small hand with my lips. Peering up at her to speak I saw that my attire, countenance, physique, general person, and twinkling contacts had had a like effect, and perhaps more. For I was the object of a possessive female gaze the like of which I had not seen before.

And her thoughts affected her person. For when she sought to speak, to say: "Arise, Sir Lenti, it is best that your obeisance be given the king, my father, rather than myself," her words came soft and trembling.

"Ha, la," I said boldly. "My very presence assures your father of my utmost loyalty. I bend my knee to you, my lady, as offer of myself to all your needs."

The princess blushed quite pinkly and the king, catching the faintest of humor in my voice, laughed loudly. "Now here indeed," he admonished Murie, "is both a gallant and a warrior beyond your taming. And I want not your knee, young sir." He had turned to me. "Rather would I have your hand. I welcome you as does my queen. And I give you our royal and fatherly thanks for the life of our daughter."

I bowed deeply to them both, making the intricate sweep of leg, plumed cap, and arm that I had made the princess four days before on the great south road. King Caronne was the bluff and hearty type—in contrast to the light and airy queen Tyndil. She was as blond as the king was dark. And I could see that though Murie favored her physically, it was her father's ways that she had taken as her own.

And Hooli was there, too. And he was not alone. He had a companion as like to himself as two toys on a rack. They sat side by side on a great fur-covered couch and watched us benignly—amusedly. Alike as two peas? Not exactly. At second glance I hardly believed what I saw, for the other Pug-Boo, known as Jindil, according to Rawl, had a large black circle around one eye. . . . I was reminded again of the dreams of my childhood.

Directly behind the seated Pug-Boos there stood a tall and patriarchal individual whom I assumed to be the court sorcerer —which indeed he was. He waited silently until we, following the king's suggestion, seated ourselves in something of a circle. The guards and the page were then ordered from the room, and the sorcerer, introduced as Fairwyn, and the king, began to talk.

"Young sir," the king began, "my good nephew, and, you, Lord Hoggle-Fitz and daughter, I bid you all a hearty welcome to Glagmaron. There is no question now that cruel and harsh winds are blowing from the river-sea. So speaks our sorcerer and seer, good Fairwyn; and so, indeed, does all that has transpired. I had not thought to see or hear of Yorns and men of Om in our fair parts. But these things have come to pass—and even a Vuun of the dark creatures. I had not thought to see or hear of vile treachery such as that which lives in Castle-Gortfin—and with such rulers as Feglyn of Great Ortmund and Harlach of Kelb, who have bowed their necks to Om. I had not thought to hear these things. But now that I have heard and have taken council with certain lords of the realm, known to my nephew and to you, Sir Hoggle-Fitz, I will say to you all that Marack has picked up this gauntlet so deviously and so cowardly thrown. . . . Know this, young sirs, and all of you: Tentatively, and prior to your own good council, we have sent couriers so that within three days Castle-Gortfin will be under siege of men and magic.

"Om has sought to use our princess in this game. It failed. But in similar ways it pursues its goal. This prince of Kelb is quite obviously here to achieve that which the dark power of the lady Elioseen could not.

"I charge all of you therefore to forbear your anger at what may be said by them tonight. The prince comes to us under the Trinity Host of Peace, and so shall he be received. For we will not show our hand." He paused then and drank from a crystal goblet.

"May I have leave to speak, my lord?" I asked.

"Indeed, young sir."

"What thought your council of the Yorns and the Vuun who passed us in the night, and who seemingly turned south in the direction of Gheese?"

He studied me carefully before he answered. He finally said, "That this force seeks to penetrate both our land and Gheese, to scout from the rear. For Om is still held in the mountain passes. Perhaps, too, they would move through us to Ferlach, for like purpose."

"And if they have remained in Marack?"

"To what purpose?"

"I know not. But it occurs to me, my lord, that they are a fighting force rather than scouts. Why else the Vuun?"

"As eyes, young sir," the king said testily, "from aloft."

"Nay, sire," I said boldly. "We—Sir Rawl, myself, and the good lord Hoggle-Fitz—have seen this force which, in all sooth, the princess and the lady Caroween did not. They were great Yorns and men-at-arms and knights. They traveled not lightly, lord, as is the way of scouts, but with strong weaponry and three hundred dottles. The Vuun, I warrant, has a purpose other than 'eyes aloft.'"

"And that would be?"

"To fly with something they have taken—out of the land of Marack; something of great value which, once captured, they could not trust themselves to hold."

"What say you, Fairwyn?" The king spoke bluntly to his sorcerer, who still stood watch behind the flatly staring Pug-Boos. I thought as I glanced to Fairwyn and caught Hooli's eye—he being the one without the circle—that he was keenly alert to all that went on. Indeed, seeing that I saw him, I will swear that he deliberately allowed a quicksilver smile to touch his furry lips.

Fairwyn had a most thin and reedy voice. It was direct,

however, and without pretense or guile. He said simply, "It seems as the runes suggested, my lord. But I would add now, in view of this young man's words, that not only is the princess endangered by this prince of Kelb—but it *is* quite possible that the Vuun is meant to carry a living human captive."

Queen Tyndil gasped. Murie's hand went to her throat and her eyes grew big. Hoggle-Fitz lunged to his feet, an oath on his lips and his hand on the hilt of his court saber. His lithesome daughter fled the arm of Rawl Fergis to move to the side of Murie Nigaard.

The king then turned again to me. "It would appear," he said sharply, "that there may be something of the Collin in you after all. But no mind. We will leave this now, to talk again when we have dined and seen this prince of Kelb." He arose, bowed to us all, and said, "My lords, my ladies. We ask that you accompany us to the dining hall." He touched a small silver bell, then took the queen's hand and led off toward the now opening doors. . . .

I would not let this chance go by. I moved instantly to the princess, offered my arm, and said simply, "My lady?"

Murie smiled, her visions of the Vuun erased. She put her small hand on mine and we fell in behind the king, the queen, and the Pug-Boos, who had somehow managed to step in front of us. I knew without looking that Rawl and his auburn-haired vixen were directly in back of us, with the towering Hoggle-Fitz and the almost ethereal sorcerer, Fairwyn, bringing up the rear.

We went down one short hall to the king's private entrance and waited for the formal blare of trumpets to announce us. We then stepped boldly forward as the great doors opened.

The banquet hall of Glagmaron castle on tournament night was a sight to see. Here indeed was the true panoply of feudalism. All that epitomized the most romantic but brutal phase of the socioeconomic evolution of humankind was present. It was dazzling; it was also tinsel and running dye. It was the absolute in insouciance for those who sat above the salt. Rank upon rank of lords and ladies, knights and squires, banners and pennons were gathered. And on the periphery of it all were even a number of tables for the graduating class of student-warriors. To say the scene was less than fantastic would be to deny all reason. . . .

We advanced down a great aisle separating a double row of tables, to the king's table. It was on a raised platform and at right angles to those below. The roars and aves for the rulers, for the princess, and yes, for me, too—for they had heard somewhat of our adventures—were deafening.

But protocol was such that I was not to eat with Murie. She sat at her father's table, to his left; the queen, her mother, was on his right. On either side of them were a half dozen great lords of the realm, including—and I stared in surprise—the lord Fon Tweel, kolb of Bist, whom I had bested prior to our abduction.

He scowled darkly when he saw me. I bowed ever so slightly and sneered back at him. Then Rawl, Caroween, Hoggle-Fitz, and I were shunted to the first table to the right, below that of the king.

Behind each diner was a liveried servant. The feast had needed only the king's arrival to begin. Indeed, at the very point of the king's seating himself a veritable parade of trays and service poured from the kitchens: great roasts and shanks of meat from all manner of strange beasts; tureens of gravies sufficient to drown a child; huge pasties of a conglomerate of fish and fowl; vegetable puddings; birds in every shape and size, and each with its feathers returned for dress-up; fruits and ices; deep-dish pies and curries. There seemed no end to it. And certainly there was no end to the varied wines and the sviss that swept like the river Cyr through that monstrous hall.

For one brief moment I felt the heavy hand of Hoggle-Fitz upon my shoulder. His voice rose, booming above the bedlam, saying, "How now, Sir Collin. We shall see if you are as good a trencherman as you are swordsman and gallant. I would beseech you to honor our God, good sir, by eating all that is placed before you—for food is truly the end product of all his works." Upon saying this, Hoggle-Fitz sat down, said grace quickly, and fell to. . . .

I was ravenous, and I ate wolfishly with knife and fingers. The roar around us subsided to a hum, with but here and there a shriek or scream to denote some conversational point or well-placed bon mot.

What with the flow of wines and such, I drank a goodly

quantity. So much so that had I not eaten as Hoggle-Fitz suggested, I would have, indeed, been drunk.

Through it all my eyes but seldom left the princess. And only then to view the table opposite to my own. There sat Keilweir, prince of Kelb, surrounded by his lords and entourage. No court gallants they, but obvious fighting men, as was the prince himself. He was tall, slender of waist, and heavy of shoulder. And, too, he was no down-faced youth. He was past thirty. His tanned and weathered features were marked with two great sword slashes. I noted that my companions were also intensely alert to the table of the prince of Kelb.

As time passed and eating died—to be replaced by drinking only—the hum increased to roar again. Here and there were shouted challenges for the morrow's games. Napkins were brought and bowls of water. We cleaned our hands and faces. Relaxed and at my ease I turned to Rawl. "What do you think of those men of Kelb?" I asked.

"That they are less of court-train and sweet reason than one would hope to see," he replied pointedly.

"Aye, and aye again," Hoggle-Fitz put in. "Where I, for one, would hope to see a royal wedding party, I see instead most hardened warriors. And, Master Lenti, the one to the left of the prince, he with the spade beard, is not of Kelb but of Great Ortmund. He is the onus of Hilless, a truly stout and resolute sword."

"Why would a knight of Ortmund be with a prince of Kelb?" Rawl asked.

"I know not," said Hoggle-Fitz.

"The Yorns and the hundred riders came, too, from Kelb's direction," I pointed out. "Perhaps they have much in common. For they are *all*, as our worthy Hoggle-Fitz observes, most seasoned warriors."

"You suggest, sir, that perhaps they are not two groups, but truly *one?*" Rawl asked.

"I do; or that if they are truly two, they will soon be *one*. If this is true, however, it may be that we can dent their power. A challenge or two for tomorrow, for example."

"Better," Hoggle-Fitz insisted fiercely, his eyes upon the onus of Hilless, "though it is somewhat awkward to do this to a wedding party, that we ask for an Onset of Fifties, and strike down half of them."

" 'Tis not meet, Father," Caroween put in bluntly. "It is against all laws of chivalry. A visiting prince who comes a-wooing beneath a flag of peace? For shame!"

"Yon pennants are peaceful?" Rawl almost shouted. "I do adore you, m'lady, but I would remind you that all is topsy-turvy now. Om is in Kelb. And the laws no longer hold."

"We could," Hoggle-Fitz continued, ignoring his spitfire daughter, "and with the help of Ormon, of course, provoke *them* to challenge *us*."

"A point," Rawl said with enthusiasm. "And it will not be difficult. I warrant there will be sufficient insult, for the atmosphere between here and there already reeks of it. Look! The prince's ambassador asks leave to speak."

Certain young knights were even now before the king, petitioning the royal favor for the morrow's assignments in tourney listings. Their pleas for redress against supposed discrimination had become quite loud. With the advance of the prince's ambassador, the prince, and two stalwarts to the place before the king's table, all this was swept aside.

A great and sudden hush seemed all-pervasive now. Those seated knew quite well what was afoot, and dearly welcomed the interplay that would ensue.

At the ambassador's approach, Fairwyn, the king's sorcerer, arose. His hands worked rapidly at some invisible web and he intoned what seemed a litany. When he had finished I was not surprised to see an intrusive skein of fog surrounding himself, the Pug-Boos, and the royal family. . . . No one so much as batted an eye. And I knew that this magic—for that's exactly what it was—was both an expected, protective thing, and at the same time commonplace.

There then began an exchange of compliments and formal folderol, including a listing of the king's lineage, that of his wife, plus the illustrious background of the prince of Kelb. This done—and while the prince was still slightly bent in protocol obeisance to the king—the ambassador began the purpose of their visit.

The bluntness of his first few words were indicative of the tactic he would follow. "And now, oh mighty sire," he said, "we do, upon the orders of our king Harlach, present his son for other than your grace and scrutiny. The prince Keilweir, of Kelb, being desirous of a bride of his class and blood does settle his choice upon your daughter, the most beauteous and demure of creatures, the princess Murie Nigaard. To firmly base his suit in something else than talk, he asks that your princess, together with a goodly train and entourage, return with him to Kelb, whereby, and during the duration of her stay, she will be made most welcome and satisfied of the person and intention of our prince. . . . We ask this in the name of Kelb and of her rightful ruler, Harlach. . . ."

No bridal go-between had ever been more curt, nor a request more terse than that. It had been, in fact, more of a directive than a request. I looked to the others for affirmation of my thoughts. A hissing of indrawn breath all around us gave voice to the silent tension. Then the silence began again so that the patter of a dubot's feet would have been thunderous had they been there.

The princess had arisen, her face white, her two hands clenched; Rawl, likewise. And two hundred others at the tables nearest us. Each great lord around the king was also on his feet.

The reedy voice of Fairwyn came floating over this baited throng—diplomatic, soothing, and deliciously negative. "We hear, oh gentle sirs," he said. "And though we be honored at your request and continence, we would suggest to you and yours that such pursuit of marriage bears thought and much discovery. We ask, in sooth, that time be spent on this. And that you, good sirs, do spend *your* time with us in likewise contemplation."

Hurrah for Fairwyn! He had managed to say exactly nothing, and say it well. But if I had thought that even he could assuage the tender skins of Marack—or of my princess—I had forgotten Camelot. . . .

Murie's voice rang out insultingly above the resultant murmurs. "Oh, gentle sir from Kelb. Would you have sufficient gogs for me to milk upon your visit? For in sooth it seems that a wife of yours must need to learn such arts and more. And tell me of your fair land. Has it plumbing for my daily bath, or would I—since you are at least in that way favored—be forced to use the open sea upon your shores?"

Her sally was greeted with a roar of laughter from all that

great hall, so that the knights of Kelb and those of Marack, too, clapped hands to court sabers.

"Most gracious sire," the voice of the ambassador called out. "We seek no quarrel here. We come in peace and good intent. Is this then to be our answer?" He waved an idle hand at the aroused revelers.

"You came in peace, and so 'tis true," Fairwyn replied. "And in like manner you may go—whatever is your wish, good sirs. Your point is made and we, in due time, will give our studied answer. A toast," he cried out suddenly, "to your good choice, Sir Prince, and to all those who, in honor, seek our princess." He lifted a frail hand with crystal cup and wine. And, the tension punctured, a thousand hands did likewise.

"Nay," Rawl muttered. "We cannot let them go like this."

I watched the others quietly—for Rawl, like Hoggle-Fitz and the king and Fairwyn, too, sensed what I now *knew*. The "tactic" was simply to provoke and thereby distract, to focus Marack's anger upon Kelb alone for whatever days would then ensue. During this time of a misdirection of energies, other peripheral and important actions would be brought to fruition, including that of the hundred riders and the Vuun. Om's methods were not only skillfully divergent but manyfold, selective, and masterful. That Om's tools were composed of lesser clay was something else again. . . .

"Well, let us provoke them further then," I suggested, above the shouting of the prince.

Keilweir, given a glass from the king's table, drank it down, recovering from the princess's sally. Refilled, he held the flagon high and said above the bedlam, "A second toast to the fairest of damsels, our princess, who I would hope will honor our request, and soon."

"Stay your glasses one sweet second," Murie called out. "For if we must toast, then let's have done with tedious gallantry. Sirs and my lords all. I would salute a truly brave and worthwhile knight without whose strong arm I would still be locked in Castle-Gortfin." She raised her glass. "To Sir Harl Lenti—descendant of the Collin!"

Well done! I chuckled mentally. My princess was, indeed, a master of the duel. While drinks were tossed I rose and bowed in the direction of the prince of Kelb, who had been put aside most prettily. His face was a storm cloud as were those of his cohorts. At that very moment Rawl chose to force our move. He, too, arose, stepped forth from between the tables, and shouted loud for all to hear.

"As one of those who shared adventures with Sir Collin [he was getting them all accustomed to the name], and my sweet cousin, I beg your leave, my liege, to speak."

The king answered loudly, brushing aside the mutterings of Fairwyn, "It appears, my nephew, that you have done just that. Say on. You have my leave."

And indeed he did. Instinctively, I think, even the sorcerer Fairwyn and the lords at the king's table deferred to those of us who knew of Om in Kelb, the witchcraft of the lady Elioseen, and the mystery of the Vuun and the hundred riders. Except for the frowning Fon Tweel the floor was left to Rawl. Indeed, there was such a deep understanding among all those close to King Caronne, such unspoken unity, that one would suspect an outside influence.

I thought of this phenomenon as Rawl began to speak. I was certain of two things, and *knew* that through some strange telepathy the others were certain of them, too. These were that the men of Prince Keilweir and the hundred riders had a purpose in Marack other than wedding feasts and scouting; and that to circumvent or blunt this effort—while simultaneously planning a counteraction of our own—we had to deal with them. We would have to do this in a way that would reflect just the usual Camelot-Fregis reaction to slight and slur; namely, with bravado, challenge, and clouted heads—and nothing more.

"My lords," said Rawl, "though all of Marack knows of the pact of mutual aid concluded between foul Om and those of Kelb and Great Ortmund, do they know, too," and he raised his voice, *"that Yorns and dead-alives are seated now in those fair lands?"*

An instant roar grew to a crashing wave around us, and all eyes were focused in rage upon the men of Kelb.

The prince's face clouded. He shouted in defiance: "This is a foul and vicious lie."

"Indeed, sirrah?" Rawl laughed. "With mine own eyes I have seen them: first in Castle-Gortfin and then last night. Last night on the great road—Yorns and men of Kelb. Where are they now, Sir Keilweir? And tell us true, *who* rules in Kelb? Your father, Harlach, or that miserable fiend from below the river-sea?"

"I say again that you lie," Keilweir screamed. "How could you know that those were men of Kelb?"

"My lord," Rawl addressed the king, ignoring Keilweir. "Have you heard? I offer now my challenge to the prince— and he will prove his insult on my body, or I on his, and *all else* who would support him in this matter."

The roar had ebbed to heavy silence, with each pair of ears strained for every word.

The ambassador, white-faced and acutely aware of what was happening, laid a restraining hand upon Keilweir's arm. "We accept no challenge, my lord," he said loudly and firmly. "And certainly not from sniveling glory-seekers with their baseless charges. It was our honorable intent to seek the princess Nigaard's hand in marriage for our prince—that only. Now, with your gracious permission, sire, we will go to the road again and leave this matter for another day."

An intake of breath like a soughing wind swept through the gathered throng. The trap had been sprung, but the baited flig was about to escape the hunter; albeit against its will, for the prince of Kelb was literally frothing at the mouth.

Whether he would win over his ambassador or not, I did not know. It was a chance, however, that we could not risk. I moved out to stand with Rawl before the king.

"Oh, sire," I asked calmly, "since much that does not meet the eye seems astir here, I beg one question of this man of Kelb."

The king glared down at me. The unity of telepathic urgings had apparently left him, for he said harshly, "We would have done with this, and now! But you, young sir, have earned your single question. Say it!"

I turned slowly to the prince, caught his eye and held it. "My lord," I said, "what I may lack in courtly knowledge, I make up for in folksy wisdom. It is known, for instance, that gentle Pug-Boos live only in the lands above the river-sea. Neither the Dark Land of Om, nor any vassal state thereof has ever seen a Pug-Boo. . . . I now submit to all within this hall that since Om has moved beyond the river-sea, there are no longer Boos in either Kelb or Great Ortmund—they have gone to whence they came. *Is this not true, my lord?*"

The quiet was heavier still. The prince was shaken. And by this very fact I knew that I was right. He finally addressed the king, saying, "It is not true, sire."

"It *is* true!" I stated loudly. "And we shall prove it on your bodies. It is written," I improvised, "that those who have no friendly Pug-Boos for the singing and the council *are less than men.* I see together with you here a hundred warriors, which in itself is passing strange company for he who brings a marriage vow. No matter. If you are less than men, then I, with this good knight, Rawl Fergis, the noble Breen Hoggle-Fitz of Great Ortmund—*and forty-seven untried students from the Collegium of Glagmaron*— do challenge the half of you to an Onset of Fifties, for that is all that is allowed. We propose—if I am right and you are less than men—to thrash you soundly. If I am wrong, good prince, if such is truly *not* the case, then we commend ourselves to Ormon, and may our God have mercy on our souls. . . ."

The roar arose again, deafening now, especially from the student tables to the rear of the great hall. I knew that upon the instant of my word they would be at dice for entry to our ranks.

Never had such a challenge been issued—students against seasoned knights. If I were wrong, though blades were dulled and points the same, we would lead our students to a slaughter. But I thought not. Already, just the thought of what I said had reached them—for, as stated, they knew there were no longer Pug-Boos in Kelb, and they were sore afraid.

Only the prince and his hundred had remained silent amid the hubbub. They knew they were trapped, and that if they failed before so unlikely a foe, and if the populace of Kelb and Ortmund got wind of it—assumed the loss of Boos to be the reason—then Om would already be less solid upon our shores. . . .

Touché! Check! And check again!

All waited for Prince Keilweir's reply. It was not long in coming. He looked at his ambassador and at his hundred lords and knights. He then stepped forward, saying simply, for he had no choice, "Oh, sire, what was a jolly wedding party is now a challenged company. We do, to clear our name, accept

70

this offer of the strange knight. And further, now, and for this reason, we do beg your leave to withdraw to choose our heroes for the morrow."

Permission was granted.

Amid the ensuing bedlam of cheers and catcalls following them through the hall, my eyes turned to Murie. Her hands were clasped beneath her chin. Her head was back, and from her throat came peal after peal of delighted girlish laughter. The fact that I, too, could easily be killed had apparently escaped her. But no matter. I was hooked. And I would not have had it any other way. When she quieted down, I grinned and winked from where I stood. She shook her head from sheer exuberance and dared throw me a kiss.

Over her dainty shoulder the Pug-Boo without the circle around his eye winked, too. . . .

When the history of Camelot-Fregis is finally written it will most definitely include the famed Onset, The Battle of the Fifties. For no more outlandish or preposterous a bickering has yet been seen in all the Galaxy. It began with magic. It may well have ended that way. But throughout the charade there was an element, too, of pure and simple guts.

By morning all of Glagmaron city and many outlying villages had heard of the great challenge. Therefore, where normally half the countryside would rally to attendance, now it seemed that *all* had come. The area of battle, the lists, was approximately one hundred yards by fifty. The tiers of seats would hold ten thousand and no more. The tents of lords were placed to north and south. But fortunately all the area to the east sloped gently up from the lists, so that the fifty thousand gathered here could also see. The king's guard patrolled the peripheral areas so that the peasants and tradesmen did not intrude upon the tents of the lords, or upon the field itself. All was carnival. All was pageantry. There seemed as many piemen, venders, sviss peddlers, and whatever, as to equal again the gathering itself.

Rawl, Hoggle-Fitz, myself, and our forty-seven chosen

students—and a choice bunch of heavy-shouldered, thick-necked street fighters they were—were gathered at the southeast point of the greensward. Kelb's forces were at the northeast. We had been given armor, a choice of dulled weapons, and shields—which we had hurriedly painted for the students with an amalgam of our three colors—and one great knobbed jousting lance each. Behind us, crouched and saddled, some belly-flat upon the grass, were our fifty dottles. We were at ease.

At quarter-day (10:00 A.M., Greenwich), the jousting and dueling would begin—but not for us. We were last on the card, the feature event. A few minutes prior to quarter the king appeared at the castle gate. With his retinue he looked down upon the dark sea of heads, brightened here and there by the garb of women and the sparkling headpieces of archers and men-at-arms. The lists, from his vantage point, was but a narrow strip of green, marked only with the banners, pennons, and flags of heraldry. A path had been cleared to the tiered stands and down this he came, followed by the queen, the princess, Fairwyn, and all the great lords of the privy council. The Pug-Boos did not attend.

Once the king was seated, to the blare of the trumpets and the roar of the crowd, the tournament began.

For those familiar with a feudal culture and its concomitant nuances, that which then ensued was by no means new or strange. Great lords and knights rode forth fulfilling certain pledges, vows, and/or in answer to some challenge or fancied insult, and battle was joined. . . . Through all the morning men in suit armor went sailing through the air at the hefty nudge of a jousting lance; were beaten to the ground by sword or mace; were pounded to a pulp by other means so that they staggered dazedly in circles—and all to the constant blare of silvered trumpets, fanatic cheers of wagering supporters, and the accompanying roar of the crowd that will cheer any onset. They fought in singles, doubles, and sixes; on dottles, in chariots, and sometimes afoot. When lunch was finally called the tents of the chirurgeons were already stuffed with those with broken limbs, cracked pates, and wounds of a hundred kinds.

It was just then that Murie chose to visit us. She came with Caroween, five pretty maidens—which set our student

crowd to roar their pleasure—and an armed guard to force
a way through the crowd. They looked a lovely sight indeed,
before us on their kneeling dottles. Actually it was the first
chance I had had to be with Murie since our arrival. She
looked delectable, as did the others in their furred and velvet
jumpsuits of varied colors. Murie's was milk white, matching
the armor she had sent me.

"How now, my lord," she said in greeting, "we meet
again." She stepped from the kneeling dottle with a certain
boldness and took my hand. The lady Caroween did likewise
with Sir Rawl; while Hoggle-Fitz, somewhat perplexed by
all this coupling, retired to sit beside his dottle. The young
student-warriors pressed around admiringly till I shooed
them off.

I looked down into the purple eyes and said simply,
"Murie, I would speak with you without the nonsense of
court and custom." I drew her to one side, to where my
dottle rested. We leaned together against its rump and gazed
out to the deserted lists.

"I am still the princess, sir," she chided me. "And it may
be that you grow too bold."

For answer I drew her gently close. She stiffened, then
relaxed, but made no move to draw away. "Enough," I said
softly. "I would rather be with you in silence for one second,
than an hour with the childishness of protocol."

"You speak but strangely, sir."

"Do I, indeed? Do you really believe that?"

"No, my lord." She seemed suddenly subdued.

"Then agree with me that our stars cross strongly. For
I think, perforce, that we will *be* together."

She pressed closer at that so that I could feel the length
of arm and thigh against me. Her voice was hardly audible.
"I do agree, my lord."

I smiled at that, looked down into the purple eyes and
elfish face, and said, "And since truly I do accept you as my
lady, am I, indeed, your lord?"

"In sooth you are."

"Well. Were we not in dead center of all of Glagmaron I
would take you in my arms."

"And I would come, but gladly."

"Great Gods," I said. Then, "Look, my princess. This

comes so sudden. After this nonsense is through—if my head not decorate a lance—I would see you alone, and for a space of time. There is much to say and I would say it."

She looked up at me and held my gaze. "That chance will come, my lord, more quickly than you think. For there is council of war of which you will be informed; 'tis said that it will encompass all our world. But other than that, runes, too, have been cast. They tell of serious danger to myself if I remain in Glagmaron. My father, for this reason, sends me tomorrow morn to the great sorcerer in the snow-lands. There in his keep, they say, lies my only safety. *You* are to head my escort, my lord—for I would have no other."

Her words prompted the possessive look of yesterday. The shock was overwhelming. That this small fur-tummied female could so befuddle my eighteen years of Galactic training in all the logics was beyond belief. But at the moment I wanted nothing else, nor would I have it any other way.

Across the field the trumpets blared again.

"You will see my father tonight," Murie said. "And you will see me, too."

"As to that last," I murmured, "I would hope for nothing else." Still holding her hand boldly, before all the others, I walked her to her dottle. . . .

Caroween had already mounted. She now sat stiff-spined in the saddle, saying loudly to Rawl, "My lord, I shall watch you closely. And if it go against you and these good knights and my gracious father, then expect me on the field. For I do not hold with ritual nonsense; and I will thrash them all who dare to win against us."

"*Have done!*" The roar was that of Hoggle-Fitz. He had just bussed his daughter roundly in fond good-bye. But even he who knew her was not prepared for this. "I warn you, Caroween," he shouted. "If you shame us, if you set your meddling foot upon yon green ere all these men of Kelb are soundly whipped, it will be your bottom that will receive the thrashing. Now think on that, and off with you."

The gathered students roared and Murie smiled. The five maidens smiled, too, and they, together with the escorts, saluted us. I stood at Murie's stirrup; Rawl at Caroween's. Undaunted, the lithe and headstrong redhead damned us all with her eyes, bent down to Rawl's surprised face, and kissed him soundly.

Murie followed suit—so swift, so soft, however, that her lips had barely touched my mouth ere they were gone. All in a flash of lively color and painted dottle paws, to the cheers of our line of student-warriors and those who had gathered to watch.

We moved together closely then, myself, Breen Hoggle-Fitz, and Rawl. They had not questioned my leadership, nor my commitment of their bodies to what might be a suicidal battle. In fact, they relished both the idea that I had made it, and that *they* were a part of it. Such was the conditioning of Camelot-Fregis. Ourselves and forty-seven untried warrior-students against the cream of Kelbic chivalry. Insanity? No one but me seemed to think so. I had said the loss of Pug-Boos would make our enemy less than men—and that was sufficient. Our students believed me—as did Rawl and Hoggle-Fitz. The deck was stacked, so they concluded. It but needed their courage now to tip the scales completely and this they were prepared to give.

We had agreed on tactics and strategy. This being to use a light armor, a smaller shield, and to avoid, but lure, their onslaught. The jousting we could do nothing about. But after, well, we would bait them to a frenzy, tire them, and then smash them down—and we had chosen blunted swords and weapons but half the weight of theirs.

A fresh breeze blew across the field, clouds gathered to our rear. And, since I had planned a bit of magic all my own, I frowned. I needed sunlight.

"How now, Sir Lenti," Rawl exclaimed softly. "It seems our time is come. Yon sortie of five knights of Glagmaron against those five from Klimpings appears to be the last."

"They *are* the last," Hoggle-Fitz said. "And I for one am glad to see it."

"Then arm and mount," I said curtly. And fifty students other than our forty-seven helped us to do just that. I wore white armor, Rawl, red, and Hoggle-Fitz, black; and all the students, green. I felt most smugly proud to see my heraldry upon their shields. It dripped in gaudy colors on my own. As stated, it was a sprig of violets upon a field of gold. Rawl's blazonry was three scarlet bars upon an azure field, and that of Hoggle-Fitz, the dainty Dernim Tulip of fair Durst in Ortmund; as stated, too, all students wore our three designs upon their shields, for as yet they had none of their own. . . .

"Once confronted with our enemy upon the green," I said to Hoggle-Fitz, when we were mounted and all in line, "I wish that you, sir, would step forward and lead us all in prayer for both ourselves and Marack."

Hoggle-Fitz's eyes, in his gnarled and craggy face, flashed gratitude for this request. "I will indeed," he said. "But also for Great Ortmund."

I nodded. "As agreed, I will take the center; yourself to the right and Rawl to the left. And, all of you would-be heroes," I shouted, standing in my stirrups and moving my great dottle out and down the line, "remember well what we have agreed upon. Strike for their weapons, elbows, knees, or throat—and in that order. Above all else, *let them attack;* protect each other. But once your onslaught—at whatever target—*follow through to the end.* And so shall we win over this weighty mess of kitchenware from Kelb!"

If nothing else my humor alone would have been sufficient inspiration for the first few minutes. With this gang, though, it was hardly needed. Rawl rode out, then Hoggle-Fitz, both standing in their stirrups. Beyond, on the field, the last of the knights of Klimpinge were either hobbling or being dragged away, while the victors of Glagmaron received gifts and prizes from the king and his lords.

We spaced ourselves along the line of students as we had planned, made a turn, and headed single-file through the swarms of peasants, gentry, knights, and archers. We all stood tall in our stirrups, gripping our lances firmly. As our first rider paced out upon the green, Rawl bellowed in a voice I never knew he had: *"For Marack! For the Collin! For Marack! For the Collin!"* Our warrior-students picked it up, forty-seven strong and lusty voices bellowing in cadence. Long before we were in line and facing north it seemed that all the acreage and tiers of seats were echoing the same—only the hundred knights of Kelb were silent, and, I thought, somewhat morose.

My interest in Hoggle-Fitz's religious administrations was anything but pious. I was still Kyrie Fern, the Adjuster. I had a bit of personal parlor magic up my sleeve. And with some luck . . . The clouds were gathering still, however, which meant my luck was bad. In fact, the very moment that the king's heralds rode forth with trumpet blare and scroll to proclaim in ritual the reason for our argument, a wash of rain swept across the field. Other than lousing up my magic it would be to our advantage, since we were the lighter force.

The heralds were through with their ritual pronouncements and the trumpeters stepped forward. But before they could lift their instruments to their mouths to blow, our Hoggle-Fitz rode forth. His arms were raised above his head, his left arm held his sword, his right, his lance. He said nothing. But the trumpeters, seeing him, stayed their horns. A great silence fell over the field. Hoggle-Fitz turned around, dismounted, placed lance and sword beside his standing dottle, and knelt upon the greensward.

And then it happened. Hoggle-Fitz's knees had hardly touched grass when, with a clap of instant thunder and a dazzling glare, a bolt of lightning struck within ten feet of him. . . . The great crowd moaned, seeing in this a mark, an omen that perhaps the question of the Pug-Boos and Ormon's grace did not favor our cause after all. Before this sighing moan had reached its end, however, an equally glaring bolt smashed down within but a few feet of the prince of Kelb.

I smiled. Tit-for-tat. Camelot's magic was indeed much in evidence. And if the power of Om had stood forth to deal the first blow, the power that favored our own—whatever or whoever it was—had matched that blow, exactly. I smiled again. For at that very moment the clouds parted and the sun shone through, touching upon my forty-seven students and my two brave knights. I seized my chance, pressed the ion-beam at my belt, widened its focus so no damage could be done, and directed it full upon the praying Hoggle-Fitz.

What I had hoped would happen, happened. All his armor, and instantly, gave forth a golden glow so that he seemed clothed in an aureole of shining light. If Hoggle-Fitz, with his tedious but pious mouthings, had ever hoped for sainthood, he had found it now. And the hissing gasps of the great multitude—crossing themselves the while for Ormon's sake—was a thing to hear. The fact that the ion-beam had simply activated the high sulfur content of the steel of Fitz's armor, causing a glow akin to that of phosphorescence, was some-

thing else. My forty-seven knelt; so did the crowds—*so did
the men from Kelb.* And Fitz glowed like the fabled, pious
Galahad of Terra, though he knew it not. Indeed of all that
gathering he alone was not to know till the game was
won. . . .

With the glowing and sainted Hoggle-Fitz bellowing aves
and prayers, I dismounted, too, and walked quickly to kneel
by the side of Rawl. I interrupted his mumbled cantos to say
softly, "We are much favored, my friend. But 'tis said that
Ormon best helps those who help themselves. Om, too, is
strongly at work here. Witness that first lightning bolt. And
more of this magic will come, though in what form I know
not. But be not afraid and pass the word that all that transpires against us *will simultaneously happen to the enemy.* If
we bear this in mind, we cannot lose."

Rawl eyed me silently. "Yes," he said finally. "I know now,
indeed, that you are not of Fregis."

I shrugged. "Ask that of my mother when you meet. She'll
quickly tell you." Hoggle-Fitz was on his feet again. I rose,
too, and so did Rawl. In back of us the forty-seven were up
and mounting their dottles. The word I had given Rawl
spread quickly down the line. And, when I glanced back at
their fresh, eager faces, I knew we had made it. I switched
off the ion-beam. Hoggle-Fitz ceased to glow and returned
to his place on the right. I must admit that the aves, mum-
blings, and the drawing of circles upon breasts, on all sides—
generated by his short-term halo—had caused him to glow
with personal, religious, stigmata that seemed for a brief
second to equal that of the sulfur-treated steel. . . . The
great crowd sighed.

And then it was time. The sun had gone. The rain began.
And there we were. The trumpets blared a soggy blast and
we went hurtling down the green.

One hundred pounding, madly *wheeeing* dottles; couched
lances and shields to the fore—two hundred yards of space.
The touch of magic continued so that even as I settled to the
job at hand the opposing, oncoming line wavered, grew dim.
But I kept my eyes focused on the prince—and saw him
hesitate. I knew then that I had been right. We, too, had
grown dim to our adversaries. Whatever. It was too late for
all concerned. Prince Keilweir's lance missed me completely.

I caught him squarely upon the shield, my knobbed lance driving him backward with such force as to snap his saddle girth and send him headlong over his dottle's rump. One down and forty-nine to go. I was conscious of a mighty cheer from the crowd. All down the line it was the same. I had expected, since the exchange of lance thrusts was our weakest area, that we would lose here. But we did not. . . . Amid the crash of splintered shafts, *wheeeing*, screaming dottles, and cadenced shouts to every saint that Camelot possessed, I could see that a full twenty of the men of Kelb were down, as opposed to but eighteen of ours. Most, on either side, were up again, afoot, blunted swords and maces hacking away in a whirlwind collage of brutal, no-quarter battle which, had the weapons been honed and heavy instead of dull and light, would have brought death to every man who fell. The prince remained prone, out of it. Hoggle-Fitz had downed his man, as had Rawl. And now the red and black crests of each were seen as the center of a furious melee.

Lance aside, I, too, used broadsword. And, I must confess, since all went well, that I held back deliberately in the first whirl of swords, light mace, and hammer. But even then it was I who hurled the lord of Ortmund to the ground, breaking his sword arm in two places so that he would not fight again for many months.

The pace grew heavy, cruel. And I now knew how Hoggle-Fitz had fought clear of all the armored strength of Great Ortmund. For with one single charge he cleared the Kelbic saddles of four knights whose surcoats and blazonry proclaimed their worth as equal to the best that Marack could produce. Rawl, as was his fortune, had in the meantime struck the prince's brawny ambassador to the turf.

There were more dottles with empty saddles now than full; knights from both sides were being pulled from the saddle to the ground. It was then I noted that the dottles, wise in the ways of humanoids, when lightened of their load would run off to the side. There with their fellows, they formed a great circle around us to watch the remainder of the battle. Being amused at the dottles I was suddenly taken unawares; many hands seized me from the rear, and a sudden blow against the side of my helm caused the world to ring and to disappear in a wall of blackness.

I awoke to find myself ringed with greaved legs and a cadenced shouting of "The Collin! The Collin!" from a dozen lusty student throats. I seized a leg and pulled myself up, helped further to my feet by willing hands. Then with no shield, but with a great two-handed sword tendered me by some unknown student hand, I laid about me and picked up the cry, "The Collin! The Collin!" Where my small group had been ringed around, we now ringed them. And the clash of sword and mace against suit armor and shield was such as to deafen all. Three men went down before my Kelbian sword in just three strokes; each with a broken rib or limb, or both; one man with a broken head—and time passed.

The rain fell hard while we strove mightily against those seasoned warriors. We were three knots of swirling blades, wet turf, and mud. All around us lay the fallen. There remained but thirty of ours to twenty of theirs, and no man was rider now. Through it all, where one would confront a foe in a panting, heaving, sweating, streaming exchange of blood and bruises, that foe might suddenly disappear, to be seen seconds later at another spot a few feet removed from the original. And, too, if one observed the expressions of one's opponent, he would note that in that same opponent's eyes he, likewise, had disappeared.

The remaining knights of Kelb fought desperately. And I thought as I stood back and leaned upon my sword that those already prone around us were the better off, since no man standing—ours or theirs—remained unscathed.

I sought to end it. I had eleven mud-covered, panting students; Hoggle-Fitz, eight; and Rawl, ten. Rawl's helmet was off, one arm hung limp, and blood bathed his face from a deep gash above his left eye.

Though they fought bravely, despairing of victory, four more of the Kelbian knights were down ere the king's heralds moved forward to blow the finish. Before this could happen, however, we had, perforce, as was our plan, to cripple more. Reluctantly then, for I would not harm good men were it not necessary, I signaled Hoggle-Fitz and Rawl for one last effort. We charged their bloody circle of sixteen knights from three sides. The blunted swords and lightened maces swung, blindly in some cases, on friend and foe alike, the rain and mud obscuring shields and blazonry. And our cheers and their screams of defiance were hoarse and wild. When the king's trumpets sounded there were but six of Kelb left standing, and twenty-two of ours. . . .

So there were twenty-two of us to stand before the king and all the pomp of Marack; twenty-four, actually, since two student-warriors with a broken leg apiece were held up and brought along by their comrades.

King Caronne then announced in the most formal of court language that we had won; therefore our cause had been proved just and our charges correct. He offered us the thanks of all Marack for our services to his crown and to his daughter. And on all sides there were cheers of admiration for the Collin, for Lord Breen Hoggle-Fitz, who though from Great Ortmund had still fought well for Marack, and for young Rawl Fergis, cousin to the princess Murie Nigaard. It was understood that a number of the student-warriors would be heggled as a result of their valor, and that Rawl and I and Fitz would name these men.

The six knights of Kelb, representing the wounded and the remaining fifty—for they alone had fought—were given the order for banishment from Marack with all their entourage: Until such time as Pug-Boos came back to Kelb and Ortmund; and this proved by those countries' kings.

Small gain, I thought as we mounted our dottles and retired from the field. Of the knights of Kelb, at least sixteen were dead; of our students, twelve. Of the remainder of both sides, the bruises, scars, and badly mended limbs would long remind the participants of the Onset of Fifties at the great tournament of Glagmaron.

Like Rawl, I, too, bled from ear and nose. Indeed, I wanted nothing now but warm water, a soft bed, some food at a later hour—and to see Murie. *Great Flimpls,* I thought, as we wended our way back to the castle, *how one does take up with the color and the substance of the country!*

Halfway to the drawbridge I felt an odd persistent buzzing

at the base of my skull and I wondered if the blow I had received had caused concussion. But no! I pressed the stud upon my belt to activate the circuit. . . .

"Well!" I said mentally. "Well, it's about time! It's damned well about time."

"Look who's talking!" Ragan's voice came from the node at the base of my skull. "You've been damped out, Buby. No fault of ours. We've tried. Great whoozits, we've tried. But you should have known. You should have . . . Look! Here we are. There you are. We've contacted a Watcher and got some information that all is not well; that things are, in fact, pretty damned *bad*. Brief us, Buby."

"Well," I began slowly, as my dottle cantered along, "it's like this. . . ."

And I told them everything, including the mental picnic with Hooli the Pug-Boo; about the maelstrom into which we had inadvertently descended; about Camelot magic, generally —and I gave my summation.

"It seems obvious to me," I said, "that what we assumed to be simple growing pains—with a singular twist which we could control or influence accordingly—is nothing of the kind. As a matter of fact, the stage is set here for one last dramatic act sans the deus ex machina. The curtain's coming down. The imagery the Pug-Boo creates—world destruction and whatever—*really happened somewhere*. I'm guessing it was on one of Fomalhaut II's three planets. I'm guessing that it can happen again.

"The indication is that the Holocaust was but one single event in the total strategy of an antagonist who remains unknown—whose ultimate goal, for that very reason, may be something other than just Camelot-Fregis. I *saw* the destruction of the planet, remember? I saw it through the Pug-Boo's eyes. Only a force equaling, or *superior* to the Foundation, itself, could wield such power."

Kriloy's voice came softly, soothing, and palliative to my intensity. I mentally pictured him and Ragan in the *Deneb* 3's "Foundation Center," as apart from the ship itself: Ragan, tall, graying, with the touch of cynicism to his voice and person that display all who have been with the Foundation for any length of time; Kriloy, dark, slender, ebullient, a facsimile of myself in that he, too, was alive to "the wonder of it all."

The starship would be positioned directly above Glagmaron city, orbiting with Camelot's axial spin. But how long had it been there? Somehow, though long-sought contact had been made, it gave me no comfort. How many times had they tried and failed? And why had they failed? It was quite possible that they served no purpose now at all; that that which was about to happen was beyond their ability to influence; that essentially, their very presence created a great and unnecessary danger for Camelot—and perhaps themselves.

Kriloy was saying: "We've not found the reason why you've been impossible to contact. We've been in touch with the Watchers of Klimpinge, but they've added nothing to their previous report, except that a deadly peril seems now to vibrate in the very air. We don't even know why we've been able to reach you now."

"Whatever," I said. "I'm as much in the dark as you."

"Sheee!" Kriloy's exclamation was sarcastic.

"All *right!*" I said. "But now that we've made contact, you'll agree that I'm in the soup, and that I need some answers, *bad.* Have you been scanning?"

"Off and on."

"What's happening? What's in the southern hemisphere— the good old land of Om? How's the traffic on the roads? The seas? The seaports? *What have you seen?*"

"No 'ghost' armies, only real ones. And no hallucinating cloud banks or dark wizardry—at least from an altitude of two hundred miles. To the south of the river-sea, as you know, it's mostly jungle and savannah until the rise of the highlands. From there on it's early winter—rain, sleet, snow. The Dark Lands are no longer dark. At the moment they are covered with fog, clouds, snow, the works. Across the savannahs, through the jungles, and into all the ports, there is troop movement, cavalry hordes of between five and ten thousand men: double that in men-at-arms, archers, and the like. Your Yorns, as you call them, are some kind of mutants; they live mostly in savannah areas. The *men,* inland, seacoast, wherever, are simply rounded up, given weapons, drilled in their use for a few days, and then marched down to the boats. Other than Om's elite, the majority are poorly trained and led.

"We suspect that the port cities are full to bursting, though many ships have already sailed north, to your area. The total figure is somewhere between two hundred thousand and two hundred and fifty thousand warriors, which suggests that you are, indeed, 'in the soup.' "

"Good God," I said.

Ragan laughed. "A few hundred thousand, more or less, shouldn't upset the mighty Collin. . . . We watched you, you know, in your little melee. I won fifty credits on you, Buby."

"You mean there was someone to bet against me?"

"We drew straws. The longs got the prince of Kelb—we know who he is now—and the shorts got you and that senior student crew with the buster-brown haircuts."

"Skip it," I said flatly. Their cavalier attitude concerning *my* bones and *my* future left me a little cold. "To get back to the south: It's my opinion that things are going to get worse before they get better. We need someone badly down there."

"Are you suggesting a Watcher?"

"Why not?"

"From what you've told us, it would be much too late to help you."

"Fine! So put one there to help *you*."

"You're a little testy, you know," Ragan said softly. "Looks like the situation's getting to you. Sure you don't want to be withdrawn?"

"No," I said tersely.

"You sound much too involved, and that's not good."

I controlled an instant anger, derived of the fact that he was reaching me because he was right. The last thing I wanted now was to risk withdrawal. "Shove it," I said bluntly. "I'm on top of it, and I've no intention of leaving now."

Ragan laughed, dissolving the tension. "We've kept a close eye on you. The vibes from you and that pussycat princess are something to feel. On the scope, it's like colorama."

I cursed them for a couple of double-damned voyeurs. "Look," I said strongly. "I'm still the assigned Adjuster, which means that *I'm* in charge. That being the case, from this moment on no scanning, no orbiting! You'll warp *in* and *out* of the Fomalhaut-Fregis matrix every sixth hour, for exactly two minutes. I'll turn full on to catch you. We'll exchange bons mots. Meanwhile, play games. One of them being that you check out Fomalhaut's binary and its three-planet system. That's an order! And you'll handle this search-and-peek job with discretion—like your next trip to Camelot-Fregis, *in* and *out*, with all detection systems given but two minutes of exposure."

"You're playing it pretty damn close." Ragan's voice held a note of anger now.

"I got a sterling hunch, children; like it's quite possible that *we* are being scanned right now."

"You think so?"

"Considering what happened to the Pug-Boo's planet, yeah."

"You through?"

"I sure am," I said. *"Fade now!"*

"Now fade," Ragan echoed reluctantly.

And they did. And I was left alone, except for the press of fifty thousand shouting, beaming aficionados from Glagmaron city. These continued to swarm like bees to see their tournament heroes—Rawl, Breen-Hoggle-Fitz (who was most pontifically distributing benedictions to everyone in hailing distance), and myself, the Collin, their hero-mythos, come to life.

I was human enough, and still young enough, so that every square inch of my bruised body was suffused with a warm and pleasant glow of self-satisfaction at this show of mass support.

Our dottles *wheeed, whooooed,* and pranced, delighted to be a part of such downright adulation. My personal charger, who had enabled me to topple the mighty prince Keilweir, was a castle mount. And his name—for dottles *were* given names— was Henery.

Henery was a male, bigger than most, heavily muscled and mentally sharp—like a Terran dog is sharp. He was also a bit of a snob. If he were humanoid, he would most definitely be a name-dropper. From time to time he would look to me possessively, prance, roll his big blue and slightly bloodshot eyes, and wave his huge doggy-dottle tail like a pennant. His fat paws matched his eyes, for they had been painted blue for the occasion.

Lackeys, I had found, were not as profuse in Camelot society as in other feudal orders. Witness the fact that prior to yesterday's dinner, Rawl and I had been left alone to take care of ourselves. Such was not the case now, however. We were very shortly being bathed and gently massaged while various oils, healing salves, and unguents were being rubbed into our bodies. This was done in a large common room beneath the castle. Apothecary bottles lined the walls, as well as various saws, knives, mallets, and whatever—the tools of the chirurgeon. The chirurgeons, lackeys, and masseurs, of course, were themselves in attendance.

This atmosphere of T.L.C. was so conducive to relaxation and sleep, that that is exactly what I did. And this time with no disturbing terror dreams from intruding Pug-Boos.

I awoke in Rawl's apartment. As before, Rawl was beside me snoring lustily. And, as before, the breeze through the stone-laced windows of the three-hundred-foot aerie was fresh, sweet, and soul-serving.

I arose and walked to the balustrade. History was repeating itself. For in the distance, I saw the prince Keilweir with his entourage, minus the sixteen dead knights. They were departing now, however, two abreast in a long line, with the prince and his ambassador to the fore. Even from a distance they seemed a dejected lot. As I watched in the swift-falling twilight, a wash of wind and rain swept the great meadow beyond the castle walls, touching the grass in such a way as to remind me of the beginnings of a squall at sea after a time of calm. . . . The prince would stop in the first village, I thought, as protection against the night and the dead-alives —or would he?

Rawl and I were ordered to the king's privy dining room to sup and to take conference. This time there was no formality; some pomp, but no ceremony.

Present were the king, the queen, the twelve lords and ladies of the realm; Fairwyn and a skinny, almost transparent young neophyte sorcerer named Ongus; a handful of hardened knights that I had not seen before; and Murie and Caroween and the two Pug-Boos.

We ate at the king's table. The hall was redolent with the smell of food; of wet flagstones and straw—all cold with the lowered temperature; of the sweet rain-washed wind which penetrated the hall to blow gently around our seated persons, pat the tapestries upon the wall, and cause the fires to roar lustily.

Murie sat directly opposite me as did Caroween to Rawl. Supping being what it was on Camelot—a literal recharging of energies so wantonly spent in brawling, arguing, and in just plain staying alive—I fell into line and began stuffing myself, too. Lord knows I needed it!

Twice we were interrupted by young, lightly armored couriers who burst in, fell to one knee, and tendered messages to the king and his lords. The atmosphere, in contrast to the festivity of the preceding night, was absolutely warlike in its tense and abrupt urgency.

The king arose to inform us of the contents of the last note. "My lords," he said. "There has been heavy fighting at Castle-Gortfin. In answer to our mirror signals the nearest garrison—in the town of Feldic—marched upon Gortfin but a few hours after the return of my daughter. The forces of my 'sister,' the lady Elioseen, were driven quickly back to within the castle walls. But this small victory cost us dearly. Indeed, the commander of our thousand, the young sir Bricht of Klimpinge, states that all this day they did but contain the enemy under siege. And that since there was little time for burial on the previous day, they were attacked last night by dead-alives. The situation is perilous."

There was a stir of alarm at this—the fact that the dead were apparently being used against us. For, though I had noted much fear of supposed dead-alives, I had yet to meet the knight or warrior who had ever seen one. I had reached the point, in fact, where I had begun to doubt the matter. But here was proof.

They fell to discussing this new event without once breaking the rhythm of knife and meat from platter to jowl. . . . Through seven courses of salads, soups, meat, and fowl, I was totally conscious of the purple eyes of my most undainty (at sup at least) princess. At times she gazed at me with the same intensity as she had used upon the first platter of succulent pasties to pass her way. I was flattered. And, since I was now fully imbued with the true Camelot spirit, I understood. I beamed fiercely back at her and she loved it, even to the point of blushing.

But yet another pair of eyes were upon me. The lord Fon

Tweel's. His stare was *not* welcome. I had yet to question him as to how he had arrived at Castle-Glagmaron while *we* wound up at Castle-Gortfin.

But time was passing, and I was acutely aware that just as I had sparked the move against Kelb the previous night, so must I force things now. There would be either a unity of purpose between the states of Gheese, Ferlach, and Marack, as opposed to Kelb and Great Ortmund, or Om would certainly prevail—and the sooner a discussion of all this, the better.

The wind had risen. It keened savagely outside and guttered the candles inside. Lackeys rushed to draw drapes over the slitted windows and to close tight the great wooden doors. I arose, wiped some kind of antelope grease from my face with a coarse napkin, and without further ado begged leave to speak.

It was granted me and I said, "Your majesty, as you well know I am new to these parts, and certainly new to court affairs and the ordering of armies. If this was not so, I would not be talking now, but would abide by protocol. But since it is true, may I beg leave to ask that we not delay one single second in approaching your neighbors of Gheese and Ferlach with offers of mediation—between the two of them—of support, generally, and of the creation of a unified fighting front to move instantly to the attack against Om in Kelb and Great Ortmund. I would ask, too, if Prince Keilweir received *proper* escort. For, since I have been given a certain task, according to your gracious daughter, I would know all of those who might chose to interfere, be they Vuuns, Yorns—or princes."

There was a rattle of laughter. The king smiled, too, and said, "Young sir, you are right in your concern. The knights of Kelb *are* escorted, even to the very borders of Kelb, though at a distance. We will know if aught transpires that does not meet our wish."

"And in the night?"

"There are ways, young sir."

"Praise be," I said. I honored them with a crossed Ormon circle. "But," I persisted, "since there is much magic about these days—of which I have truly had my share—is it not possible, considering the stakes, that dark sorcery will aid the prince Keilweir again?"

A great lord arose from his striped skin-bedecked chair. He had been introduced to me as Per-Rondin, kolb of Blin. His hand was raised to the king. Caronne nodded and Per-Rondin spoke. His voice was strong as were his features. He was Hoggle-Fitz's double in height and girth. "Young Collin," he said—and his ready smile was friendly. "You have traveled far from your dour province of Fleege with its moors, its snows, and its dark forests. I knew your father, young sir, though I remember him as a slower man than you. You honor him well. But to get to it. The ways of war are such that we oft lose much by panic and too hurried judgment; likewise, though studied countermoves are made, we cannot always foretell the movements of our enemies. You speak of magic. Well, so it has been. We cannot negate this phenomenon. So let there *be* magic!—magic on all sides. And if we are so fortunate as to have this magic work for us, we will truly thank our God—as you should thank him for his aid to you this very day. Conversely, if the magic of the cursed Kaleen prevails over ours, then we will fight him with our blood and with our hearts alone. And thus will we *still* prevail!

"We are entering into a bloody war, young sir; of a scope such as has not been seen since men first formed cities in this great world. All information brought by you, our noble cousin, Sir Rawl Fergis, and the great lord Breen Hoggle-Fitz, is substantiated. We shall decide now, with your counsel, for you have earned it, what we will do. With my lord, the king's permission, I bid you welcome to our deliberations."

Per-Rondin bowed deeply. And there was such a smattering of handclaps that, since Rawl and Fitz had both been mentioned, they stood up, too, to take their bows with me.

And then we talked and talked—and talked. Great quantities of sviss were drunk and certain wines, but not enough to boggle our minds. Most of the women left. Not so Caroween and my princess; nor the queen and two or three of the wives of the lords, including the lady Brist, wife to Lord Per-Rondin. In the ensuing discussion they proved by their brains and their courage that they were by no means mere chattels of their lordlings. The Adjuster in me welcomed this fact as a sign of health in the Fregisian body politic. . . .

The two Pug-Boos, Hooli and Jindil, sat silently watching. And there was such a feeling of well-being around us, of peace, and, yes, of *protection*, that I wondered if, perhaps it was not their doing; that this was the thing they could best provide, if one were but within their proximity—a sanctuary against evil. But I remembered Murie's abduction, and knew that it could not be . . . and yet . . .

Despite the drapes and the closed shutters we were made aware of the mounting storm without by an absolute crescendo of lashing water, causing a rumbling thunder throughout the mains of the castle. And there developed such a howling of wind as to almost prevent the exchange of ideas about our plans for total mobilization. But we persevered.

And once, between the rise and fall of the wind's howl, a voice—like Hooli's, like my own—spoke softly in my ear. "Go not to the snow-lands, Harl Lenti. For your life—go not there!" I looked instantly to the Pug-Boos. But there was nothing in Hooli's shoebutton eyes or placid, smiling mouth to tell me that it was he who gave the warning. Then the voice was gone, as if it had never been.

I was given command of a wing of the center army, which was to march immediately upon Kelb. This task I would assume upon my return from having delivered the princess to her place of sanctuary. No one suggested that I be replaced as escort to Murie—in view of the urgency of the move on Kelb—not even Fon Tweel, which I thought was passing strange. I was obviously in no position to make such a practical suggestion myself.

There would be three armies. The first, of twenty thousand men, was to advance upon Great Ortmund, with the Marackian warlords of the provinces of Keeng, Fleege, and Klimpinge in command. Breen Hoggle-Fitz, lord of Durst in Ortmund, was appointed to the council of this army, and was to reenter Ortmund with five thousand men in advance of the main forces and rouse the countryside against the false king, Feglyn. This he accepted with great gusto. The second army, also of twenty thousand men, would advance directly on Kelb. The lord Per-Rondin, of Glagmaron, would command it. Two other lords, the king, and myself, the Collin, would be his war council. It was expected that I would arrive on the scene long before the crucial battle had been joined. As this army advanced it would settle Castle-Gortfin's hash as an extra bonus. . . . Lastly, an army of thirty thousand was to march in the direction of Gheese. It would be under the direct command of Lord Fon Tweel, with a staff of three warlords of the southern provinces. Their objective would be to seek an immediate truce between the warring parties of Ferlach and Gheese, and to then direct those forces, concurrently, upon the flank of Kelb and the hordes of Om.

There were thirty thousand men-at-arms, archers, and knights in the proximity of Glagmaron at this moment. Twenty thousand of these would be assigned to the first two armies, who would then complete their muster with border troops and levies gathered along the way. The call for muster had gone out by courier and mirror two days ago, upon Murie's council with her father. Fon Tweel was to wait in Glagmaron with the remaining ten thousand until his forces were augmented to full strength by levies from the countryside.

And finally, Sir Rawl Fergis was given the unenviable job of riding on the morrow with the entourage of but one hundred knights and students—he had especially asked for some of those who had fought so bravely with us against the knights of Kelb—to Ferlach. He would act as direct emissary of King Caronne, and would petition the highly respected Draslich, king of Ferlach, to also desist in his altercation with Gheese, and to join in the final effort to drive the hordes of Om into the river-sea.

As the finishing touch to our deliberations, it was decided that the Marackian fleet, smaller than those of Ferlach or Gheese, would sail down the west coast from Klimpinge to Ferlach, to join with that country's ships in the assault. . . .

And thus did we deliberate.

And it seemed to me, while we did this, that there was no longer any starship, no Foundation—and no influences, malign or otherwise, to affect our course. When I spoke—and I spoke loud and often—I imagined myself as a lord of the house of Plantagenet, during the Terran feudal wars, about which I had studied. It was as if our world depended upon our council, our deliberations, and upon our ability to carry them out. Thus, I imagined, too, would those who planned crusades have acted and, conversely, from the Mohammedan point of view, thus would those have also done who sought courageously to defend Islam from the depredations of the heathen.

Then it was over and we retired to our quarters through corridors wet with the rain's penetration, and cold with the touch of the north wind.

Once there, Rawl said gruffly, grinning the while like an idiot dubot, "Well, I'll leave you now, sirrah! You may plague but yourself this night, with your snores. . . ."

"How so?"

His grin became almost ridiculous. "Because I seek fairer company than you, great oaf. I would remind you that you are not the daintiest of bedfellows, and," he finished slyly, "admit it. You serve me no purpose between the sheets."

"I wish you well," I said, laughing; thinking, too, that he was off, perhaps to pleasure some serving wench with his boots on. "But turn me a jug of milk," I admonished, "before you go. I'll then be reminded that you *do* serve a purpose."

He looked at me owlishly. "Well, hey and *hey* then! 'Tis, perhaps, for me to tell you, Sir Collin, that did I remain in this room you would hate me beyond all reason. I do but leave to guarantee—among other things—your undying affection."

"You speak in riddles."

"Then divine them. Good night, Sir Lenti, Sir Collin. I wish you the pleasantest of dreams, though I doubt not that that which will happen in your waking moments will be the better."

I shook my head. "Have done then. And since I see the jug already holds my sviss, I have no need of you at all."

After a quick shower and a change of clothes, he bowed out, still grinning. And, I thought, seeing him go, and showering myself with the now freezing water from the castle pipes, it was hard to believe that but ten short hours ago we had battled to exhaustion upon the field of Glagmaron. My skin felt unbruised. The shallow gash upon my forehead was well on its way to healing—a testimonial to the salves of Camelot not derived of magic but rather from her budding science. All this I pondered, then doused the candles and retired to the great fur-covered bed.

I deliberately left the windows undraped. The keening north wind in and around the aerie was of the proportions of a baby hurricane.

I loved it.

I had but clasped my hands behind my head upon the pillow when I sensed the presence of someone else in the great room. My sword hung from its belt by the bed's coping—an awkward position. I instantly flung myself toward it to draw.

"Stay your impetuous hand, m'lord!"

The voice was softly intimate—as intimate as the instant and total caress I received from the small body of Murie Nigaard as she dived from wherever she had been hiding into the welter of furs and bedclothing to seize me in an embrace that was truly awesome.

I responded in kind. It was as if all Camelot's magic, white, black, and piebald, had united for one great web of rainbows. I had experienced nothing like it. I instinctively knew that I would probably not experience its like again—except, perhaps, with Murie. Humanoid women have the ability, if they but dare to exploit it, to so weld the male of their choice to them that said male will seek no other. To say that I welcomed this fantastically warm bundle of sweet-smelling female pulchritude would be the understatement of the millennium.

Murie, all one hundred and five pounds of her, was mother-naked. Though, if one be softly furred in the most peculiar places, this may come under the heading of quasi-quasi. Whatever. I was quasi-quasi, too, and it was the kind of nakedness that dreams are made of, if one but has the imagination.

"Hey, my lord?" Murie had finally straddled me between clutches and was holding me by the ears and looking down into my eyes. "You look surprised. Did you not expect me?"

"No, I did not," I said.

I reached up to pull all that squealing, squirming, sweet-scented, soft-fleshed mystique down upon me again.

There was no moon, or moons; only clouds reflecting the strobelike flashes of blue lightning to silver the room and our faces. In all the Galaxy, I thought, there could hardly be a more romantic setting than this. I was eighteen again, and it was senior prom with the scent of girl-flesh and Venusian Kablis. . . . I was a number of things, each representative of everything "great" that had ever happened to me. Then, finally, I was again Harl Lenti, the Collin. I was a knight, a warrior, a feudal lord, a mythos come to life, so that small furry creatures such as the one I now held in my arms would continue to people the green vales and wine-dark mountains of this so-fair world of Camelot-Fregis.

I looked down into her purple eyes—she was beneath me now, held strongly against me, and holding just as strongly. "My princess," I said, "I know naught of palace dalliance. But if you were to repeat but a tenth of this—even in thought— with anyone else, I would flay, stuff, and mount you, so that you would ride forever on my dottle's rump, as Pug-Boos do. For know you well that I am the possessive type. And she who I most desire above all women, having come to this bed of her own free will, may not just leave it at her pleasure." I was only half teasing. I gripped her tighter still and buried my face in the soft curve of her neck and shoulder.

"Oh, Sir Collin." Her voice came muffled. "You think yourself possessive? I would warn *you*, sir, that the women of our family love fiercely or not at all. They choose not idly either. And when they do, the lord of their choice had best not yearn for chambermaids and bar girls, else *he* be flayed, tanned, and worked into a greatcoat for winter outings. You have my love, my lord, and that is that." At this last she reached up and covered my mouth with hers, held for brief seconds, then slipped down the length of my throat to sink her small white teeth into my shoulder.

Above my instant yell she said, "And *that* is my mark. Do you likewise upon my body, so that I may know that you love me."

I sat up aghast. "Murie," I said. "I cannot. I'm not an animal. I would not hurt you."

"Nor am I an animal, stupid oaf. But I do love you. And if you have forgotten that in these brief seconds since the making of my mark, I will do it again—and again—*until you love me.*"

And so saying she gripped me with arms, legs, and teeth, so that I was driven somewhat wild with the absolute sensuousness of it all. And we became what we truly were. And the great, fur-strewn bed was a welter of Murie, the Collin, and sundry remains of various pelts and treated skins. It was like nothing I had ever experienced. And in the end I knew, at least from one point of view, what it was to *love*. I would learn of other ways in the perilous days ahead. But of this night I learned that which few are given to know—and in the end she had her teeth-marks. So help me, Ormon, but *she had them!* And we lay back then, her curls in the curve of my shoulder, arms and legs thrown across my body, and all around us the screaming of the wind and rain and the blue-white lightning of a primal sky such as only the Furies themselves could create. . . . A fitting stage, I thought, for this welding of myself and the elfish princess from a world that was now mine, too.

We talked. We murmured nonsense. We made love. Caroween, Murie told me, as I worried one of her slightly pointed ears with lips and teeth, was even now with her cousin, Rawl. And it was because of this that he had suspected that I, too, would be so honored.

"And what of your father?" I murmured against her breast.

"That you are my chosen."

"He was not opposed?"

"Opposed?" She leaned upon a dainty elbow, her eyes but a lash's distance from my own. . . . "I would think you not of Marack, my lord. Why oppose? I am his daughter. Were I not so in fact, then it would be otherwise. But I am. And that, too, is that."

I pondered her statement. I said mildly, "But are marriage vows, at least, followed by certain ceremony? In our case, since you have arranged this joining, am I to assume you have arranged that, too?"

"In good time, my lord," she said, and kissed me. "We are at war now, however. But since all will know soon enough that you are to wed me, it will be sufficient for the moment."

"Gods!" I grinned, and she grinned back at me.

I felt just slightly off-balance, though. Without a doubt prerogatives had been used without my gainsay. I said softly again, "It would appear, my most delicious tidbit, that though my counsel is sought in war, it is not sought in matters of our personal union."

"Which is as it should be," she answered pertly. "The question of marriage is the sole province of women, plus the ordering of the household—or has this news not reached that frozen mudhole wherein you claim your birthright?"

"Whatever," I said. "One thing's for sure, and that is that my 'mudhole' will see no more dull moments." I bowed to her without getting up. "Your servant, m'lady. . . ." Then I ran

my fingers along the length of her instantly reactivated body
—and tried to hold her. "You," I exclaimed, panting, "are like
a bucket of eels."

"Eels, my lord?" She wriggled deliciously. "What are eels?"

"Small fish," I stammered. "In the north, in my province
of Fleege."

"I know not of them." She looked at me closely and stopped
her sexy squirming. "Which suggests again the matter of the
mystery in you—a thing of the Collin, that you have hinted.
My cousin, Rawl, has said that you are not wholly of this
world, though what he meant, I know not. He told this to his
love, the lady Caroween—and she to me."

"In due time," I said gruffly. "Be patient and know one
thing, which is that I do love you, and that all that I do is
a part of the love I bear for you."

She raised above me again, stared into my eyes, then seized
me in an embrace to equal all that had gone before. Finally
there were but three brief hours till the pearling of a Fregis
dawn. So I cautioned her, and wrapped in each other's arms,
we slept. . . .

She was gone when I awoke. Yet, when I met her later in
the gray and storm-lashed courtyard, she was as fresh as a
babe. Only the intimate sparkle in her eyes remained to tell me
of our night's adventure. We spoke but briefly, though she
leaned to kiss me upon the cheek before all that gathered as-
sembly—and thereby established our relationship for all to see.
She was with Caroween, which was surprising since I had
quite expected the good dame Malion to be her journey companion. But, as it turned out, the dame was sore ill, and of a
sudden, so that Caroween took her place. They were both in
light armor, dainty surcoats, and furred capes against the cold.
They looked most appealing upon their quietly kneeling dottles. The skinny sorcerer neophyte named Ongus was with
them. He, too, was dressed warmly for the journey. Other than
a bag of tricks, herbs and such, he also carried a musical
instrument consisting of a series of small pipes and a bellows.
I had heard a similar one but yesterday, upon the tournament
field. It had a strange, monotonous, and skirling noise—
somewhat hypnotic.

The great flagstoned courtyard was alive to men, mounts,
puddles of rain, and the shouts of hostlers and lackeys. I was

all business now. I had but three days to deliver Murie to her sanctuary—three days to cover four hundred miles, and three more to reach the king's army on the frontiers of Kelb. The ground-eating lope of a dottle was at twenty miles per hour, so this feat was not as impossible as it may seem.

Rawl and Hoggle-Fitz joined me in a brief inspection of our men: Rawl's hundred in one corner of the courtyard; mine in another. I had been granted but ten men-at-arms and ten students. All were a menacing panoply of leather, steel, and weapons. I matched them in grimness. Even Rawl remarked that in the dawn's light I looked most huge and black and evil. His statement seemed molded somewhat by his surprise at seeing Caroween with Murie. Indeed, since they, too, had spent the night together, I had no doubt that he had planned to keep her with him.

Griswall, a member of the king's own household guard, and a heavily bearded knight of many seasons, commanded my men-at-arms; Charney, a blue-eyed, red-furred scamp of a youth, led the students. I learned later that Charney had listed among his ten, three of his brothers. All had participated in the melee. I welcomed them, shook each proffered hand in turn. We were twenty-six in all. We had a herd of a hundred dottles, five of them burdened with foodstuffs, baggage, and the like.

There were no trumpets to hail our departure, only the muffled martial cadence of kettledrums, echoing hollowly to the padded beat of our prancing dottles' paws. The fulsome clouds lowered still further so that a most evil and penetrating mist seemed to descend upon us. I led off, with Murie at my side, down the distance between the walls and through the outer gate to the great meadow beyond. The mist was sleet, actually, akin to the cold of my own, supposed, northland. I reached across my dottle's middle—I was riding Henery—to touch Murie's hand, wondering if the snow-land to which we traveled was like the hell of the ice-world of Fen in the Cygnus system, where I had spent a most miserable six months.

Once through the portcullis and across the moat, we bid good-bye to Rawl and Fitz. We clasped hands and arms to do this, leather and armor all a'tinkling. I even felt somewhat choked up as I received the "sainted" Fitz's blessing, and wished him well in turn. After all, the chance that I would see them again soon, considering, was questionable.

Caroween clung to Rawl for the space of minutes, tearful, feminine; her natural, warlike aplomb was now worn to a nub. Hoggle-Fitz stared fiercely and paternally at the both of them, but said never a word. . . . I wondered, at that last moment of parting, about Hooli; why he was not with us. I had not asked, for I was sufficiently suspect in that area already. But still, as our dottles broke into their first long strides, I remembered the voice of last night and became obsessed with the premonition of a gathering fate wherein the web had suddenly gone awry. . . .

All that day we thundered north and west, stopping only for the four-hour, midday dottle browsing period. We crossed the Cyr three times along its sinuous course until it fell away to south and east. Some miles beyond Glagmaron city the forest began again in earnest, thick, impenetrable. At one point great rock falls lined the winding road that paralleled a tributary of the Cyr. The middle-aged knight, Griswall, led the way with his group of ten. He, like his men, was familiar with the road, having been born in those mountains bordering the plateau of the snow-lands.

With the steady drizzle, the advent of early summer, or "late spring" as some would call it, seemed premature. The rain-filled clouds were no harbingers of sunshine. Great birds flew overhead, waterfowl and predators of the winged variety, while all around us in the underbrush, outlined on wild promontories, and sometimes in the very road itself, was the fauna indigenous to Fregis. Some were sabertoothed, carnivorous, and *almost* ready to dispute our passage. Though, at the very last moment, if they were in the road, they would stand aside, or if watching us from a close deer-meadow, they would turn and disappear into the brush. One great animal resembled a Terran grizzly, but was six-limbed, as, seemingly, were most animals of Fregis. The thought caused me to wonder at the dominant humanoids with their *four* limbs; for suddenly it was something to think *about*. The "grizzly" was larger than the Terran model. He stood at least fourteen feet. He rose from the heavy grass beside a small stream to watch our passage with tiny eyes of a bright and laser red. He made no move to approach our thundering herd, though. And our dottles streamed past him with rolling eyes and bared teeth.

In the late afternoon the road wound between low hills and rocky promontories. It began to climb more steeply. Three times we passed hard-riding couriers, their dottles wild-eyed, dripping swaths of foam and sweat. Twice we passed large contingents of cavalry, archers, and footmen with heavy hardwood spears and pikelike weapons. There were at least two thousand to each contingent. Their captains saluted us gravely, bowing their heads briefly in obeisance to the princess. On one flat and rocky mass of crisp, short grass and wind-gnarled trees we found a crossroad. It led east to another road that, I knew, would meet one which would lead to my own, supposed, province of Fleege. To the west it wound down to Klimpinge province and Klimpinge city, on the shores of the western sea. One hour beyond the crossroads, and in the light of the fast-setting sun, we made our camp. Again we were ringed around with dottles against the night.

Murie and Caroween slept to themselves, though Murie came to me briefly before retiring. We leaned against the bole of a great tree, and I held her closely and we talked of Marack and of Fregis, and of ourselves and what we would do when the forces of Om were no longer on the northern shores. And once she spoke of strong sons to further our cause in distant battles. And while she talked I thought myself possessed of a veritable Valkyrie. I wondered, too, since my mink pelt—its growth had been artificially stimulated—was what it was, just what she would think of our somewhat "shorn" progeny. Then I walked her to her tent.

We—Griswall, Charney, and I—set pickets for the fires and as watchers. And in this we included ourselves. During one of my hour-long stints—it was almost the time of the false dawn and the clouds had disappeared and the second moon shone whitely—I dared to walk beyond the kneeling, sleeping dottles to a stony outcropping that overlooked the road we would take on the morrow. As I stared out along its length and then up to the fast-hurtling moon, I saw what seemed to be the great bat wings of the Vuun, skimming low, away from the mesa. Had it been here? I wondered. Settled and watching from across that silvered road? Or over there, perhaps, in that large grove? Then a slight breeze stirred and a smell of carrion, *of rotting human flesh*—I knew this because of the sick-sweet stench of it—touched briefly upon my nostrils.

My sword sprang instantly to my hand, and with never a sound, so well-oiled had I made both sheath and metal. A great boulder, half again as tall as a man, lay on the downslope of the hill. I approached it stealthily and rounded its prominence to come face to face with three creatures. They were as tall as myself, white-furred, muscular; naked, except for a leathern harness with sword and dagger. But the resemblance ended there. A single look into their eyes told me that they were what I had not believed to exist. The eyes were white-filmed, the mouths open, slack. . . . It was from these open mouths that the foulest of carrion stenches came. They were dead-alives, and they had been named correctly.

I drew a quick breath, crouched, knees flexed—and waited. Were there others in that far grove; behind the boulders strewn around? Then they advanced upon me, awkward, hideous, stumbling, pulling their swords from their sheaths with stiff and labored movements. I did not wait for their clumsy assault. In as many strokes as it took me to do it—and with an indescribable repugnance for the job—I literally slashed them limb from limb. Two final strokes and I had hewn the white arms from the last one's body. Then I cleft the head down through the shoulders to below the waist, from which there poured entrails and sundry putrescent effluvia containing a second life of maggots and yellow filth, to drench its knees and lower parts until the whole tottered and toppled. I did the same to the carcasses of the remaining two, so that, but for a few still jerky movements, they were reasonably dead a second time.

I stood apart from this moon-splashed scene of horror to find that my sword and legs were splashed with a reeking, stinking mass of pus and matter. I couldn't stand it. I backed away, retched, and gave the contents of my stomach to the ground. Were I again attacked in so defenseless a position, I would indeed be easy prey. My mind was dazed. The smell, no longer encapsulated by the cadaver containers, had reached the sensitive nostrils of the dottles some three hundred yards away, and they were up and *wheeeeing* in horror and fear.

I woodenly retraced my steps toward our circle; saw Griswall, Charney, and the others. They were armed and staring white-faced through the ring of dottles.

"Stay your weapons!" I cautioned. "There is naught to do now. Those who would walk the night are slain again. Bring me water. And bring it outside the circle, for I would not subject you to the filth of the things I have destroyed." I stood some fifty feet from the *wheeing* dottles as I talked. They brought water but hesitated to come beyond the circle— even Griswall. But Murie, who had awakened, snatched a bucket and said, "I come, my lord," and walked bravely out to me. The others sheepishly followed.

Of the fact that I truly loved her, there was no doubt; that I loved her then above all else was as true as the stars of our Galaxy. I disrobed before them, threw my clothes to the ground, cleansed my sword, my belt, and my body and walked back naked through the circle, with Murie most proudly at my side.

"The dead-alives," I announced, while one of the students fetched fresh clothes, "were brought here by the Vuun; for what purpose we can only guess—certainly not for spying since the Vuun itself has better eyes for that. Have you *seen* dead-alives before?" I asked slyly, knowing full well that they had not.

"Nay, my lord." Griswall was the first to answer. "They are passing rare. But whenever one appears it is usually to seize upon a captive to be spirited to the Dark Lands."

"This I know, except for the spiriting. I warrant that those three out there are dead-alives from Marack and not from Om. The Vuun is their transportation. They are brought to life here—as at Castle-Gortfin—by sorcery of the Kaleen. The Vuun then takes them to a place where one of ours can be captured. It is that simple. It was said last night in council that those who had fought and died *and not been buried* at Gortfin were up to fight again that night, though their weakness was such that they were but stumbling blobs of flesh. . . . Be not afraid of them," I finished bluntly, "for they are mindless, weak, so that any man here could easily carve his way through a thousand. Indeed, sirs," and I laughed, "their stench is their greatest weapon."

My arrogance was sufficient to the task. And it was a pleasure to see that Charney and Griswall and the others who, but moments before, had been terrified of something unspeakable, horrible, now frowned, chagrined, and walked out to the cadavers by the boulder to see for themselves, unafraid.

They returned, gasping for breath. And Charney said, "You are right, most noble sir, in that their greatest weapon is indeed their stink. Chivalry gains little with such opponents."

The true dawn was showing again, and with a promise of bright sun. I gave the order to break camp and prepare to march. We would breakfast, I told them—with nose held high—in some other spot, for I had, in sooth, lost all stomach for this one.

We rode out in silence and the rocky mesa changed swiftly to the lower slopes of a great range of mountains all covered with a dense forest of conifers. At breakfast, on a grassy mound by a fast-flowing stream of cold, sweet water, we talked of the Vuun and what its presence meant. And it was then that I questioned Ongus, the skinny sorcerer, as to his purpose with us.

"The key, my lord," he answered shyly. "The *word key* for the opening of the circle before the keep of the great wizard. Without it we could not enter."

I looked to Murie. "Is not the wizard informed of our coming?"

"How so, my lord?"

"Has Fairwyn no magic? No crystal balls within which to send and receive thoughts? Are there no mirror messages?"

"I know naught of crystal balls, my lord. And the snowland is a land of mists and clouds, usually, where mirrors do not work. . . ."

"Birds," Ongus put in. "We have sent a carrier bird to Goolbie. But he might not have successfully flown the distance."

"Enough," I said, and then to Griswall and Charney, "Have you truly never seen a dead-alive before?"

"My lord," Griswall replied, and he looked me squarely in the eye for doubting him. "In all my forty years I have met *none* who have seen one, let alone fought with one. No one would, of their own accord, leave the confines of a dottle circle."

"But since the dottles also fear them," I suggested slyly, though with a straight face, "why cannot these walking bladders of putrescence just walk right through a circle and cut you down?"

"But it is *written*," Charney quoted, brimming with student lore, "that no dead-alive will cross a dottle circle."

"True," I said tersely. "But it occurs to me that the reason may be other than mystic. For example, those who manipulate the dead-alives may be aware, even if you are not, that if the creatures entered the circle they would then meet their true end; for despite your fear, I warrant you would destroy it— just as those at Gortfin were destroyed. And you would find it passing simple, as Om would know full well. As agreed, other than its ability to instill terror, and thus prevail, the single weapon of the dead-alive is its stink. Now what think you of the Vuun?" (I had briefed them all the previous night as to the coming of the hundred riders.)

"The question would be," Griswall had said, "are they in pursuit? Do they lie ahead in ambush—or are they after us at all?"

Now Charney said, "It would appear that the Vuun, alone, does follow in our tracks."

Griswall said, "That makes sense. The Vuun is their 'eyes.' He has told *them* of our presence on this road. They have created dead-alives for the Vuun to take to us—in the hope, perhaps, that the creatures might succeed in a job of abduction."

I smiled.

"But there is the chance of treason, too," Charney put in. "Black betrayal. How else would the hundred riders know of our specific whereabouts, or of our purpose?"

"Do you think they seek to stampede us back to Glagmaron?" I asked softly.

"The question then is who will be in Glagmaron tonight. The king marches for Kelb. Only Fon Tweel remains in Glagmaron." Griswall's question and answer were rhetorical.

"Then"—Murie's voice came strongly above the sound of the rushing stream—"if only Fon Tweel is in Glagmaron city, I am for the snow-lands. I will not return to Glagmaron."

I think she sensed what I now knew. The others sensed it, too. Something was rottenly awry in the state of Marack. "Good sirs," I said. "The sun rises fast, and we should follow the thinking of our princess." So saying, I arose and walked her to our waiting dottles. We mounted up. I was on Henery again, Murie on a lovely female. We waited for the somewhat glum Caroween to join us, then followed Griswall's ten up the ascending mountin road.

The wind from the northeast blew strong. And when we had thundered still farther over the ever-rising path, it seemed snow-laden, with the frost of glacier and perma-ice. We rode with our cloaks raised to our eyes, and our furred caps to below our ears. The lush deer-meadows soon disappeared. We stopped in the last one for a full four hours. In this way the dottles were allowed to fully browse while we rested.

There would be no stopping at all tomorrow for the simple reason that there would be nothing to stop for. All would be ice and iron-stone; all would be bare and windswept. A reason for the limited size of our party was that, though forage was kept in readiness at the keep, it was only enough for a hundred dottles at a single entry. Other than that, they would go without food for one full day—coming and going.

I asked Murie, as we rode, to tell me something of the sorcerer Goolbie, and why he had chosen the cruel isolation of the snow-lands as opposed to the court or the Collegium. "He is old," she said, "almost two hundred years." (I would point out that a Camelot life-span is well over a hundred—the first eighty years, what with cold steel, and all that, being the hardest.) He had asked her grandfather, King Iblis, Murie explained, to create the keep of the snow-lands as a place of purification, meditation: where the great ones of the realm could seek the peace of quiet and tranquility, if so desired. He, Goolbie, sought the same thing but for different reasons. According to her father, Goolbie searched "for the meaning of it all," why magic worked, especially his own, and from whence came Ormon and the Gods.

"A most noble research," I said, "for a man to question the Gods themselves, and his own abilities." And we left it at that.

The pace was a bit slower now. From twenty miles an hour, we fell to fifteen. At one point, and for a period of two hours or more, we literally clung to the side of a great precipitous canyon from which the road had been hewn from solid granite. Below us, on the final stretch of this perilous nightmare, was a sheer drop of well over five thousand feet to a roaring, boulder-strewn maelstrom of frothing water. "A freshet"—Griswall smiled—"from the snows above."

We were silent in the last hours of the day, laboring mentally with our dottles as they pounded ahead. They would not deliberately slow their pace unless absolutely forced to. To them, it seemed that all ground was a challenge; that the distance between two points was forever to be shortened and conquered by forging dottle paws. Toward twilight I was once again mounted on Henery. And his great, smoothly co-ordinated muscles had carried me across the hump, as it were, of the crest of the pass. Great snow peaks still rose on all sides. But now, too, there was an endless expanse, a desert of snow and ice before us that seemed to go on forever.

We had brought fuel for the night. We camped and set up our cooking pots. All around us were broad patches of wind-whipped snow, hard black earth, and equally black boulders. Goolbie, I thought, had certainly chosen a most Ghast-forsaken bit of terrain to call his personal fief and keep. But, despite the piercing cold, the night was pleasant. We made a wondrous stew of gog-meat and vegetables, its aroma enhanced by our labors of the day. We sat and talked for a while, cleaned our weapons, and prepared for the morrow. I sat with my arm about Murie. Caroween had perked up somewhat, the sudden loss of Rawl put to one side. We relaxed, while in the deepening darkness our skinny Ongus played upon his pipes and bellows to produce a wild and blood-charging rhythm of notes and sound. He then recited in singsong, poetic, minstrel cadence, the saga of a great court of knights and ladies who had sacrificed themselves in gigantic battle with sundry ogres, dragons, fiends of Ghast, and warlocks in that time when the world of Camelot-Fregis was still young.

I fell asleep, being reminded of the Terran chronicler Mallory, in the question and sequence of "who smote down who, and when. . . ."

Just before I kissed Murie soundly and retired to my heavy saddle blankets—we had again put our pickets out for the night—I was pleased to see one of our first guards, a student of Charney's ten, step boldly beyond the dottle ring for at least a hundred yards to show his courage. I waited until he returned. He was grinning broadly. I grinned, too, and went to sleep.

And Hooli came! And it *was* Hooli. I know it now, though at the time, what with my mixed-up imagery of dreams, irrational thoughts, and whatever, I was not sure. Just the voice, that was my own, as before; no starship, no picnic, and no fat-fannied honey-bear floating in air with a motarboard on his head. The voice announced itself once or twice, intruding like a candle's flicker: "Collin! Collin! Beware again. . . ! You are alone and there is great danger, and I cannot help you. Turn back! Turn back for your life's sake!"

I awoke again and, as before, in a sweat, trying to string the words together as they had come to me. Had it indeed been Hooli? If so, why had he not appeared as strongly as before? Was it rather a manifestation of Om—such as that moon-gibering hysteria of the previous bout? If so, did Om wish to drive me back to Glagmaron and Fon Tweel? Conversely, if it was really the Pug-Boo, did he, indeed, wish me to withdraw from the protection of the sanctuary offered by Goolbie? Why? I woke Charney, Griswall, Murie, all of them. I ordered everyone to sleep with chain-mail shirt and weapons at the ready, and I gave them no explanation. I asked, too, that each man sleep by a single saddled dottle, and that Murie and Caroween sleep next to me. I was curt, taciturn in my orders, so that even Murie frowned. We slept fitfully again, rolled tightly in our fur blankets. This time there were no dreams.

We awoke to a slow-moving wind, raw and bone-piercing. We were all glum, silently preoccupied with our gear and our saddle-cups of sviss. It was as if a spell had been cast upon us. I finally managed a smile for Murie, and she one for me, and that was the extent of it. We mounted, and once again were off.

And now the road, if one could call it that, was one freezing monotony of bleak ice and rock-hard earth. The dottles set a truly mile-eating pace, as if to make up for the delay in the climbing of the mountains. Early morning had seen bright sunshine. By noon clouds had gathered. We halted briefly to heat sviss and to mix hot snow-water with honey as a treat and an instant energy jolt for the dottles. We rested for minutes, then went on. I was quite sure by now, and the others concurred in this, that there was neither pursuit nor ambush in the offing; concomitantly, since there had been nothing behind, nor along the way, the chance of anything ahead seemed small.

The terrain, as stated, was generally flat, but with great snowcapped peaks always to the right and left, and to the rear. This flatness, however, did not exclude an occasional hill over which the road passed. To either side, too, there were sometimes low-lying hillocks of stone and snow, and with here and there an ice-locked gully.

It was late in the afternoon when we mounted the rise of a last hill. For on the other side, almost at the epicenter of a mile's square, shallow basin, we sighted the keep of Goolbie, the great sorcerer. It was still a few miles distant. But even in this camouflaged stillness of stark whites and blacks, we could see that it was by no means small.

It was well engineered of stone and mortar. It had a great wall, a drawbridge, portcullis, and gate. Above and beyond the wall two towers arose. Upon one of these flew the blue and white banner—strewn with an abracadabra of cabalistic signs —that was the chosen heraldry of Goolbie. A haze of blue smoke hovered above the towers. We assumed by this that Goolbie and the Pug-Boo, Pawbi, were alive and well on stone mountain.

We drove ahead with the clouds falling lower and random snowflakes twisting cottonlike through the now still air. The dottles had began a running prance again. They sensed rest, forage, and warmth, and stretched their six pairs of thumping legs accordingly.

Since we had come over the slight rise precipitously, we could not tell if Goolbie's pennant had been run up specifically to greet us, or whether it had been there all along. Five hundred yards from the raised drawbridge—it, too, spanned a gully like the one at Glagmaron—we were forced to halt. Griswall had recognized the two large stones, similar to Terran menhirs, which stood up-end, facing each other across the road. And beyond these, according to Ongus and he, we could not go without the *words*.

I held up my hand, moved instantly to the fore, and to the utter horror of Ongus, stepped deliberately between the two stones, touching a stone of my belt as I did so. I felt what could be likened to a magnetic field in that the metal of my mailed shirt heated instantly with resistance. The stone registered a plus category. I withdrew and put my arm back into the field, sans any metal. I then experienced a mild shock, which I knew would be far more intense had I not warped the field slightly with my belt's stone. On either side of the menhirs the effect was the same. So, satisfied that Goolbie had created a magnetic field of no mean proportions as a protective device against intruders, I then withdrew. It was notable that, though the road led to the castle and beyond, a side road made a perfect half-circle to the far side, paralleling, I surmised, the actual periphery of the field.

I returned to the others. Murie and Caroween were smiling. They had long since ceased to wonder at my audacity. My men were grinning, too. Only Ongus remained somewhat miffed.

I nodded and he stepped forward to the double menhirs. He clasped his hands, over which were draped a string of opaline beads, and began to chant. I listened intently, noting that the chant had a pronounced staccato rhythm. He did it once. He did it twice. He did it three times; though I thought he had actually cracked the field on the first time. He looked awfully young and intense as he stood there muttering. I thought, too, that his sorcery, linked finally with Ormon, as all magic is to some deity or other, gave him a feeling of power; of control, such as his slight body and almost feminine gestures could not gain for him in any other way.

"Praise be!" I said loudly and suddenly, as Ongus returned to mount his dottle. "Now let us be to yon friendly shelter. For though we no longer fear dead-alives—and any of those would most certainly freeze solidly here—yet would I like warm food, rest, and baths for my lady, and for us all. . . ." So saying, I leaned smartly across my saddle and kissed Murie's cheek as a sign that the journey was well done. We had only to go those last few hundred feet.

A light swirl of snow swept gently across our path, but quickly subsided to intermittent flakes. I ordered shields to the fore as we cantered two-by-two, in cadence, so as to present the usual Marackian military splendor and readiness for battle. For we *were* a military guard. Griswall led out his ten. Then Murie, Caroween, and I to the center, with myself in the lead. After me, shields hugged tight to furred cloaks, came Charney and his students.

As we approached the walls, the bridge across the gully dropped, snapping icicles with brittle, glasslike *pops* in the still air; the portcullis raised, the double-gates opened, and we set up a cheer.

We streamed across the bridge and entered upon a courtyard that, though large, was still less than a tenth of the size of Glagmaron. We bore to the right keeping close to the inner wall, moving toward the entrance to the main hall from which the lights of many candles shone, since the doors were half open. Without, it was still daylight, though dusk was fast falling; within, what with the clouds, it would be darksome indeed. Halfway to the entrance—and we riders were all within the courtyard now—the great gates slammed shut and the portcullis rattled down to its teethed position: this with our herd of unmounted dottles still outside.

At that very moment, I, like the others, instinctively halted my forward movement. In our few brief seconds of entry one thing was certain: no single soul had come forward to greet us, and the slamming of the gates seemed done by unseen hands. We turned our backs to the wall and faced toward the entrance to the keep. I motioned to Griswall and that hoary knight stood high in his stirrups and bellowed: "Ho! Castellan! Lackeys! Great Sorcerer, Goolbie! Is this the manner in which you greet your princess? Step forth, and *now!* For we are weary and sore in need of sustenance and roof!"

His voice echoed above the metallic *snick-snack* of broadswords plucked from their sheaths at my signal. In the immediate and continuing silence I also ordered all to dismount, upon which we sent our dottles with whacking rump pats to the protection of the arch of the gates. A Fregisian custom is not to have gentle dottles slaughtered needlessly. . . .

And there we stood and waited, all shields to the fore. We drew close in a tight line in that cold and ice-bound courtyard.

Then, like wraiths, beyond the fall of sporadic snowflakes, there appeared a group of warriors to our left and from behind an arch across the yard. Simultaneously a second group moved forward from the protection of a similar arch to our right. Then the great doors of the hall's entrance were thrown fully open and there issued forth a company of heavily armored men. They ranged themselves across the broad steps facing us. The deep breathing of my twenty-two warriors at this ghostly challenge was a thing to hear. Our silent adversaries stood quietly. Great Yorns were with them. This I could tell, despite the fact that features and bodies were, at best, indistinct.

Murie and Caroween, swords also drawn, thrust forward on either side of me to join our line. But I instantly thrust them back to stand with Ongus, who was now fingering his set of pipes and frowning. Sweat stood out upon his pale forehead. I said to Murie, who angrily pushed back against my restraining arm, "Nay, my princess. If all this be what I think it is, the battle will eventually come to you, never fear! For there, finally, are the one hundred riders—*and more!* And we are but twenty-three. So hold back, and now! And you, my lady Caroween, guard her, as is your vaunted prowess."

We, our line of twenty-three, shuffled closer, forming a half-circle around the two maids and the sorcerer. Then the silent company of warriors before the entrance parted to allow two others through.

Both were resplendent in heavy mail and flashing, jeweled swords. One strode before the other and stopped at twenty paces from me. I was not at all surprised to see that it was the prince of Kelb with his ambassador.

"Greetings, oh mighty Collin," the prince said loudly and sarcastically. "We meet again. I to collect my bride-to-be so that Marack will then join with Kelb; you to pay the price of insolence. . . . If you surrender the princess now, sir, we, on my honor, will grant you a quick death. If not—and remember, in battle you risk the princess, too—when taken, you and yours will wish for death a thousand times before you die."

Murie's sibilant whisper came instantly to my ear. "Do not surrender me, my lord, for I would die with you; and if taken I would end my own life. Trust him naught in any way."

But I sought time and knowledge. His men drew nearer and I could see that a goodly quarter of them were Yorns. I called out sharply, "Stay! All! Or you will meet your deaths before your appointed time. I will speak now with your master —this boasting traitor to true men. . . . Hey, now," I said directly to the black-browed prince, while a smattering of chuckles ran down our line. "I take it Vuun passage brought you here; perhaps with only remnants of your entourage, since I see that though the original hundred riders are here, this is not true of yours. . . . Now tell me: Where is the sainted sorcerer, Goolbie, and his familiar, the Pug-Boo, Pawbi? And where, too, are the retainers of the castle? Before I die—if die, I must—I would have knowledge of how the magic of the dark Kaleen did prevail against that of Goolbie."

The slowly encroaching line had halted upon my ringing command. They looked now to their leader. Their numbers were evident. There were one hundred and fifty men and Yorns arrayed against us. The prince's features, while I talked, grew blacker still, assuming a Ghast-like look. And he seemed suddenly not the same man as had appeared at the council hall of Glagmaron. He seemed possessed.

"The magic of your sorcerer," he shouted, spittle flying from the corners of his mouth, "was powerless before that of Om and the Kaleen." He seemed to grow visibly in stature when he said this and his voice had the ring of insanity. His eyes, too, I thought, flashed fire. . . . "Just so were the powers of the wizards of my father and of Feglyn also brought to naught. You ask of the castle retainers . . ." He half turned to his warriors who then joined him in what I assumed was a mutually shared joke, in that they all roared with laughter. "Know you, you sorry oaf, that the three you destroyed the other night were but a part of the castle's fifty retainers who, but for poor timing on our part, would *all* have been upon the spot to do *then* what we do *now*. Our regret is that even the Vuun, who waits in yonder stable, is not sufficient carryall to hoist an army. And of the Pug-Boo, Pawbi? Where else do 'sainted' Pug-Boos go, who are but a form of rodent after all? To holes stupid sir—to holes and away, and that is that. If he were here, and if you lived, you would no doubt have time to find him. But since you will not, you will not. And that, too, is that. . . . Enough! Will you surrender the princess?"

I stared straight into his eyes for the space of seconds,

looked quickly then to right and left and back to him again, and said loudly in the crisp air, "I will *not*, sir!"

I had caught Griswall's and Charney's eyes. During all the shouts and threats, except for a first long sigh, then the deep breathing of a warrior entering battle, they and the others had not flinched. They stood stoutly, legs apart, well grounded, with room on either side to swing: a solid shield wall. I continued, louder still, baiting them: "So come all, sirs and gentle Yorns. But know this well: We do not ask for quarter —*nor will we give it. . . .*"

My bold statement had its designed effect, for some in the now advancing line hesitated, and some fell back. To face an outnumbered and terrified enemy is one thing; to face potential berserkers who are absolutely not afraid to die is another. It was then that Prince Keilweir decided for them. He turned, faced them, whirled his sword around his head just once, and screamed, "On them! On them now! Or you shall suffer such a fate at the hands of Om that death itself would be a thousand times more pleasant. On them! On them *now!*"

Only thirty paces separated us. It took but three seconds for them to cross it. Instantly, all was a hellish maelstrom of swords, shields, and clanging armor. I cleaved my first man's shield in half, hacked his surprised head from his squat body. I whirled then, full circle for added sword weight, and caught my first great Yorn square on the shoulder, and cut him to the heart. Not pausing, even for a single breath, I plunged still forward, my sword a glittering sweep of absolute death for anyone within my reach. For I knew full well that could I but achieve what I sought—an instant and deadly fear of me —my men who fought for their very lives would not only take heart, but might even sense a possibility for victory, far-fetched as that may seem.

I killed ten men in as many seconds—and saw the entire Kelbian line fall back before our swords in abject horror. In all, twenty of theirs had been slain, and but two of ours. Their charge had been hysterical; our defense the cold calm of hate. Griswall had slain two men; Charney, a Yorn, pulling his sword from the creature's throat even as the others withdrew. My lusty students and warriors had accounted for the other seven—and more, since severed limbs and great gobbets of blood remained upon the flagstones to tell of wounded who would not fight again.

I pursued our advantage.

I stepped ten paces out before my shield line and yelled a personal challenge—knowing that our opponents were still men and Yorns of *Camelot,* and therefore conditioned by their very manhood to respond accordingly. I then killed five more. The first, the ambassador of Kelb himself, when I beat his shield to his knees and with one lightening blow cut him in half at the waist. A second knight, who charged straight forward blindly, was dispatched with a simple, iron-hard chop. My third opponent was a Yorn, of more intelligence and skill than most. It availed him naught. I treated him as I did the second opponent; I shortened him by both legs, so that he toppled over and filled the courtyard with his bellowing. The last two came at me together, dazed by their own temerity. I killed them both so quickly that I surprised myself. They had not the heart for it. Their arms and legs were leaden with their fear. I took no pleasure in their slaughter. Then no more came forward. The Prince of Kelb stood back to watch me, white-faced, trembling with hate and anger. My men, emboldened, also challenged. One student was answered, as were Griswall and Charney: each killed his man. And the space on the flagstones to our front ran crimson with blood. Only the torches gave us light now, for the sun was almost set.

"Come, my sweet Keilweir, prince of Kelb," I yelled, thinking to lure him out against his better judgment. "Come taste the magic of the Collin's sword which defies you and calls you coward!" But he would not come. Indeed, at no time did he actually enter battle, but rather stayed behind his line to urge the others on.

At a signal, they doused the torches and charged again. Their onslaught, despite their superior numbers, was one of desperation now. For, psychologically, *we* were superior and acted so, whereas *they* were sore afraid. The second assault was a fantastic melee of grunting, sweating, hewing, howling men and swords and shields and armor. Again I killed to right and left in the half-light, as did my stalwarts. Once I slipped in a reeking mess of blood and entrails; heard a shout from the enemy who charged over what they thought was my fallen body. But I arose mightily and cut down those who had made it beyond me—all but one, who had seized Murie, dropping his shield to do so. I need not have feared for her. For simultaneously with Murie's shortsword to his heart, my other Valkyrie, Rawl's shield-maiden, Caroween, drove her sword, with both hands, straight between his eyes, so that it stood out a hand's-breadth beyond his skull.

While we fought I heard Ongus's pipes. The bellows began suddenly, at first low, then rising quickly to a shrieking skirl so that the very wildness of the music set our blood afire and lent a rhythmic cadence to our blows. We hacked, slashed, and butchered until the bodies around us looked like a charnel house. There were so many upon the stone that I gathered my remnant, formed a circle with Murie, Caroween, and Ongus in the center, and moved out across the courtyard.

There then began a thing that passes all belief. Two of the hardened veterans that followed Griswall—and we were but twelve now, with four of Griswall's men and five of Charney's still standing—began the death chant used only when some great warrior is borne to his grave. They chanted for themselves, I knew. And, considering the circumstances, they had earned the right to do this. We, all of us, picked up the hoarse, soul-smashing beat of the words—"*A*-la-la-la! *A*-la-la-la! *A*-la-la-la!" And over it all came the wildly shrieking, screaming, skirling, maniacal pipes of Ongus.

We cut our way through them and back again. We killed till our arms and armor and surcoats were literally drenched with blood. We marched through them again and again, hacking and slaying—we drove full around the inner circle of the courtyard and none stood against us. . . . "*A*-la-la-la! A-la-la-la! *A*-la-la-la!" And the accompanying skirl—always the skirl. We crossed the flagstones, mounted the steps to the very entrance, and came down again. And the snow fell, and the torches, relighted, dimmed so that, finding it more difficult to see, we slaughtered the wounded, re-killed the dead, and destroyed the living alike. We were no longer human.

They ran from us and we sought them out and killed them. They bore down upon us screaming their fear—and we hacked them to the ground, those Yorns and men of Kelb. Until finally, when there seemed no one left alive within the court-

yard, we paused in its very center and leaned upon our bloodied, steaming weapons.

There was a great stillness. There had *been* a stillness,
really. For our chant had ceased some time ago, and the
sound of Ongus's pipes had died. The last minutes had seen us
kill silently, horribly, with the detachment of cold fury. . . .
The snow fell gently as we gasped and panted until our hearts
slowed, until we were once more in possession of ourselves.
But four torches placed in niches remained to illuminate that
carnage, that abattoir of the courtyard of Goolbie's keep.

Prince Keilweir and eight men were all that survived of the
one hundred and fifty who, but a short hour before, had so
confidently sought to take our lives. They stood in sheer
terror now, huddled upon the steps before the great hall.

And we? Though conscious of a thinning of our ranks, I
had had no time, or reason, to look before. I did so now. Griswall was alive. So Charney. But both were sorely wounded. Of
Griswall's men, *all* were dead; of Charney's, only one red-
headed brother named Hargis was on his feet, plus a troll-like
student-warrior named Tober. Tober, squat and heavily muscled, now leaned upon an ax. When I looked at him he
winked and whispered hoarsely, *"Now* are we indeed safely
arrived, Sir Collin. And I would take that bath and rest we
spoke of, and eat my fill."

I nodded, mutely.

Our piper Ongus was no longer with us. He lay across the
courtyard, skinny figure in monkish garb. His still white fingers clutched the now silent bellows and pipes. The bellows,
like his very heart and body, had been pierced with many
sword thrusts. And finally I looked down to see a fierce-eyed
Murie Nigaard, whose shield still linked with that of the read-
head Caroween. Murie's small sword was, and had been, at my
left side. It, too, was red with blood. They had been a part of
our "circle" in our last charge, and I knew it not. I thanked
whatever gods that watched over strong-willed, stubborn fe-
males that they were still alive.

My single mistake was my last mistake. And it was simply
that in pausing now instead of dispatching them all, we gave
Keilweir, prince of Kelb, time to do that which he could not
do before. . . . Perhaps he could have, on second thought.
But there had been this to say him nay: If he had made a

plea to the Kaleen for help while he still had thrice fifty warriors at his call, the shame would have been too much. But now, indeed, when all were dead, it was not so.

And I stood stupidly—yes, *stupidly*—drugged with the smell of death around me, and let it happen.

He said his *words!* He screamed them aloud before my very eyes, and I made no move until it was too late, until there came a thrumming in the air and the first touch of numbness to my body. I knew instantly that all that had been won was lost, and that the magic of the Kaleen, if not opposed, would bring my death. But how oppose? The others, just as I, now knew it, too. They, with Murie, looked to me with frozen horror.

I had no choice. I pressed the useless stud of emergency contact upon my belt, though I knew full well that unless the *Deneb-3* was directly overhead there was no chance—and damned little if it was. I mentally shouted across the void: "Ragan! Kriloy! Ragan! Kriloy!" But there was no answer. I knew with a fast-sinking heart that there would be none. I cursed the fact that the powers that lay within my belt were useless. I could not destroy—for I would first *be* destroyed.

And then, in the very second of the first needles of paralysis, the weak but steady voice of Hooli—or his facsimile—came to me. "Be not afraid, Harl Lenti. You will not die here. You will lose the princess, for in that I cannot help you. But neither you nor those now living will die here."

I closed my eyes, breathed deeply, then opened them again. Then I echoed the words of Hooli, softly, briefly, to the others—not fully believing, not fully disbelieving. It was simply that I had no other recourse. But they believed me! And a measure of peace came to the stricken features of Griswall and the students. And as great thunder rose and blue-white lightning flashed to signal the absolute arrival, the presence of the untoward, the unexpected, I had time to look into Murie's terror-filled eyes and say with the slowness of near paralysis, "Whatever happens, be not afraid. For if I live and I am with you, I will win. And if I am not, and live—I shall come to you. Wherever you are, I shall come to you. Remember that."

Tears sprang to her eyes and her lips moved. And though I could no longer hear, I knew that they formed the words:

116

"I do believe you, my lord—and I will wait." And I was satisfied.

And now all the castle courtyard with its dead and its blood was filled with a strange and unreal blackness. It was as if a shroudlike, ebony patina lay over all. Black figures moved toward us, the men of the prince of Kelb. And through the great arch to the left of the massive keep came the Vuun, dragging its ponderous, stinking hulk, its leathern wings held tight to its hairy sides. As it moved across the bodies of the slain, its monstrous head, with reddened eyes like the pits of Best itself, turned slowly this way and that. And our craven dottles, hiding within the dubious protection of the arched passage to the portcullis, screamed and moaned their terror.

We lay where we fell, Griswall, Charney, Tober, Hargis, and I. And the prince and three others lifted the bodies of Murie and Caroween and carried them to the Vuun. The four remaining Kelbian warriors approached us, swords drawn.

So now, I thought, *we shall truly know the proof of this proverbial "pudding." For either I hear voices and am insane, or I hear A voice, and am sane. And If I am sane, then I must indubitably have a date in time with a certain miserable Pug-Boo*. I thought this, for at the moment I cared not *who* or *what* the Pug-Boo was—or what his role, if any, in the unraveling of the skein of fate of Camelot-Fregis. I knew only that if he did have the power—and still allowed my princess to be taken—then indeed we had a date in time. . . .

I had noted that when Keilweir and the others carried Murie and Caroween to the Vuun, the very act of contact caused their movements to become somewhat sluggish, as if contaminated by the spell of Om. So it was with those who sought our lives—but more so.

My would-be executioner—and he still stared fearfully at me—had thrust his trembling sword toward my throat. But it touched me not. In his very closeness to me his movements had become awkward, weak, without control, so that his weapon was like a straw in his hand and could harm nothing. I doubted that he could successfully part my hair with it. So was it likewise with the others.

They shouted back to the prince, their voices trembling, that the magic of Om was truly great in that the enchantment reached out to touch them, too.

"Then leave them," the prince screamed, "for they will be long dead of cold ere ever strength returns. Come! We must not tarry longer."

At that the great Vuun slowly spread his leathern wings, which when fully expanded measured two hundred feet or more. Those who would have killed us left and ran to him, and climbed the webbed harness around his middle, to which the others clung and to which Murie and Caroween were tied.

And it literally leaped into the air, a full hundred feet or more before the first thunderclap of monstrous wings seized upon the leaden air to drive it skyward. . . . Then all was quiet.

The snow fell and the black patina waned and died. I wondered if the prince of Kelb had not been right in that we would soon freeze to death in the now bone-biting chill. We could not even whistle for the protective warmth of dottles, which were clearly peeking at us from their archway. No doubt they thought us dead.

And then, within the space of the opened doors of Goolbie's keep, a small figure appeared. The candle, torch, or firelight from within outlined him perfectly where he stood: small, brown-furred, inoffensive. It was the Pug-Boo, Pawbi—a mirror image of Hooli. And as he casually walked toward us and the tingling nerve paralysis waned, I thought, *You little bastard. You miserable, fat-fannied cowardly little bastard. . . .*

And that, for the moment, was the end of it, for suddenly I, and the others, too, were encompassed in a veritable aura of well-being and encroaching Lethe, bringing clouds of relaxed "goodness." But before I fell into line and accepted it completely, I had time to hear the Pug-Boo's voice inside my head. He said bluntly, "You're not so smart yourself, you know. Indeed, in my book you're something of an idiot. . . ."

It took but seconds for release from the sorcery of the Kaleen of Om. The accompanying memory lapse was negligible; the therapy, excellent. It was as if we had awakened from a long sleep, refreshed, rested—and famished.

We arose, the five of us, from the bloodied flagstones, to

stare curiously, almost in awe, at each other. For we knew what we had accomplished, and that now there was a bond between us such as few men would ever know. We grasped hands, gave each other the arm-to-shoulder simile of the Terran embrace. Words would come later. The smell of blood, despite the cold, still lay heavy upon our nostrils.

Then we whistled the wide-eyed, skittish—they had thought us dead—dottles to us, retrieving our saddlebags and furred cloaks. Henery trembled when I touched him and he would not meet my eyes. Dottles most definitely possessed a much higher intelligence quotient than most animals. But though they had the average destrier's modicum of courage, to face a Vuun, or the carnage all around us, was something else again.

I gave Henery a friendly pat on the rump to help assuage his guilt. Then he trotted off with the others to the warmth and food of the stables. The muscular Tober offered himself as dottle-warden. He held them in the courtyard until he had opened the gates so that the remainder of our herd could join them.

In the hall we found tables laid for a feast. And indeed, such would have been the case had we simply surrendered our throats to the fal-dirk and allowed the princess to be taken without a struggle. Our coming had caught them at the very moment of dinner, for the table groaned with still warm tureens of gog-stew, vegetables, bread, and sviss. . . .

We staggered then to the great room of the Chirurgeons, masseurs, and gnostics—and found what we had hoped for: baths with heated water from great ceramic cisterns. We soaked, bathed, and tended each other's wounds. Mine were a shallow gash across right forearm and shoulder—our armor was slashed, torn, and otherwise in sad shape—and a deep sword thrust through the thigh muscles of my left leg. It was just now beginning to stiffen. The soaking, the mutual massaging, and the salves and unguents—plus, I am convinced, some of the Pug-Boo's juggling about with our cell structure and blood chemistry—did wonders for all of us. Tober and Hargis had fleshwounds like myself. Not so Charney and Griswall. Besides bleeding from a dozen gashes each, they had also sustained a number of dangerous sword thrusts: Charney, through chest and body; Griswall, a deep thrust to midriff, and an ax bite to sever the shoulder muscles of his left arm.

. . . We were dexterous indeed with gut and needle. No seam-stress, I thought, had ever sewn a neater line than I in putting Griswall back together; this after all cuts had been cleansed, treated, and salved. Neither of the two complained of internal bleeding—only of a soreness, which was to be expected. And again, I thought, *This is the Pug-Boo's doing*. Since, if it were not, both of them would be well on the way to being dead by now.

The proof of the pudding here, I think, was that after these attentive and thorough ablutions we went straight to the hall and quite deliberately sat down to table to eat our fill.

There were three draped and fur-strewn chairs at the center table which, I thought, had doubtless been the seats of the Prince of Kelb and his favorites. Pawbi, the Pug-Boo, now lay on his back in the seat of the center chair. His little round feet were draped over one arm, his head against the other; his little raccoon-teddy-bear arms were folded across his fur-dimpled belly—and he was sound asleep.

Tober, coming from the stables, made a point of brushing snow from his surcoat so that we would know that a storm now raged without. He quickly returned from the baths to join us. We continued to eat in silence. I had the most pe-culiar sensation, as the warm stew entered my belly, of being recharged with energy. It was as if my stomach and sundry auxiliary organs were miraculously converting the gog-meat to "instant blood."

After that we retired to the fire-blazing warmth of an ante-room, replete with fur-blanketed couches. We built up the fire with dottle briquettes and then, without further ado, and regardless of the fact that the fire might die so that the cold of the storm would penetrate each nook and cranny of our retreat, we slept.

I awoke a number of hours later. I knew this, for though it was still dark beyond the heavily draped windows, the fire had been replenished more than once. Indeed, the stack of dottle briquettes had dwindled considerably. I felt possessed of a fantastic euphoria of well-being. The fire, my relaxed state, the added warmth of the sleeping furs, the knowledge that we had survived and that our myriad wounds were as pinpricks in the rapidity of their healing—all served to enhance this feeling. Then I thought of Murie and what I must do; though, indeed, my thoughts had never left her. I had made no idle promise. I still had the lifeboat from the *Deneb-3* hidden at the spot where I had first met them on the road. True, it had been damped from temporal space. I had but to say the numbers aloud—Hey! Ah, hah! the numbers—the words—the *words!* Hey! and hey again. . . . Sleep had *indeed* cleared my brain! I had, perforce, found Camelot's Rosetta Stone, and more, perhaps. And now in effect, and for sure, Kelb, Vuun-land, the Kaleen himself—whoever, in fact, held the princess Murie Nigaard and the lady Caroween in thrall—would have a visitor, and soon.

My newfound knowledge spurred me to instant action. I sat up on the couch, thrust out my sword-pierced thigh to find it not so stiff at all, and stood up. I tested the leg. Good! There would be no problem there. The sleeping couches of my companions, illuminated by firelight only, for we had doused our candles and our oil lamps, were still occupied.

We had changed to fresh, warm clothing after bathing and dressing our wounds, so that I was fully dressed now. I reached for my cloak, drew it tight around me, attached sword and scabbard to belt, and silently left my companions to continued, healing sleep.

In the hall and in the center chair at the great table, Pawbi was now wide awake. I marched directly forward to confront him across the boards. I said deliberately, "I would visit the rooms of Goolbie, the great sorcerer. I would see the place where he died."

Pawbi merely stared at me.

"No more games, you little bastard." I grasped my sword's haft. "I would visit Goolbie now!"

Pawbi then leaped to the flagstones and rushes, where he remained on all fours, though I knew he could just as easily walk erect. For minutes he darted this way and that, as a puppy would, or a kitten with a plaything. He even stopped once to worry a gog-bone, staring stupidly up at me over knobbed protuberances. I simply waited.

Then suddenly he stood up and left the hall. I followed. We went by a narrow passage directly to the south tower where we climbed a spiral stone stair without handrails to the very top of its hundred-foot height. The room we entered was small, round, with two windows, open now to the chill of black night and white storm. The room, or study, included a sleeping couch with furs, a desk, a chair, a table, and sundry shelves with all the paraphernalia of the practicing warlock, the sorcerer, the alchemist. Other shelves around the interior of the walls were lined with books.

And there was Goolbie!

He lay where he had fallen, beneath the eerie dark south window. His corpse was blackened, twisted. He looked as if he had been hit with a hundred thousand volts. The room still stank of ozone.

I wasted no time. I had none to waste, and Goolbie helped. The information I sought was a part of Goolbie's treasure: the last thing he had touched before being blasted by the Kaleen—his Great Book. His findings. His conclusions and summations.

It lay now upon the table, opened to the very page of his last entry. I risked laser heat from my belt to light two lamps and to get a fire going. I did this in Pawbi's presence. There was no time for tedious flint and steel and shavings. He had seated himself upon Goolbie's couch and his eyes had slitted; he dozed.

I pulled my cloak around me and settled to the contents of Goolbie's book.

He had given it a grondoise title, typical of the times. It was something like: *A historee and an encyclopeedee of the Fregisian world and the inhabitants thereof; and the Two Lands and the Great Water. And all that otherwise therein do dwell and do have converse and effect, one to the other—plus the Gods and the things of magick and from whence it comes. . . .*

Goolbie was, without a doubt, Camelot-Fregis's first librarian, first true encyclopedist, and first true "Webster," since, unlike the few Fregisian notes or signs I had read to date, his spelling had some consistency.

He had divided his great book into what he presumed were pertinent and specific sections. The sections were subdivided to points of information in alphabetical order. Each subdivision remained incomplete, however, indicating that he was still adding to everything.

I spent the remaining time between black night and pearling dawn studying Goolbie's work. I journeyed through his eyes and thoughts, to Gheese, Ferlach, the Seligs of the river-sea, the great jungles, and beyond those far Dark Lands—to the world of Om. The two great continents, north and south, which spiraled around the water-world of Fregis-Camelot, were landmasses to be considered. Marack and the countries to the north ranged three thousand miles from snowcap to river-sea tropics. The sea—or section of the total ocean dividing the two continents—was another three hundred to five hundred miles in width, with a myraid of islands dotting its expanse. Then came the two lands of the southern continent's northern shores, Seligal and Kerch, each a thousand miles in length and breadth. They were mostly jungle. Beyond them were the savannahs, the mountains, the moorlands and tundras of Om. . . . From the river-sea to the southern pole, another three thousand miles could be counted.

The history of Fregis was the history of its wars and of its trading ships: most of this but recent, in the last thousand years. Like most worlds of plus-ten sentients, it was most difficult to spearate myth from fact and Goolbie's depiction of things was a most wonderful admixture of both. . . . Had Om always been the center of evil? No. Only in the last three hundred years or so. Men of the north had been to Om; those of Om had sailed to the north. The river-sea itself precluded, at least in the past, any truly large-scale war. Cities dotted the lands of Om, Seligal, and Kerch, just as they dotted Ferlach, Kelb, and Gheese, and the island empire of the Seligs. Most all, at one time or another, had been raided by war parties, fleets, and armies, so essentially all knew of each other as either the looter or the looted. Only Marack and the lands of the north, however, had shown the first faint signs of a socioeconomic evolutionary process—the Collegiums and the rising tradesmen and guildsmen. Beyond the river-sea there was little or none of this. And each time such possibilities arose—philosophers creating schools of discourse; artisans going beyond the accepted craftswork: daring to invent, to explore, to indulge in primitive research—*all* was destroyed. The god, Ormon, was but one of many in Seligal and Kerch. But in Om itself there ruled the living god, the Kaleen, seen by no one; administered to only by his priesthood and the subordinates of his governing class, themselves kings and princelings and petty lords. . . . The Kaleen ruled from the Dark Lands, so named, according to Goolbie, because of the black earth, moors, fens, and mists of its great rolling hills and deep valleys. The Kaleen ruled in Hish, city of silence, city of priests, of warriors, of slaves; wherein all that was planned for Om and Fregis was brought to fruition, and where the thoughts of the Kaleen prevailed above all else.

Despite Goolbie's reference to the cities of the world of Fregis, imparting to the gentle reader a picture of a great and metropolitan world, such was not the case. I knew this better than he, for I had seen the greater part of it. Fregis-Camelot was simply a water-world of two great continents, each with but a few million humanoids at best, and each a generally savage, unexplored, and primitive world of endless forests, mountains, and dark rivers. The great cities of Goolbie's book were, like Glagmaron of Marack, populated at most with fifty thousand people. And if a dozen of these existed, inclusive of Hish in Om, all else were villages, seacoast and river-mouth habitations, dependent upon trade and a minimum of agriculture in the hinterland.

All below the river-sea were controlled by Omnian warriors and Yorns, plus the dead-alives of the priesthood, and a black pall of death-dealing magic—*which I now knew was but the adroit manipulation of the planet's magnetic field.*

For how did Goolbie handle this fact of Fregisian magic—Omnian or Marackian? " 'Tis a thinge," he wrote, "of sounde. For if one do not saye the words aloude, the effect of the witcherie is not sooth—'twill come to naught. . . ."

He had truly hit upon the secret. For, as I myself now knew, other than the admixture of simple chemistry to the *words* and their proper pronunciation, Camelot-Fregis magic was just so much mishmash. That it existed at all was because of its singular role in plans formulated across the ages—in this case by forces which were active now. Right now! The Kaleen was but a part of it all. What, or *who* was behind it, I had yet to find out. The answer, in part, was obviously the Pug-Boos. But could one really trust the obvious? Could not that other power simply be using the Pug-Boos as the medium whereby its will or plan, or counterplan, was put to action? After all, what, really, was a Pug-Boo? I looked up to check the sleeping figure of Pawbi, that fat, furry, daintily snoring "rodent," as he had been strangely called by Prince

Keilweir. He continued snoring, but in my mind's eye I remembered him walking toward us through all that horror of the courtyard, and the feeling of goodness and protection that accompanied his every step, when all seemed lost.

I remembered, too, the voice of Hooli, soothing, assuaging. Why Hooli? Hooli's voice was also my voice, though it was *his*, too. Could the voice have been Pawbi's? Was Pawbi, Hooli? Were there any other Pug-Boos than the ones we knew to exist? Could they somehow be a single entity, a collective? It was obvious that they knew of the Kaleen and, in their way, opposed him. Did the Kaleen, in turn, know of Pug-Boos? I was willing to bet, remembering the prince's statement, that the Kaleen did not. So then, in the midst of this world magic, created by the Kaleen, worked as a series of events operative when the proper sounds were emitted. As a result whole fields of force, matrices of energy, were rearranged in finest detail: water became wine; gog-milk became sviss; force fields protected kings from harm; material and living things were atomized and recreated according to their original structures; the transmutation of metals became a fact; the dead were activated; love potions in the form of hyperactivated genitalia were real; storms were childish games. And in all this the equally powerful (?) Pug-Boos remained hidden. . . .

Why had not the Kaleen prevailed over these many centuries? After a period of pondering, I almost had the answer to that, too. I had learned a lot, enough to know where I must go now, and what I must do and how I would do it. I woke Pawbi, took his paw in mine. Together we descended the winding stairs of the great tower and made our way through the deserted hall to the others.

Outside was a white hell of howling wind and snow. Despite this we managed to bury our dead with honor. And we erected a great stone cromlech to mark their heroes' graves. The Yorns and men of Kelb were left for another time. They would keep well in that natural refrigerator of a courtyard.

Then Tober fetched our herd, brought forage for the dottles while we provided ourselves with foodstuff for our journey back. Pawbi rode behind me on fat Henery's rump. I marveled that the cold seemed not to bother him.

The ride was a nightmare. If we had averaged twenty miles per hour before, we did better than half again that speed this time. The dottles literally flew through the storm, pausing only to shake the ice of the keep, with all its horror, from their paws. The road across the white wastes and down the precipitous stone-hewn path of the mountains was a maelstrom, a madly flowing stream of dottles. We did in one day what had taken us two days before, so that at the end of our first day we were again beside the stream where I had re-slain the dead-alives.

And it was the sixth hour, Greenwich, and I was as ready as I would ever be. I had sought the excuse of needed privacy. It was granted me by the others who, I suspect now, had long concluded that I was truly something other than a man of Fregis-Camelot. . . .

I moved out some three hundred yards from the fires to a series of upright stones and seated myself upon one of them. The time was right. I would make contact in exactly two minutes, no more. I, myself, had arranged it. Not that we would be reduced to but two minutes message-wise. They would have taped what there was to tape—I likewise. This information would be fed instantaneously back and forth to be checked later. The two minutes were for us. By my ring chronometer the countdown was now thirty seconds. I pressed the appropriate stud and waited.

"In!" It was Kriloy's voice, flat, curt, and mechanical.

"In," I echoed him, resigned to proper formula. "Question. Are there Pug-Boos anywhere else on Fregis?"

"Certainly! The woods are full of them in Yorn territory. They live in family groups, spend most of their lives in select trees, and are about grade '0' on the I.Q. chart. Question. Can you be prepared to leave, spaceboat-wise, at emergency signal?"

"Nope. I've signed on for the duration. Question. Is the planetary mag field broken in the area of Hish?"

"Yes! Question. Is your presence in your true capacity now known by the 'baddies'?"

"No! Question. Can you release me from penalty of equipment use?"

"No! And you damn well know why."

"Question. Have you included coordinates from Vuun territory in your tapes?"

"Yes! Time's up. Contact in seventy-two hours, Greenwich. Fade now."

"Fade now."

And that was that. I had brought a small skin of sviss with me. I put it to my lips and downed a full third of it. Then I relaxed on the stone to hear the message.

The receiver was also the belt, the circuit attuned to the node at the base of my skull. I activated the circuit. The message began:

Aboard the *Deneb-3*—Fomalhaut I, five parsecs from Foundation Center: We came into the atmosphere of Fomalhaut II's third planet (call it Alpha) counterposed to its axial spin; this, within two hundred miles of surface so that, atmospherically, there was but little resistance to temporal mass. A planned circumnavigation was made within the two-minute span, all systems open. The following information is hereby listed for general application to existing problems, excluding the normal, standard trivia.

As previously noted the planet is bereft of life, with the effects of a nuclear holocaust most evident. What had not been noted until now is that the planet is also completely sterile. No single amoeba, spore, bacillus, in any form, exists. Previous life is evidenced in that the shells of great cities and other marks of a humanoid civilization abound—metal bridges, canals, great roads. The marks of forests also remain, though, as stated, no life exists in any form. The planet is an absolute anachronism in that it has an atmosphere and land and great oceans—but no life. It is also extragalactic in that it *has no magnetic field*.

Jack-pot on that one, I thought, and continued to listen.

Since there is no magnetic field, Fomalhaut's Alpha can be said—in terms of temporal space—to be non-existent or, to put it differently, to exist simultaneously in hyper *and* temporal space. Fomalhaut's Alpha can therefore be likened to a window, a way station, a *bridge* from somewhere else to *here*—to this galactic island.

Whatever the reasons, the facts of planetary destruction, the absence of life, and a consequent and total sterility must play some vital role—*somewhere*.

An instant conclusion is that extrauniversal, alien contact may have been made; may even now be working through this way station; and further, that according to information from you, Camelot-Fregis may even now be involved. You are therefore directed by the Foundation to proceed with caution. Under *no* circumstances are the life-forms of Fregis, in opposition or otherwise, to be aware of your existence. This directive is final until we have exact knowledge regarding the question of Alpha and/or of the tie-in with Camelot-Fregis.

Latest data on the movement of Omnian forces is that a fleet of some three thousand ships, mustered in the port cities of Seligal and Kerch, have embarked for the north. They should arrive in Kelb within two days. It is estimated that some two hundred thousand warriors and twenty thousand cavalry comprise these contingents. Few dottles were seen boarding ships and it is estimated that the twenty thousand Omnian cavalrymen will receive their mounts in the subverted areas of Kelb and Ortmund. . . .

The message then continued and ended with a lot of trivia —interesting, but most of it known to me.

I returned to the campfire and Pawbi. We didn't post a guard. Somehow I knew that with Pawbi around we had a small degree of protection—this, despite the fact that Hooli had been with the princess at the time of her abduction. If the Kaleen had a mind to check us out, I was sure he would be met with sufficient interference to come a cropper—which he would attribute to natural causes and switch his attention elsewhere. This didn't mean that Pawbi would step in if the Kaleen's interest was sufficient for a complete effort. Ununh! The way I had it psyched, the Pug-Boos, for whatever their reasons, would interfere only to the extent that their efforts would not be recognized as such. Example: It was quite true that the Kaleen's magic at Goolbie's keep was sufficiently strong so as to encompass all who fell within its focal area. We have noted already the slow movements of the prince and his cohorts. It was absolutely insufficient, however, in that it did not allow the prince's men to kill us. That's where Pawbi played his game. He simply added to the Kaleen's own strength so that those who would have killed us were powerless to do so. He did this in a way that no outside force would be suspected. In effect, the Pug-Boo's game was to influence, to control, to perhaps direct. But not at the expense of exposure. And they would continue to work in such a way that their presence remained hidden, until . . . Well, that was the big question. And it remained exactly that. Who and what was the force of the Kaleen? Who and what were Pug-Boos? Was I really, by siding with Marack and the countries of the north, on the side of the angels? I continued to think so. So much so that I knew in my heart, as we pounded the last few miles toward Glagmaron on the following day, that I would not heed the directive of the Foundation to proceed with all caution.

I had concluded that I knew better than they what the developing "something" was. And that I, better than they, could best thwart, or otherwise provide the quite necessary fly in the ointment.

We rode into Glagmaron city at dusk, or rather we rode around it, taking the granite road above the Cyr to the castle. I wanted above all else to avoid a meeting with Lord Fon Tweel.

"An additional caution, sirs," I told Griswall and the others as we approached the castle drawbridge. "We must see that our rooms are next to each other's. For it may be that with the lord Fon Tweel in charge at Glagmaron, we might have to fight our way from this courtyard, too."

Griswall rode ahead to talk to the commander of the gate. All of the palace guards, a skeleton remnant now, were friends of Griswall. He was told that the lord Fon Tweel was camped on the great plain to the east of the city. The roster of his thirty thousand men had been completed yesterday.

But Fon Tweel had yet to prepare for the ride south to Gheese and Ferlach. Griswall cautioned the commander, in the king's name, to make no mention of our presence. And, since he was their senior, and also well liked, they promised to do this.

I had dared the castle for one reason: This night there would be three Pug-Boos together—Hooli, Jindil, and Pawbi. I meant to have converse with the three of them.

We took Rawl's now vacant apartment, and another next to that. Charney and Hargis stayed with me. Tober stayed with Griswall. We dined in an adjunct to the great hall, were massaged and bathed in the room of the chirurgeons, then retired to our beds for much needed sleep—or so my men thought.

But it was not to be that way. "Sirs and friends," I told them in the hallway, "these last days have seen us sworn to the king, to the princess, and to Marack. From now on and to the end this will be totally so. Be ready then," I admonished, "to ride this very night. For I promise you that such things will happen soon that if you live your deeds will be saga and song throughout the ages in every hearth and hall in all our land. Sleep now and I will wake you."

Griswall asked bluntly, "When, my lord?"

"I do not know as yet."

"And will you sleep, Sir Collin?" Charney's concern was obvious.

I smiled. "I mean to do that."

We clasped hands and entered our rooms. Charney and Hargis took the great bed and were almost instantly asleep. I chose a fur-covered couch which I pulled close to the stone-laced windows and lay down and closed my eyes.

But not to sleep—to relax, yes! To prepare myself for a contact that I could only hope would come.

And it did. The doors were finally opened to what had been hidden. In the end I knew that if my message to my stalwarts had suggested song and saga whether they lived or died, so now I knew this to be true. Above all else it *would* be true.

We had doused the candles, and the largest of the two moons, free now from the rain-filled clouds which had fled to the far horizons, peered curiously in at me. I stared back, unwinking, until my eyes grew tired. *Relax. Relax*, I told myself, breathing deeply of the scented night air. *Relax, and let that which will be, be. . . .* Time passed, and I felt a slow "goodness" then, throughout my body. It was as if each muscle were suspended, individually, free of tension, nonexistent, every bit of me free, so that my mind no longer had a body—so that my mind, too, was free.

I closed my eyes.

And Hooli came, and Pawbi and Jindil, and their voices were as one voice, and that voice, as before, was my own. . . .

"Collin!" the voice called. "Collin! It is time now for you and for us. And you were correct to think that we would come to you. A page has been turned, Collin, and a step has been taken. It matters not if the step was ours or *theirs*—it is irrevocable."

"At what point are we, then?" I asked. My question implied a knowledge that I did not possess. Beyond the blackness of my closed eyes I could see them sitting in midair, out beyond the lace of stone—three pairs of legs flat out, pudgy paws over pudgy tummies. . . . Their shoebutton eyes seemed to gleam in unison and three pink tongues made a circular swipe around the blunted laughter of three brown and grinning muzzles.

"Your question has no answer, Collin," my voice echoed back to me. "Since you know neither the beginning nor the end—or even the *now* of it all. You are here for a single purpose, and the time for *that* has come."

"Oh?" I said. "And who are you to say this?"

"We sent for you, Buby."

"Did you now? Really. Just how did you do that?"

"Through your Watcher, my dear."

"The soothsayer and the crystal ball at Klimpinge?"

"Yes!"

I sighed. "But when you first appeared—when I was a prisoner in Castle-Gortfin—you asked me where I came from; who I was."

"We would know if you knew or suspected us."

I sighed again. "But *me*. How did you know you would get *me*?"

"We didn't. Whoever! It would have made no difference. It makes none now."

"I see," I said slowly, though I didn't, really. "But the

131

variables—myself, the princess. How could you know? What if I had been killed at Gortfin, in the tournament, at Goolbie's keep?"

"The chances were that you would not. As for the keep . . . well, we tried to warn you."

"The chances that I would be killed at the keep—they, too, were slim?"

"Yes."

"That's hard to believe. But say I was killed—"

"There are always alternatives."

"Another page?" I asked sarcastically.

"Something like that."

"And perhaps another thousand years?"

"That, too, is possible."

"Great Gods!" I exclaimed in irony. And then, "I know of you. I suspected, and now I know that there are other Pug-Boos on Camelot-Fregis."

The three of them just smiled.

"All right," I said. "Then tell me what I am to do, since you've arranged it all. I will then decide whether to do it. But first check me to see if I've psyched you properly. To begin with: You are not of Fregis and you have taken the form of Pug-Boos for the simple reason that they alone are the most harmless and inoffensive of Fregisian mammals. You do this to conceal your presence from the force of the Kaleen —and, simultaneously, to gain entry to the presence of the kings and lords of the northlands as harmless pets. This gives you entry to their council, to their thinking, and to all that will transpire by their hands. All this you use against the Kaleen. . . ."

The Pug-Boos smiled.

"Except," I continued, "that you act as the people's minstrels, too. Your music tells them of their past—the past of Fomalhaut's Alpha. Therefore they know and love you, and see you as something other than simple Pug-Boos. . . ."

"Not true." The Pug-Boos smiled. "They hear the sound of music, nothing else. Have you ever been told by anyone of ths history which *you* read into the music? It remains solely in their subconscious. We do but serve to keep it there so that, genetically, it will be as an ingrained memory pattern, to be used—someday."

"But don't you risk discovery in the playing of this music?"

"The listeners are shielded at the time of the playing and nothing remains in their conscious minds. As of this moment, friend Harl Lenti, in all of the north there are no memories of a Pug-Boo's song."

I tried another tack. "I would know," I asked, "if the Kaleen, too, is an animal or humanoid of Camelot-Fregis, possessed perhaps by another alien force, but in opposition to your own."

"The Kaleen is a force unto itself. It is but a fragmented part of the whole, but acts for the whole."

"And are you but the fragmented part of a whole, so that you, too, act for it in the guise of gentle Pug-Boos?"

They eyed me solemnly, then their voices came again: "Have done, Sir Collin. You shall be told so that you will know in part all that you need to know. Though we are of a common galaxy, ours is a life-form older by millennia than all that you know. We have long known of the force called the Kaleen on this planet which you have humorously dubbed Camelot. We deem it a force beyond your present power to comprehend; beyond, in part, even ours. It is extragalactic, of another universe whose gateway is the planet Alpha of Fomalhaut II. Beyond that gateway, in that other universe, a battle has raged for uncounted millennia. The force is but one of the antagonists; of its opponent, we know nothing. Suffice it to say that the force sought an escape, a way perhaps to avoid final destruction. The unthinkable energies of an entire galaxy were directed to the single purpose of creating a warp through hyperspace, to seize upon a single planet in a single system, and to substitute itself for the life-form of that planet, and so escape the holocaust that pursued it.

"Alpha, the planet of Fomalhaut, was chosen. The space warp was created. So, too, was the life-form of Alpha selected for transmigration. . . . But we, born of this galaxy, came to know of the warp, and our powers were such that we transferred all that was sentient life to Fregis Three, and destroyed by sterility all that remained on Alpha. And thus, though the gateway remained, its potential for exploitation was in part destroyed. We say 'in part' for the simple reason that in the transfer, a single element of the force, dormant in the body of a sleeper, was also transferred. And it is here

133

now. It is weak, without the strength to recross space to the gateway; with strength only to stay alive, to maintain contact, and to prepare for the time when a path from Fregis to Alpha is created so that the potential of the gateway will again be available. Then will the life of Camelot-Fregis— survivors of Alpha—be utilized again, as the force had intended in the very beginning."

"But how," I asked, "were they not aware of your interference, of your creation of a sterile planet? Surely they must have suspected?"

"The answer lies in that simultaneously with their invasion —for this took place across the space of a hundred Galactic years—nuclear war broke out between opposing factions on Alpha, along with first attempts at space travel. The resultant Holocaust, though falling short of complete planetary destruction, presented a logical reason for the sterility. As for Alpha's remnants, taken to Fregis-Camelot in the few ships available . . . well, we destroyed their memories; this, so that they would not again return to Alpha until such time as a solution had been found to the problem of the intruder, the force. We would point out that in the absence of a magnetic field, destroyed by the force in the creation of the space warp, sterility was easy to achieve."

"And it was not aware of your interference."

"All was attributed to both the warp and the nuclear Holocaust. From that, they supposed, came the sterility."

"In Hooli's music there was a hint of galactic destruction beyond that of just the single planet, Alpha."

"This was a suggestion of the struggle in terms of that other universe; a suggestion of what may well happen here if the force in the long run was to prevail."

"Sounds pretty pat."

"It is pat."

"All right," I said. "Here comes the big one. Why have you not just destroyed the gateway and the force, yourselves? You, seemingly, have the power. . . ."

"That is a question, Harl Lenti, Sir Collin, that we are not prepared to answer. Think what you will—that we are weak, that we have other games to play. We say only this: That our goal is a Camelot-Fregis free of the force; a planet Alpha fertile and with a proper field; and a gateway closed until such time as controls can be instituted over any contact with that alien universe so as to guarantee the safety of our own. . . ."

"There is a lot unanswered."

"And so it will remain."

"You know, then, of us, of the Galactic Foundation?"

"We do."

"What if *we* isolate Alpha for total destruction, as a precautionary measure?"

"We would prevent you. But your Foundation will not do this. For you cannot tell them what we have told you."

"I already have—an instantaneous tape at my last message period."

The Pug-Boo's smiles were wider still and their auras halolike. "There was no message. Your tape was blank."

"You bastards."

"And also, Sir Collin, what you now know of us can be imparted to no one either. Such an effort, in your idiom, would boggle your mind, bring on an instantaneous mental paralysis. We caution you not to try it."

"You dirty bastards," I said again. Then finally I sighed. "All right. You sent for me. I've been subjected to a thousand bits of nonsense. Now let's have done with it. What's the denouement? What is this 'simple' job that I am to do, that you cannot do?"

"There is nothing that we 'cannot do.' We simply prefer that you do it—for our own reasons."

"Great Gods!" I said glumly, and to no one in particular. "Six years with the Foundation, the rank of Adjuster, and I've just been reduced to the rank of a pawn on the chessboard by a trio of teddy bears. . . ."

"But," said Hooli—and I knew it was he, for he leaned toward me and winked in the saying—"the pawn has already taken the princess, who will someday be queen. Is not that single thing worth all the rest to you?"

"You sure know how to reach a guy," I said. "Yes! It damn well is worth 'all the rest' to me. Now speak up. What's the pawn's next move. . . ?"

"Exactly what you yourself already intend doing. Rescue the princess. . . . You will return to your small ship and thence to the mountains of Ilt. The Vuun has most wisely, after returning Prince Keilweir to Kelb, kept your princess and her companion as hostage in *their* game with Om. While rescuing the princess you will also dissuade the Vuuns from participating in the coming battle. This will be a disastrous ploy against the Kaleen, who counts heavily on their support."

"And how does one explain my ability to fly through the air?"

"The Vuuns need no explanation. They are as old as time. They know of space travel—and more. We even suspect that they know of the Kaleen's true origin. As for the princess— well, 'tis magic that you practice, sirrah! What else?"

"You're just the greatest." I sighed.

"We think so, too," Hooli said.

"And all of this is to happen just like that?"

"If you don't blow the game, Buby."

They had begun to fade, so I shouted mentally: "Thanks, you bastards. Thanks at least for the healed wounds. Maybe that's what you really are—a bunch of small-planet pharmacists. . . ."

"No trouble," Hooli's voice came faintly. "It was no trouble at all."

The relaxation came again. An hour of it, two hours. Every fiber in my body—as in those brief moments on the flagstones of Goolbie's courtyard—was washed with a "goodness" of peace, a rebuilding of tired and weary cells, a replenishing of bright red blood. . . . I let it happen.

Then I arose and woke Charney and Hargis, who awakened Griswall and Tober. And we dressed, attending to each other's armor. Fresh surcoats, underdress and padded long-shirts, buckled swords and fal-dirks. We made our way through the dark halls to the yard and the men-at-arms around the gate warden. I asked for but ten dottles, including Henery. My stalwarts were surprised at this, for they did not know what I knew. Then we rode out across the bridge and into the silvery night. And the gate warden was surprised at that, for he still feared dead-alives.

The path took us down from the field before Glagmaron

castle and onto the "Great South Road." As we came off the castle hill we could see to our northeast, spread before the walls of Glagmaron city, the rows of tents and dottle rings of the gathered army of the lord Fon Tweel. Fires blazed so that the field seemed an acreage sown with flaming embers.

My men asked no questions. I told them nothing. That is the way it had to be. We had but twenty miles to travel. We reached the area of the starship in exactly one hour. I led them off the road and up the bluff to where, but a short ten days ago, I had awaited the coming of the princess Murie Nigaard and entourage. At the top, in a small hollow at the base of a stand of trees, I asked them to unsaddle their dottles and let them forage, and to gather around me.

They did this, and the second moon illuminated our little group in such a way that we were as statuary in a wild and primitive garden.

I made use of the one weapon—if one could call it that—allowed me by the Foundation: the weapon of hypnosis. It was a simple trick of misdirection, of concentration, and of final control so that within the space of minutes they lay around me in deep sleep. I made them as comfortable as I could then, wrapping each in his saddle blanket against the cold of the night and the heat of tomorrow's sun. The trees would offer some protection, and the dottles would stay close. Whatever. They would be here for some time—until I was ready for them.

Then I went to the back of the hill where I had left the ship. I pressed a belt stud to activate the field around it. Once done I gave the numbers, *aloud* and *strongly* (shades of Camelot): "Three-seven . . . two-nine . . . four-one–" I waited, and slowly, slowly, before my eyes the little starship took form, first wavering, then becoming solid. And there it was, all thirty feet of it, snub-nosed and competent. . . .

A simple movement in time; a shift in perspective. It was like coming home. . . . I entered, and once again I was Kyrie Fern, Adjuster. Damn the Pug-Boos to Hell—and the Kaleen, and all the controlled variables that dared to name *me* pawn! I had played the game all the way. What had the Boos done to date? Other than a propitious Band-Aid, all achievement had been *my* doing—mine and the Foundation's. And why should I believe them in their claim to power over the Foundation—though I recalled that they hadn't exactly said that. I then chose in my anger to forget that my death had been somewhat delayed in Goolbie's courtyard; that in all that had happened the Pug-Boos' manipulation had indeed been shaking the web. In one thing, however, I was right. My quite positive contribution so far was based on my own initiative. Whatever the Boos were up to, without me and the Foundation that first page might never have been turned at all. So let it be then, I concluded. There was still a job to do, indeed, "a world to win," as in the old cliché. But I would play it my way—as if there were no Boos at all.

I settled into the contour seat before the control panel. Within seconds I was a shimmering, silvered dot above the brooding green of Marack's forests. I followed the great road, scanning, enlarging wherever a point of interest appeared, but checking each aspect of that well-traveled path. Camelot-Fregis looked more beautiful from aloft, if such could be possible, than from the ground. I had not appreciated it before. I did now. I would not run to my princess immediately as the Boos had suggested. For though I truly loved her I thought her sufficiently strong to stand Vuun stink for a few more tens of hours. I would apply the Foundation Adjuster Kyrie Fern-Sir Collin finger to the now baking pie in my own way. I would tie the strings of our far-flung battle lines together, first. The Kaleen saw the board as a whole. The forces of Marack did not. I damn well intended to provide that service despite the cautioning of the Foundation to retreat to the game of hide-and-seek, and the smug suggestion of the Boos that I play the game as *they* saw it.

Best damn them all! I would indeed by the hero-mythos Collin, and that was that!

Over forests and rivers, across villages, fields, and sparkling lakes. The ship was a silvered blue with a metal skin of chameleon potential. I could see and not be seen.

Smoke rose over the dour aerie of great Castle-Gortfin. I learned later that it had fallen because those of Caronne's loyal subjects within its walls had taken and held the gates in aid of an attack from without. The Yorns and soldiery pledged to Lady Elioseen had fought to the last for each room, each stair, each cavernous hall beneath that great stone mass. The magic of Elioseen had been evenly matched by that of the king's sorcerer, Fairwyn. The magic of Camelot, created by the Kaleen, and known equally well by north and south, had canceled itself out again, and the lady Elioseen was now a prisoner. The gates to Gortfin were open, too; the drawbridge was down. A few hundred men had been left to garrison the walls, and the banners of the king floated from its highest towers. The Marackian army had moved south as of four days before; they had not waited for Gortfin's fall. When I spotted them, they were breaking camp (it was still early morning). Pickets were out. Small parties of cavalry were already moving through the countryside. They were many miles from Gortfin.

I then passed over many a Kelbian town and village, a great plain ringed with rocky hills and one burned-out small volcanic cone known as the plain of Dunguring, and finally the main port city and capital of Corchoon. The mixed Omnian-Seligian-Kerchian fleet had not yet arrived. This I knew by the rather sparse shipping in the quite beautiful, natural harbor. But a Kelbian army was encamped on the flat and grassy plain to the west of Corchoon. I estimated its strength at twenty thousand. And the herds of fat dottles to their rear spoke of a numerous cavalry.

Focusing on the royal Kelbian tents, I spied King Harlach and Keilweir himself, all aglitter in silvered armor. Two companies of Yorns were camped on their right, along with an equal number of Omnian soldiery. They were calmly playing at stits, a game of balls and spears and shields. Their appearance suggested that they hadn't a care in the world. This, despite the fact that their spies must certainly have told them of the advancing Marackian army.

I studied them closely and saw that their lines were well disposed for either attack or defense, depending upon their strength and strategy.

With Omnian forces arriving shortly, the deck was definitely stacked. Om's muster of two hundred and fifty thousand men, plus this twenty thousand of Kelb, plus whatever Great Ortmund would bring to bear—plus the possible participation of the Vuuns—all of it together boded no good for Marack. One would be a fool to think otherwise. I suspected that all this force would move forward to that great plain of Dunguring for the final confrontation.

I sent my little craft to north and west then, over the lush coastal valleys and plains, and inland. I crossed the borders between Great Ortmund and Kelb at some three hundred miles from Corchoon. Already masses of Ortmundian warriors could be seen making their way toward Kelb's capital. Then more towns. More villages. And finally, Janblink, capital of Great Ortmund. Like Corchoon and Glagmaron, any town that could be called such was protected by a castle. Janblink castle was a thing of absolute beauty, an arras, a sculptured totality of all things medieval. Perched on a granite hill overlooking a rushing river, with a dozen great turrets, a monstrous encircling ravine with a veritable "bi-frost bridge" as an entry to portcullis and gate—I could only marvel and stare.

Further scanning revealed it to be well defended. And I knew that the Marackian warlords of Keeng, Fleege, and Klimpinge would make no attempt to take it, but rather would bypass it for a later storming.

Like a gadfly, I zipped further inland. Ten miles to the foot, beyond Castle Janblink, I came upon the beginnings of a small battle. Lord Breen Hoggle-Fitz's five thousand had caught the Ortmundian rear guard with its back against a craggy pass. They were deployed on the fields before this pass now. And Camelot's rising sun, Fomalhaut, shone upon a scene in which Hoggle-Fitz was preparing to advance against them in classical array: a wing of archers to either flank; foot soldiers and men-at-arms in the center, and a phalanx of heavy cavalry to the front—with Hoggle, himself, at point.

I could see that the Ortmundian rear guard would meet them with a smaller force, but similarly deployed—or so it would seem to Hoggle. From my mile-high vantage, however, I knew better. To Hoggle-Fitz's right, hidden in a small valley, were additional squadrons of heavy cavalry, half of them Yorns; easily sufficient to turn Fitz's flank. His archers could never sustain the charge they would mount. The ground sloped down from the valley in such a way that the horde's momentum, at the point of impact, would be terrible indeed.

A small creek split the field, shallow, easily forded, with banks about five feet from water level. It was about forty feet wide. It would present no obstacle to a force prepared for it. Since it was closer to Hoggle-Fitz's array than to that of the enemy, it was clear that his entire line would cross this creek long before contact was made.

I had twenty minutes at best to interfere. Two of them were used in landing behind a ridge in a grove of broad-leafed trees. I damped the ship, and moved off, carrying my colors with me. I noted as I topped the rise above Fitz's base camp that a number of animals were also on the ridge. They had chosen this vantage point to watch the battle. All Camelot's mammals seemed to possess this curious proclivity. I grabbed a likely looking dottle from the herd, had him saddled by the herd-master, chose a lance from a sufficiency of such at Hoggle's armory, attached my colors to its tip, and rode off to smite the heathen. Since the event of Glagmaron's tournament was still fresh in the minds of the Marackian warriors, I even received a smattering of cheers as I rode through the first ranks on the right flank of Hoggle's now advancing force. The commander of these five hundred archers with his small covey of men-at-arms welcomed me warmly.

"Ho-la, my lord," he said, laughing. They were in good spirits. "You come in good moment. We are about to force yonder pass, which should take but a fistful of minutes. Indeed, sirrah! Though we welcome your prowess, we need it not. Rest here, sir, and from this vantage point you may observe all that will come to pass."

I raised a steel-gauntleted hand. "Two things first," I cautioned. "Send a message to our lord Hoggle-Fitz that you will hold to this side of that little creek, and that he in turn should allow the right wing of his center to lag somewhat. This will present a front to a few squadrons of cavalry which will come at you from yon"—and I gestured—"hidden valley. With this precaution, and with your archers positioned to feather their hides with your shafts from *this* side of the creek, their disposition will then be upset. And the advance you speak of will then continue without peril. . . . Hurry! For there is little time."

He didn't bother to ask me how I knew this. He just shook his head and grinned. Within seconds two riders were streaking to the center van where Hoggle-Fitz's pennons waved arrogantly.

We drew up to the creek and positioned ourselves, passing the word down the front of our thousand. I focused my contacts to as many magnitudes as were necessary for a clear scanning of the valley mouth, and waited. The newly risen sun being against us, our young commander—I found later that he was Sir Mordi Tornweedi, nephew to the lord Per-Rondin, captain of the king's center—was shielding his eyes now. His riders and archers did likewise. And the dottles, sensitive to the situation, stamped their paws and *whoooed*. Then I saw the enemy squadrons. They emerged from the hidden valley at a slow but quickening gallop, so that when a full five hundred riders had come into view they were already streaking toward the flank of our advancing army in a thundering, shrieking froth of leveled lances and swinging swords. They were indeed a beautiful sight. They wore heavy armor, most of them being heggles mixed with Yorns. There would be, I thought, no stopping them short of a matching force. But that force was there.

"They *see* us now," I said to young Tornweedi. "But it is much too late. They no doubt thought us lax in spirit so that we held behind. Now they are not so sure. Look, you! They slow even now to guard against us."

"Aye," Tornweedi answered exultantly. "And look, *you*, my lord. Fitz of Great Ortmund has swung his flank to hold."

And Hoggle-Fitz had done just that. In those few short minutes we reversed what could have been a signal defeat for Marackian arms. The charge across our front slowed, since they saw too late that we had not moved, and did not know whether to face us or to continue on. Their momentum lost, they were easy prey to the flights of arrows loosed in good order by our bowmen, to the shouts of the sergeants. From five hundred bows there flew as many arrows, and then again, and again, and again; each flight taking but five seconds for the notching, the draw, and the release. The distance was at some two hundred paces, a goodly shot for an archer. But though ours, like all Fregisian warriors, were careful so as to target riders only and not gentle dottles, the distance was too great for accuracy. The sun, too, was also an obstacle. This being true, tens of riders *and* dottles were already down and screaming.

Fitz's flank did give somewhat at the impact of the Ortmundian charge. But it held. And because it did, that was the end for Ortmund. By slowing his center almost to a halt the bulk of Fitz's five thousand had remained outside of arrow range. Om and Great Ortmund had but one meaningful alternative then: to fling their remaining three thousand in headlong assault of Fitz's superior mass. They were confused. They hesitated at a time when to waver meant certain defeat or death.

Then we, too, moved forward, crossing the creek in a long green line; loosing flight after deadly flight into the dwindling ranks of the Ortmundian-Omnian soldiery, so that when the bulk of Ortmund's rear guard could no longer contain themselves at the slaughter of their own, and moved against Fitz's center and left, it was far, far too late. We moved with the men-at-arms and archers. We were approximately one hundred dottles and riders strong. Once through the screen of archers, we smashed into the melee with its remnants of mounted knights and men-at-arms. They were courageous, those warriors of Ortmund and Om. Either that or possessed of the sorcery of the Kaleen. They asked no quarter and gave none.

Through all the great dust cloud of battle, the *wheeeing* of the dottles, the death shouts of men, and the screaming of the wounded, I held back. I fought only to defend myself, keeping to the side of the young nephew of Per-Rondin. Strange paradox that I could not keep him from his death. He had, after bearing himself bravely in the hacking fests, been challenged by a hulking Yorn in armor of bronze and steel chain. He accepted the challenge. And, as was Fregisian custom, those who were not battling in close proximity stayed their weapons to see the outcome.

Tornweedi chose to rely upon his quickness and the point of his blade rather than compete in the hefty broadsword exchange of shattering blows, and the pate-cracking thump of mace and hammer. It proved his undoing in that after they had circled with a fast exchange of steel, he bent beneath his shield for a thrust of point to the armor chink between breastplate and greave. He missed in his forward lunge, and the Yorn, a huge, white-browed, and intelligently evil specimen, brought his great sword from across his left shoulder in one whistling sweep to dash the head from poor Tornweedi's body. He then bent, ran sword through waxen cheeks, and shook it mightily above that bloodstained field for all to see.

I could say here that I avenged Tornweedi. But it would not be true. I didn't have to. Indeed, I was not allowed to. The Yorn was attacked from all sides. And though he slew three more, he was brought down—as were all the others of that fated troop. They had asked no quarter. They received none. And, in the end, when the field was won and the pass open, I saw that at best there were a hundred prisoners. The field, for a full fifty acres around, was littered with the bodies of Marackians, Great Ortmundians, and Yorns alike.

It was high noon when the battle ended. Strange how time plays its tricks on the threshold of death. There are periods which are but minutes, but seem like hours. There are others which seem as minutes—such as our fighting before the pass. But four hours had gone by since the squadrons of cavalry had first burst from their ravine.

I accompanied Tornweedi's guard to where the lord Breen Hoggle-Fitz waited on that stricken field. He leaned from the painted saddle of his great dottle to grip my hand and place an arm about my shoulder. His helm was off, his mop of gray hair a wrathful aureole. There were tears in his eyes, too, and he stank of blood.

"By Ormon, most noble Collin," he shouted, to those hardened, black-furred warriors around him, as well as to myself. "By Wimbily and by Harris. Bless them! Blessed be their names! Bless them! And bless us all who have survived this field! And bless those—" He seemed carried away with himself again and I said softly, interjecting, "Ah, m'lord and most courageous companion, my confessor—" He beamed at that one. "I have bad news of the lady Caroween."

His face paled. It was the first time I had seen this happen, a sure sign of where his heart lay. He took my arm. "Say you so? But how, and where?"

We rode back toward the base camp and I told him as we rode. Tears rolled down his rugged, blustering face to such a degree that, I must confess, I was touched and shed a few

144

myself. In the end I boasted of Caroween's prowess in that battle of the courtyard, so that he called all to gather around and bade me repeat the story to his warriors.

As I told the tale my voice took on the cadence of a minstrel. And that which came from my mouth as prose became poetry. Before the ending of it instruments accompanied me —a lute and a set of pipes such as Ongus had used so well. And all this in the bright light of Fomalhaut and its far binary. It was a strange thing, too, in that I spoke to men who had themselves just fought a noble battle; yet here they listened to salute the courage and prowess of another.

Then we held a war council and I told them what I had come to tell them in the first place: "Go not to Janblink city or Janblink castle," I admonished them. "For the armies of Great Ortmund are not there. The king Feglyn is on his way now with all his host to join with Harlach before the gates of Corchoon in Kelb."

"To which site there goes our noble king Caronne," a doughty young warrior shouted.

"Aye," I said. "And to which site, too, there now comes from across the river-sea the greatest horde of Omnian soldiery that the world has ever seen."

No one asked me, "How do you know this?" They asked instead, "How many?" And I told them.

There was a great stirring then, and a silence while all pondered. The first puffs of an early afternoon breeze blew around us, bringing a scent of wet earth and spring wildflowers to cancel the blood of the field and the smell of the sweat of our bodies. A flight of tuckle-birds flew over, too, with a spate of melodious chirps—like raindrops. The whole scene was highly incongruous.

The lord Hoggle-Fitz, in full command of the knights around him, then said, "It seems then that we go now to Corchoon or, as young Collin would have it, to the plain of Dunguring by the oblique south road beyond the pass. We shall of course send to those who follow, the lords of Fleege, Keeng, and Klimpinge with their fifteen thousand, that they do likewise—and instantly."

"I would indeed suggest that," I echoed him, smiling.

"And what of our lord Fon Tweel?" Fitz eyed me keenly.

"We will see, sir," I answered softly. "And I promise you

here and now that his thirty thousand will also be at Dunguring."

Fitz stared hard at me, then lowered his eyes and his voice, and said simply, "We will await them."

The others, too, looked at the ground. But no one questioned me. . . . I had their attention and they were waiting, so I spoke up and told them what they needed to know. "There will be a great battle," I enjoined them. "It will be soon. Tomorrow, the next day, the day after. . . . It will last for as long as is needed to drive the hordes of Om from the northern shores of the river-sea. Your twenty thousand—inclusive of the fifteen still to arrive—will join with the twenty thousand of our Marackian king Caronne. You must then hold until the full force of the lord Fon Tweel, plus the warriors of Gheese and Ferlach, arrive upon the field. Even then you will be but one hundred and ten thousand against perhaps three times as many."

If I had thought they would be frightened, I would have been less blunt. But I now knew Camelot and its warriors. All around me eyes had lifted. They literally sparkled with a fierce and warlike joy. "And so then, Sir Collin"—a young knight spoke up boldly—"in no other battle could ever such glory be found. And this for us only; not for them, for we are the fewer. I, sir, would have it no other way."

"Nor I! Nor I!" A full hundred voices shouted. I looked at the beaming countenance of Hoggle-Fitz and smiled.

He said, "Indeed, I join with them, Sir Collin. I would that my sons were alive to see this."

"Well, sirrah," I assured him, "though *they* be not there—*your daughter will be.*"

Tears sprang to his eyes, for he remained what he was other than a warrior of some courage and skill—namely an emotional, fanatical, and lovable old fool. I stepped forward and put my arms around him again. The others took this as some sort of signal in that they instantly moved to disperse. The camp came alive again with the saddling of dottles, the striking of tents, and the packing of gear. I walked then to my dottle, and Hoggle-Fitz followed.

"Do you not ride with us?"

His question was rhetorical, and he knew it.

"No," I said. "I go to fetch the princess and your daughter.

146

The lord Rawl, who has given your moppet to my safekeeping, would not forgive me were it otherwise; nor would the king—nor would you, my good friend. . . ."

"You are wrong, Collin. And I shall pray for you. For though I know not where you go, of a certainty, wherever it is, there lies great danger."

"As stated," I said, "I think the battle will be fought on Dunguring plain. If so, it is there that we shall meet again."

"So be it, Collin." Fitz stared after me as I kicked my dottle's belly with both heels so that she pranced off through the camp to the south and east, and up the small hill and beyond to the grove of broad-leafed trees. . . .

Strange, I thought, as I dismounted and slapped her rump so that she would return to the others, the animals that had gathered to watch the battle still lay about, hypnotized by the man-made carnage. Were any of *these* of the planet Alpha? Had just one of those fleeing ships been, perhaps, an ark? Then I said the *words* to phase in the starship.

I lifted straight up for some fifty miles; a high parabola. The city and castle of Glagmaron were directly below on reentry. I hovered at one mile, scanned at sufficient magnitudes to be almost at ground level. It was as I expected. The great camp had *not* been broken. Fon Tweel's thirty thousand were at ease. They played at skits and flats, they gambled away their mustering fees, and they dueled in the sun. And that was about the extent of it. As expected, Fon Tweel had no intention of going anywhere; neither to Gheese and Ferlach, to impress upon the rulers of those countries the urgency of their joining with Marack against Om—nor to Dunguring before Corchoon to the aid of King Caronne. Those loyal in the camp—and I supposed these generally to encompass the whole—would not know of his treachery until it was too late.

So be it. I would return, for I had a most simgular message for Fon Tweel. . . .

I maintained an altitude of one mile, sweeping over the terrain in a southerly direction at slow speed. I had time. The countryside continued wild: great forests of oak and pine, wide rivers and serrated mountain chains which swept, I knew, down to the river-sea. These I naturally rose above, and down again until finally I had crossed into Gheese where its border joins both Marack and Ferlach. It was here, I knew, that a battle was being fought. And it was here I hoped to find Rawl, hobnobbing with Draslich, Ferlach's king; waiting, perhaps, until Fon Tweel arrived, to do the same with Chitar of Gheese so that, impressed with Marack's call to common cause and the strength of Fon Tweel's army, a meeting of conciliation could then take place.

I was right in only one thing. Sir Fergis's blazonry topped a field tent in the proximity of King Draslich, with both on a broad and boulder-strewn field overlooking a sparkling stream. Across that stream was a second army. The colors of the king of Gheese, Chitar, stretched for fully a mile over an equally grassy and boulder-strewn field. Here and there on both banks spears and lances stood erect in the ground, marking the spot where a fallen hero had been buried. From my vantage point I could see additional hundreds of unburied dead. The inconclusive fighting had been going on for quite some time. I brought the starship down as before in an area surroundered by wild clumps of bracken and heavy forest, careful so that I would come to ground on the far side of a hill.

It was done. I took time to bathe away the sweat and stiffness of the morning's battle. Then, armor reburnished, surcoat and furred cloak most carefully cleaned and spotted, plus sundry other preparations—and I must say that I had the time for this since I had no intention of springing myself upon Rawl until dusk fell—I stepped forth. Again I was fully armed, with fal-dirk, shield, broadsword, and small mace. I waved the starship back to its exclusive warp and walked to the crest of the ridge.

It was most pleasant, like that first day when I had awaited the coming of the princess on the south road. The thought of Murie now—and that she was alone and miserable in a Vuun cave, awaiting my arrival—made me somewhat ill.

Oh, that magic *did* prevail, I thought. For then it would truly be that best of all worlds so sought after by humanoids across all space and time. A release from needed knowledge, from the constant search for the why and wherefore of it all. How simple life would be if that were so—no "Constant H," no law of inverse squares—to be surrounded forever by the world of childhood with its ogres, its fairies, its sleeping princesses, and its never-never lands. . . .

I lay myself down on a broad and heavy spread of grass overlooking the martial camp of Ferlach's king. Herds of dottles foraged below me. Beyond them were tents and cooking pots and fires. Above, in the bowl of a still azure sky, was a vast pattern of cirrus-cumulus clouds. Flights of strange birds and flitterings of smaller winged creatures were all around me. At one point during the afternoon's progress I felt eyes upon me and clapped hand to sword and sat up smartly. Peering through a clump of heavy foliage was the double-horned head of a massive gerd, such as Hoggle-Fitz had used as a steed. He seemed possessed of a strange intelligence.

Then I dozed, to be awakened later by a blast of trumpet upon the still air. I noted with alarm that the sun was setting fast. I arose on both elbows to peer over the ridge. Of the two river fords visible from my vantage point, a group of knights were gathered at one—and this on the Ferlach side. From the tents of the Gheesian army, a line of mounted knights and warriors were trotting to the ford. At the head of the line were the banners of Chitar and sundry lords of Gheese. And, to Chitar's right, waving splendidly and bravely on a single lance tip, there flew the three scarlet bars upon an azure field of Rawl Fergis. Good lad! I mentally cheered him. He was not waiting for the strength of Fon Tweel. How he had managed this tête-à-tête, I knew not. But he had achieved what I had planned—set the stage for a meeting between Chitar and Draslich. Even as I watched the royal banners of Draslich—an oak tree against a blood-red sky— moved out to greet the black-swan pennons of Chitar in midstream. Protocol, I remembered, demanded no less.

There was another round of trumpet blasts then, and a cheering and hurrahing. And someone, perhaps, flipped a Ferlachian obsol, and Chitar lost so that both sides then retired with all pomp and ceremony in the direction of Draslich's war tent.

As stated, I had dozed far too long. Dusk was falling. It was obvious that they feared no dead-alives in such war camps as these, nor treachery either. For Camelot's chivalry and its code said that Chitar would stay with Draslich and no fal-dirk would find his ribs in the small hours.

Below me, and in hailing distance, was a small group of

149

foraging dottles. I whistled shrilly and they looked up and wagged their doggy-ears and tails in unison, peering anxiously around them. I stood full up. Darkness was gathering so rapidly that just as the camp itself was dim to me now, I was, perhaps, equally dim to the dottles. I whistled again and they advanced toward me. One fat-tummied female approached me brazenly, her big blue eyes inviting nose pats and friendly thigh rubs. They gathered around and I spoke gently to them and mounted the female after tossing my furred cloak over her back for a saddle, so that my armor would not hurt her. Then we led off, and pranced our way down to the great camp with its teeming warriors.

Aboard the starship I had touched up the heraldry upon my shield so that the sprig of violets against its field of gold now glowed with a most delightful luminescence. Two other things had I done: One, the creation of a null magnetic field about my person which, if I had had the wisdom to use it before, might well have protected me from the power of the Kaleen at Goolbie's keep. I doubted it on second thought, however, since Pawbi would not have allowed such an overt indication of the presence of an anti-Kaleen power. Two, I activated the ion-beam upon my belt and turned it upon myself so that my armor, like Hoggle-Fitz's at the great tourney, glowed with a silvered brilliance. To say that my arrival in the camp of King Draslich evoked a measure of interest would be an understatement indeed.

I rode straight and tall, glowing shield slung from my back. My left hand was buried in my dottle's fluffy mane to guide her. My right hand was on the hilt of my great sword. They fell away from me in awe, first cooks and helpers, then whole coveys of archers and men-at-arms. Most made the circle and the cross of Ormon; some kneeled and bent their heads. Finally, at the great block of tents surrounding that of the king, I was given escort. Knights and lords not summoned to the council ringed around me—not closely but at a distance. Nevertheless I *was* ringed. And I wondered if, despite their magic and/or gods, they would attack me if they deemed it necessary. The answer was undoubtedly "Yes." For, as the lord Per-Rondin had said, "And if their magic prevail over ours, then will we fight them with our blood and with our hearts." And so it was on Camelot.

As I neared the entrance to the king's tent, those in front turned around and ranged themselves before me, swords drawn. They would defy me. Inside, the kings' council, attracted by the hubbub, sent forth certain lords to inquire as to the reason. Needless to say, the guard of Chitar, also in the proximity of the royal tent, drew their swords, too, in defense of aught that might befall their king. I sat my small dottle silently, stared boldly at the lot of them. Then I dismounted, shooed my petite one off, turned around, placed my two hands upon my belt, leaned back my head, and bellowed: *"Now hear me all! Great lords, knights, and warriors! I am the Collin of Marack, come to have converse with your kings and with my friend, Sir Rawl Fergis, who is even now within that tent. . . . In this last respect, I would have him forth, and instantly!"*

The name of the Collin was known throughout the northern lands. Indeed, it was a mythos owned by all above the riversea; therefore my presumption struck home. Some fell back and some drew sword in anger at my quite, to them, audacious claim. One knight stepped forward, threw back his cloak, held his sword in readiness, and demanded loudly, "How dare you, sir, to take the name of *Collin*, and to approach us thusly? Speak out and clear yourself, or I shall clear your head from your body despite its glowworm shine."

He was a brave man and I didn't wish to kill him. I didn't have to. . . .

"Leave be!" The voice was Rawl's. He had stepped from the tent's interior followed by two broadly grinning students of the tournament of Glagmaron. I noted then that there were others of Rawl's hundred scattered through the crowd. They made way for him, my saffron-furred friend; even the lord who had challenged me. For Rawl was the emissary of Marack, which gave him much stature and substance. He came directly to me through the line provided, stared me fully in the eyes, his own half twinkling at my shining, half fearful of what he did not understand. He asked simply, "How now, my lord?" and fell to one knee before me. His students did likewise. Then he arose and faced the others. "Whatever you may think," he cautioned them bluntly, "this great warrior *is* the Collin! He will now join me in council, and I offer my life in forfeit that he comes in goodwill; that no harm but rather sooth shall reign throughout for the fact of his presence here. Now make us way, my lords."

"Indeed make way!"

The voice was strong and came from a giant of a man with black eyes, a great curling beard, and a mop of ebon hair with rampant fur to match. Thus had I heard Draslich described. "I would see this Collin," he continued, shouting, "about which our young lord of Marack has spoken so well. And so would my bold companion here." He nodded in the direction of a squat and heavily muscled torso topped by a leonine head with piercing eyes. This I took to be Chitar, king of Gheese. Behind the both of them two tall, cloaked figures stood: kings' sorcerers by their garb. Though their presence canceled each other, I had time to wonder whether they would try their tricks on me. I was glad for the slightly ruptured field around me, for if they tried they would soon see that all their wiles would come a cropper.

Rawl reached to take my hand, felt the strange dissonance of the field, and dropped it sharply. "Fear not." I looked him in the eye. " 'Tis but a passing thing." He nodded and Draslich bade us enter the tent, so that he led off and I followed.

All and sundry had been at sup. And, in true Camelot-Fregis style, after I had seated myself between Rawl and Chibu, one of our newly heggled students, the meal commenced again. I truly think that if the Kaleen himself had joined a Marackian, Gheesian, Ferlachian, Kelbian, and Great Ortmundian dinner, naught would be said about sundry quarrels and differences until after the final course of fruit and sviss. I was indeed hungry. My slight magnetic rupture hindered in no way the passing of gog-meat to gullet. . . .

I noted, too, that neither of the Pug-Boos, Mool of Ferlach or Riis of Gheese, were present. Then I remembered that Pug-Boos did not go to war.

There had to be an end to the feasting, however. And when it came, King Draslich wasted no time in dissimulation. He simply arose, begged Chitar's permission, as was proper, and spoke directly to me.

"Sir Collin," he said—and there was no hint of sarcasm in his voice. "We have heard something of you from yon young emissary of our brother, King Caronne. So we think that we know you, somewhat. . . . We are gathered here this night —with our common sport most sadly interrupted." He looked around the seated host at this sally, for expected applause, and got it. "We are gathered here at the call of your young lord who, we might add, is most persuasive. He has told us on the one hand of a threat to all the lands above the river-sea. He has also suggested that there be forces from Marack on the way here which"—he smiled broadly—"could add influence to a settling of differences so that Gheese and Ferlach would see Marack's wisdom in asking for unity in the face of a common peril. To date, Sir Collin, and you, Sir Rawl Fergis, though we are aware of the danger from the forces of the Kaleen, we have yet to see the arrival of our brother's thirty thousand under the lord Fon Tweel. In fact, if the circumstances were not what they supposedly are, we would find it difficult to forgive our brother king this overt pressure. In short, sirs, though we have been told of deadly peril, we still see only this young man with his command of youthful knights and squires—and now you, Sir Collin, all aglow, to emphasize Marack's concern. Perhaps now, Collin, you can inform us further of the intricacies of these strange happenings—inclusive of your arrival upon a saddleless dottle—and where, mayhaps, all this will lead."

He sat down and there were shouts all around, friendly and otherwise, making me aware, and strongly, that this was not the feast hall of Glagmaron, but the campaign tent of two warring kings. Rawl looked to me anxiously, as did his Marackian student-heggles. I smiled benignly back at them to give them confidence. I rose slowly. When fully on my feet I moved from the table to the open space within the large inverted "U" of wood and trestled tables.

Again I placed my hands on my hips and stared them straight in the eyes; not with arrogance, but with an intensity and a seriousness which I hoped would serve to set them all on edge. I began: "My good king of the land of Ferlach, my good king of the land of Gheese, my lords all, and knights, and all true warriors within my voice's range—hear me. Just as there be traitors in Kelb and Great Ortmund—and I speak of the kings Harlach and Feglyn—so are there others in Marack, and perhaps in your own tight domains. In Marack's case, I refer specifically to Fon Tweel, lord of Bist. Six days have passed since decisions were made in Glagmaron castle. The armies of Marack have already been in battle, at Gortfin, and this day, too, before the Veldian Pass in Great Ortmund. King Caronne's major forces are even now deploying before the great plain of Dunguring in Kelb. But even now, forsooth, I, too, see no king's emissary—other than Sir Fergis—at your council; nor do I see this emissary's minions camped beyond the hills. Nay, sires! The lord Fon Tweel is *not* here. And he will not *be* here. For his forces have yet to decamp from Glagmaron—and there is no longer time. I say to all of you, therefore, that this is treason of the foulest sort; not just to Marack, as you shall see, but to all the lands of the north."

I took a deep breath and held them silently with what I hoped was a steely, commanding glare. Adjusters are, above all else, consummate actors. "So be it!" I then announced firmly. "It is enough that you now know that King Caronne, his sorcerer Fairwyn, the great lord Per-Rondin, and sundry other councillors were most wise in sending our gracious young knight, Sir Rawl Fergis, to implement the diplomacy of Fon Tweel. Perhaps they knew of Fon Tweel's leanings. And Sir Fergis, it appears, has done his job, and well.

"But now I say to you all, Sir Knights and my lords and kings—*there is no more time to waste!* For at this very moment there comes to our northern coasts, to the great harbor of Corchoon in Kelb, thrice one thousand long-ships—with two hundred and fifty thousand Omnian warriors; among which are some fifty thousand Yorns with sundry cavalry. This force, added to that of Kelb and Ortmund—an additional fifty thousand men-at-arms, archers, and belted knights—should be something for all to ponder."

A murmuring swept the assemblage inside the tent and beyond. . . . "And confronting this mighty host, my lords," I continued, "barring the road to Marack, and to Gheese and Ferlach—and, yes, to the domination of all our foes and northern shores—there now stand but forty thousand noble warriors of our brave Marackian king." I paused again, then said, "And this is it, my lords—and I be blunt and brief. You *know* the enemy. You know now the stakes—namely your lives and your countries! Will you sit idly here in dalliance with but sundry games of flats across yon creek while this greatest battle of all time is fought? Will you, indeed, when all is done, present your necks like idiot gogs at slaughter time for the Kaleen's pleasure? *Will you allow this glory to be Marack's alone—if victory comes and you be not there to share it?* What say you to this, my lords?"

I stepped back, raised my two hands, fists clenched dramatically, and slowly pivoted to face them all. The yelling was thunderous. And some were against me for what they said was my insulting tone. Their hands even went to sword hilts, but others held them back. Outside the tent, the word having been passed instantly with the telling, additional howls mixed with shouts of approbation, and defiance of Om came like waves from the farthest perimeter of the camps.

The sorcerers of Ferlach and Gheese had arisen. And as they moved around the tables the yelling quieted so that an equal wave of silence followed their gliding figures. They were of the same mold as Marack's Fairwyn and Goolbie, skinny, ethereal, self-contained, wary—and curious. Their hands were upraised. And thus the silence. They approached to within a few feet of me and halted. One could have literally heard a dubot squeak. . . .

They looked me in the eye, and there was no fear in them. "The auras," the tallest of the two said finally and in a clear, high voice, "are most evident here, my lords. But there is *no* evil. This young man, who glows with the light of Ormon and Harris, seems not quite of this world."

There was a muttered roll of "ahs" and "ohs" at that and the shorter of the two stepped one pace forward. Apparently they had arranged some test between them for, just as they had thrown a field of force about their kings and another around themselves, they sought to do some *thing* to me. This second sorcerer—he was of Ferlach and his name was Gaazi, and his taller companion was called Plati—began his *words*, to be joined in measured cadence by Plati. They watched me sharply. I smiled evenly back at them. Their own protective aura was something other than the null magnetism I was using. What they intended was powerful, though not deadly; this I found out later. Whatever it was, however, did not work. After the required number of seconds, so that they would know they had been given every chance, I smiled and stepped back. I then bowed in the graceful sweep, swirl,

155

dip, and general genuflection which was Fregis's gesture of respect and, in some cases, obeisance. . . .

"It is not wise," I said to them, "to tarry longer with your enchantments. They will have no effect on me, though I know not why. Indeed, as our good sir Rawl Fergis will tell you, there are things about me that I do not know at all. Perhaps 'tis true that I am possessed, that in this time of need and peril for all a part of that ancient Collin's power has been given to me. And perhaps 'tis true that for this special time I am as I did proclaim—the Collin."

At this last—said somewhat more softly, you may be sure— I dropped my head in a most humble attitude, and all began to cheer again.

Draslich arose, tall, black, and commanding. He waved a hand and a cushioned chair was brought to me. A flagon of sviss was brought, too, and I drank. "Sir Harl! Sir Collin!" the king said. "My lord Gane of our great city port of Reen" —and he gestured toward a black-furred grinning giant— "tells me that you fought bravely with him some three years ago against the Selig pirates. He says he remembers you as a loudmouthed, courageous youth with much spirit and few brains. He informs me"—the king smiled—"that you are much changed."

Laughter spread around like summer rain, and I joined in. "Refer me kindly to my lord," I said. "He may still be right. Indeed, when this affair is over I just may revert to being as addle-pated as before. If such the case, or otherwise, I would still call him friend, and he but call me his." I basked in the resultant smattering of applause.

Chitar arose then, red hair a flaming aureole about his equally flaming face. He paused to finish a draft of sviss before speaking, then wiped his lips with a sleeved arm. "I would simply ask," he said quietly, "how you know all this. I have seen much magic in my day. . . . I doubt not that the Kaleen prepares for battle, nor that your king, Caronne, intends to oppose him. But how know you, sir, the scope of the present fighting? And how know you of the ships and men of Om, and of the mustering of the warriors of Kelb and Great Ortmund? How know you all these things?"

"My lord," I answered bluntly. "I know not how I know, except to say that with these eyes I saw the force of Marack

156

and Kelb this very morning. And if perchance you were to meet the lord Breen Hoggle-Fitz of Durst in Great Ortmund at some future date, he will tell you that I fought at his side on this very day before the pass of the Veldian mountains. Think on that. But not for long. For if I know not the answer, sirrah, how can you?"

At that exact moment I caused the ion-beam to intensify so that my armor glowed more brilliantly. Then I let it die; but not before a chorus of "ohs" and "ahs" came from my audience at both my glowing and my words. . . . And this, too, in a growing candlelight, since all without was total darkness now.

I stood up again to continue—strongly, as if in anger and frustration. "There is this, too, oh great king of Gheese. If your warriors do not leave in haste and at once for the field of Dunguring, then, come what may, to Marack will fall the total honor. And if we go down to bloody death—alone— *yours* will be the shame, in that the countries of the north-lands were put in Omnian chains by *you*, for all eternity."

There was a roar then from those inside and from the others beyond the tent. And some were for instant departure. And some were for personal battle with me. I stood silently until finally, above the crash of sword on shield and pike butt against hardened earth, the voices of Draslich and Chitar prevailed. Draslich, after short consultation, summed it up in one brief paragraph. "We shall go to Dunguring, Sir Collin," he said. "Together we are a host of forty thousand. We shall arrive on the eve of the third day, for 'tis a full six hundred miles, and even noble dottles cannot travel faster, though we mount all our men as is our wont."

"If it will be three days," I said solemnly, "you will most likely arrive to a stricken field. Om and the Kaleen have counted on the fact that the five countries of the northland be split; that if they do join finally in mutual pact, that it cannot be implemented in sufficient time to matter. Marack stands before Dunguring *now!* It marshals its array for battle, *now!* Our king has but twenty thousand men. The lord Hoggle-Fitz rides to him with the lords of Keeng, Fleege, and Klimpinge, and another twenty thousand. They will join in two days. However, my lords, the forces of Om will land in Corchoon on the morrow. And I suspect that on the *third*

157

day a great joining of battle will take place. And if *all*—including *you*—can hold through that *third* day, then will *I* arrive with the thirty thousand who now camp before fair Glagmaron under the false lord, Fon Tweel."

All at the tables had seated themselves again, since council had seemingly begun in earnest. Chitar, chin cupped on palm, asked curiously, trying to probe behind my eyes, "You have not said, Sir Knight, how we may cross six hundred miles in but two days. I would be apprised of this."

"You have sufficient dottle herds for hard riding?"

"We do indeed."

"Then, my lords, you ride at night as well."

"At night?"

"Aye."

"Are you some fiend of Ghast? What are you, truly, sir?"

"I am the Collin! And if you truly seek to aid the north, then, great sirs, *you will ride at night*—"

When I think back on it now, I am sure that not until that very moment were they fully aware of the seriousness of the situation. That I had asked them to ride at night brought it home. All were silent, their faces strained and white. I called for sviss. The others did likewise. And the quiet continued. It was as if we were in the eye of a great hurricane. Then Chitar glanced at Draslich and Draslich nodded and Chitar arose.

"My lords all," he began solemnly. "Bear with us for we are your liege lords. It would seem from what the Collin has told us that all that has been will be as naught, do we not follow where Marack leads. It is also true that our northland will not survive our absence from the field of Dunguring—if it survives at all. Therefore would we be there to lift our swords against the might of Om. It promises to be a battle unlike to anything our world has ever known. And it will be a place where—thinking on some future time—all who now call themselves men will curse their absence, whatever the reason, did they not go to Dunguring. So finally, noble sirs, if this be sooth—then, in the matter of the dottles and the night, what, indeed, is one more broken shibboleth?

"That we will truly fight the might of Om should first be seen in that we dare to ride the blackness of tomorrow's night. . . . For we *will* ride tomorrow, sirs, and on tomorrow's night, and the day after! And in that way will we arrive

for one night's sleep, and to battle on the third day's morning!
And if we hold, as this young man prays we do, then on the
morn of the fourth day will we receive the thirty thousand of
Glagmaron for the battle's end, whatever that may be. . . .
How say you now, sirs? *Stand up and give me voice!"*

If there had been clamor before, it was as nothing to the
shouting and hurrahing that now arose. A great fever, akin to
an almost religious frenzy, swept all the tent and the massed
warriors outside. I learned later that Chitar's twenty thousand
had even marched to the river bank to hear the news from
the shouted words of men strung down to the water's edge. I
knew then what holy wars were like—crusades, and the
infantile idiocy of the call to "flag and country." In Camelot's
situation, however, the stakes *did* have merit. In effect, and
even the Boos would agree with me, whatever our means—
they would most certainly be structured to envision dire
and perilous *ends*. . . .

I switched off the ion-beam and instantly ceased to glow. I
glanced at my two sorcerers; they smiled back at me, too
caught up in the emotion of it all to notice my fall from
purity. I was about to cancel the null magnetic warp, too, but
thought better of it. Though harm would no longer come
from the sorcerers, the Kaleen still loomed large on my
personal horizon. I signaled to Rawl, arose, and went to my
original place at the great table. Then, while Draslich and
Chitar and the great lords of the two countries planned their
march—a full one-hundred and twenty-thousand dottles and
forty-thousand men in a thundering charge across six hundred
miles of mountain, plain, and river—I told him of his lady,
Caroween, of our trip to the snow-lands, and of the great
fight in the courtyard of Goolbie's keep. I put my arm around
him when I came to the loss of his lady, and my own. And
well I did. For in the telling he grew hot eyed, clapped a hand
to his fal-dirk, and in his anger would have sought some
quarrel with me had not my presence and his reasoning
prevailed.

"Well, what now then, Collin?" he asked bluntly, his anger
hardly assuaged. "Where go you now? With us? To
Glagmaron? To Vuunland? Where go you, sir—for I would
go there, too."

"You cannot."

159

"Indeed?"

"Aye, indeed! The Marackian fleet of some five hundred ships, come down from Klimpinge, should be off Ferlach's port city of Reen now. You will ride with your hundred to join it; to tell of all that has transpired so that they will know; to see that all remains well in that the greatest unity is forged then with the fleets of Ferlach and Gheese, so that—and they should number at least two thousand, all gathered—when you appear off Corchoon four days from now, the Omnian fleet will know your strength. It is desired," I improvised simply, "that no ship of the Omnian fleet will ever see the southern continent again."

"I am no sailor, and I would go with you."

"You cannot."

"Collin," Rawl said softly, and his purple eyes against the bold saffron of his fur were deeply unhappy, "I was not born to tread the planks of ships. I would fight Vuuns and rescue Caroween and your lady. I believe you in that you did this day fight in the battle of the Veldian Pass. I would go with you to Vuunland, for I know you go there, though I know not how you go."

"It cannot be," I said again.

We were being ignored now by the very dynamics of the situation, and therefore jostled by the shouting, milling throng around us, with couriers coming and going and all the marks of a great movement beginning to develop. The two kings were no novices in the marshaling of armies. "It cannot be," I repeated. "But I promise you one thing, good friend."

"Which is?"

"That you will see me again—and that after that you will be with the lady Caroween and the princess Murie Nigaard, and Lord Hoggle-Fitz, and all the great lords of Marack *on the plain of Dunguring*—if all goes well."

"What mean you—if all goes well?"

"Why, simply that despite what things may seem to be, I am as human and therefore as vulnerable to death as you, sir."

Rawl clutched my arm then, hard. His eyes gleamed fiercely, with joy of my knowledge. "Well then, Collin—see, sir, that you stay alive. We, all of us, have a stake in you. And, too, sir, mayhaps there will be much to do—even beyond this war."

I frowned. "And what means that?"

"That if we win there is still a great and unknown world beyond that river-sea. And the Kaleen is *there*."

I laughed. "Let us win here first."

We were interrupted by Rawl's two student guards. They had heard my orders to Rawl, that he was to go with the fleet from Reen in Ferlach to Saks in Gheese, and thence to Corchoon in Kelb. They liked it not; nor did the remainder of the hundred. "Do not deny us, sir," they begged, "the privilege of Dunguring."

I could not say them nay. "Cast lots," I told them. "The ten of you who lose will accompany Sir Rawl to the fleet; the remainder will join my lords of Gheese and Ferlach for the ride to Marack and Dunguring."

We left them to go joyously off to gamble while we joined the two kings at the great table. I cut the null magnetic field so that where I touched but the faintest tingle would be felt. This for my continued safety, and their surprise. We shook hands. The eyes of Draslich and Chitar lifted in astonishment, and amusement. . . .

"You have indeed summoned a *something*," Draslich said. "If it be the Collin, I know not. But I will call you friend, withal. For I think you good liege to my brother king, Caronne."

Chitar mumbled similar kudos and then asked sharply, "And do you ride with us, Sir Collin?"

"No," I said, and stepped back a pace or two. "No, m'lords. I go to another place, and now—and then to Glagmaron. Recall? I said to you that I would bring all Fon Tweel's thirty thousand—plus his head—to Dunguring."

Draslich took my cue. He asked, smiling, "You make as if to leave us now?"

"That I do, m'lords—with your permissions."

"Or without them." Chitar grinned. "Nay, nay!" He raised a muscular arm while laughing. "Let the deliberations of kings not delay you, oh Collin. . . . Just do your promised thing, and bring us the thirty thousand—else, I warn you, sir, you will answer to me when next I see you."

I bowed deeply, saluting all with the intricacies of sweep, swirl, and dip. Then I pressed the ion-beam to glow again, walked with Sir Rawl Fergis to my fat and *wheeeing* dottle (he had ordered a dottle saddled for himself), vaulted upon her fur-cloaked back, and bid the gathered throng within and without the tent a hearty farewell.

In a sense what followed was like running a gauntlet. Though the long double line to the edge of the cooking tents brandished no clubs, they did hold swords and spears aloft, which they then brought crashing down upon their shields in thunderous cadence. The cheering was deafening, too. And I kept my arm raised in salute as I rode, my armor all ablaze.

At one point a herd-warden—by the insignia upon his jupon—yelled over the clamor all around him: "Where did you find my lovely dottle, Zelpha, Great Collin?"

" 'Twas she who searched for me," I shouted back.

"Then keep close rein, withal," he cautioned loudly. "For like my wife, she tends to stray."

The ensuing roar of laughter was followed by more "hails" and "aves," and Rawl and I continued on. At the edge of the tents, and therefore at the edge of darkness, we halted. "I would leave you here, Sir Fergis," I told him.

"Just like that, m'lord?"

"Exactly."

"So let it be—if we meet again at Dunguring."

"We will," I said. "And mayhaps before. I promise you." We shook hands and I turned and left him there; and beyond him all the others who had ringed the fires to watch.

As I kneed my dottle, Zelpha, toward the darkness of the grassy fields and the small hill beyond, I damped the ion-beam so that I would begin to fade; so that in their eyes I would now slowly disappear. . . .

Minutes later, at the top of the hill, I dismounted and gave that overly friendly Zelpha a rump pat to send her on her way. I was not surprised when she swiftly turned her head to give me a quick blubbery kiss such as Pug-Boos oft receive from dottles. Then she clicked her heels and ran off to the herd. . . . I wiped my face with the hem of my surcoat and smiled.

I slept in the starship, insulated from Pug-Boo probes. They had suggested one thing; that thing I would do. Still I was not about to accept interference from them, on any level—or from my cohorts on the *Deneb-3* either. I was tired and I slept well. Toward morning, since controls had been set, I was gently massaged by bed-fingers. More, I was bathed and oiled with a healing flesh unguent, so that when I actually did get up, it was as a phoenix from one's proper fire. Erstwhile Terran fanatics would call it being born again. I, too, clicked my heels, like dainty Zelpha, and went to breakfast.

It was still night. Vuunland was next—Vuunland and Murie. And now that all else had been done, I allowed myself to think of her; of that elfish, piquant, great-eyed face; of that small body that was so fantastically feminine that even now, were I to dwell upon it, I would develop one damn large pain in my gut. . . . "All right! Shield-maiden!" I exclaimed aloud to the control panel. "Your bold and brilliant lover is on his way."

As I plummeted south across the night side of Fregis-Camelot, I seemed to follow the path of Ripple, the second and smaller moon. And it, in turn, seemed to trail the wake of Capil, the larger and brighter.

Again I had time. Requested data about Vuuns and Vuunland had been given me in the instant tape from the *Deneb-3*. Though the creatures had long been thought extinct by those of the northern countries, Watchers had known of their continued existence through pirates, prisoners, and the few Selig tradesmen who dared the sea to the northern cities. One had but to go to where they once held sway, and that in the great mountains to the east of Om, itself. Thrice two thousand miles the distance was. How fast, I wondered, did a great Vuun fly?

I dropped low in the protective darkness to skim the waters of the river-sea. I passed over many hundreds of tropical islands, then a calm; then a raging storm with the visible fury of great phosphorescent waves.

Then I was over the continental landmass of Kerch, and beyond that country to jungle and high savannah and teeming river life such as was not listed in Watcher data, except for mountain Yorns. Fregis-Camelot possessed a myriad of life-forms, of which the great Vuuns were but one.

Om began with the high ground, the plains, and the lofty mountains in chain on chain. I regretted that I had no time for all that night-bathed grandeur. My goal was the eastern-most alps called Ilt on our maps and matrix. There were only trackless wastes below. Indeed, other than the few paths from

Omnian cities to the northern ports of Kerch and Selig, across thousands of miles of plain and jungle, the southern continent, like the north, was virgin territory. I had time to wonder what truly lay in all those massive, forested wastes that was of Camelot-Fregis alone—and not derived of the tragic refugees of Fomalhaut's Alpha. . . .

The Vuuns, I had learned, were telepaths which, when you think on it, should have told us something. Whatever. I was keyed to contact with them. I slowed the starship so that to ground view I would seem as a floating, baubled facsimile of St. Elmo's fire. . . . I relaxed wholly in the encompassing contour chair before the ship's screen, letting my mind be open, receptive to all that might come. Though I had tried this once before, thinking the Pug-Boos would seize the opportunity for contact, nothing had happened. I thought now that it would be ludicrous indeed if those same Pug-Boos chose to intervene at this point. Even the Kaleen might join in the hookup, were he aware that such existed. But he or "it" did not, and I had no fear that he would. Instead I received the first glimmerings, half-formed pictures and disconnected thoughts of lesser Fregisian creatures; for all simple animals in their formative, evolutionary years, have the potential for telepathy. But finally, to my S.O.S. of, "I would speak to you! I would speak to you!" there came an answer.

"*Who speaks!* Who on all this world save us, and that which lies in the tomb of Hish, has the power to speak thusly?" The projected thought-words were icy cold, insistent. They formed an alien web to seize upon my mind so that I felt a sudden, abysmal, soul-choking fear. I didn't reply at once. Instead I ceased my probe and listened, regaining composure. Again the question: "Who speaks to us? Who speaks to us who have known the world forever? Say again, and now—and know that your life will not be forfeit."

I then said boldly, "I speak. And I would meet with you, and would you tell me how and where."

"Who are you? *What* are you?"

"I am one of those of which you are informed. But I am different. I would have council with you. I would not, nor could not, harm you; nor you myself. But there is that which you should know which only I can tell."

"How know we that you cannot harm us?"

164

"I am a man of the northern world. Can such harm you? Look now at me and all that I truly am." I then projected a self-image so they would know. "How can *I* harm *you?*"

There was a great silence which seemed to last and last, so that I became afraid they had broken contact. "Hear me!" I said again, peremptorily. "Hear me! I would speak with you."

"Oh, simple man," the thought came through and strongly. "What would you say to us who have lived forever? Why do you come at all? Well we know that we are the horrors of your dreams, the dragons of your play in childhood. What want you now of us, who have brought you naught but death before?"

"I would speak," I said calmly, "of that which lies in Hish, and of what it plans for you. For though it be true that I cannot harm you—no Vuun now living will survive the thing with which you now enjoin, if you continue in your path."

"You are aflight!" The thoughts came again, and almost in excitement. "We see you as a glowing thing in darkling skies. Why should we not now strike you down, and end our new-found fear of you?"

"You could not do that."

"Then you *can* harm us."

"No. I cannot, for I am prevented by a force stronger than yourselves. But that in Hish, for which you now do service, can truly bring you naught but death."

"And so have we begun to think. Yea. We will see you. And do you harm us, we have two of yours that likewise will be harmed."

"I know this," I said bluntly. "Now through my eyes I see the following—and it is for you to guide me." And I told them of serrated chains of mountains and chasms, all covered with snow, since it was winter in this southern clime. They then gave me directions so that I selected one great valley with giant conifers at its bottom, and implanted with stunted, twisted growths of evergreens on its precipitous slopes and craggy ridges. I went full up its length to where white water sprang from a high precipice, beyond which lay another, tighter valley of barren blasted rock and night cliffs. In contrast to the wintry white of snow and gray-white granite, the great surrounding peaks were volcanic. From them poured an empurpled mass of flame, so that the dawn sky was laced with a kaleidoscope of hellish colors.

I was told to enter this shadow valley, which I did. At its farthest end there arose great cliffs to the height of the final base of volcanic peaks. These, other than their glowing cones —from which I was pleased to see there came no lava—were snow-girt and perma-iced. Three quarters of the way up the sheer black cliffs (some six thousand feet) at the valley's end, were the mouths of great caves. These were indented somewhat in that before them was a ledge; full circle for some ten miles. To left and right were other cliffs and ledges and caves, so that I knew that here indeed were the homes of Vuuns.

"Where are you, then?" I mentally asked. "Of all these caves, I know not which—and further—he or those with whom I talk must have authority for decisions. For in what I do there is little time. I would not waste it idly."

"We are three," the voice of the great Vuun replied. "We are council *and* authority."

"Then one thing more. Bring the two of whom you spoke, for I would see that they are unharmed."

"Indeed?" The voice grew colder still, and held the fine edge of insult. "Are you some miserable mating animal, then? And is that, perhaps, your real and total purpose?"

"It is *not!*"

I landed the small craft beneath the direction of the great Vuun. We came to stony ground before a cave mouth of a full six hundred yards in width. Indeed, the ledge itself was a full two hundred yards from mouth to lip. I stepped to rock, damped out the ship, and instantly moved toward the entrance. I was dressed lightly, though warmly, in green shirt, padded jacket, and breeches and furred knee-boots. I wore my belt and sword and nothing else. I stood stock-still before moving to enter the cave.

"And now I must caution you," I said strongly. "If any harm comes to me from you, and I enter yonder cave, you and all the dwindling handful of the life that you represent will rue it to your last great stinking breath; for I tell you now that I bring you years of peace—but that without me, *for you there will be nothing.*"

"Enter the cave mouth, Man," the great Vuun answered, "and stop your mewling. As for the stink you mention, know you this and know it well: it is the smell of life to us; whereas 'tis you and the likes of you that bring the stench of flesh and carrion. . . . Now! Enough! Come to us and you will not be harmed!"

Despite my bluster I entered that cave with an understandable degree of trepidation. Again, I was encompassed with a null magnetic field against the Kaleen. It would avail me little, however, if the Vuun and all its cohorts sought to squash me —one flick of a monstrous claw and that would be that.

The clouds, snow-filled and gray, had been low outside, therefore the light within was meager. I found a gigantic, seemingly endless hall whose dripping walls rose to a great ceiling beyond my sight in the semidarkness. Its depths disappeared before me in like manner.

To the left and right, at one hundred yards within the entrance, were raised platforms of some semitranslucent and softened substance. They could be likened to great green and glowing pillows. Upon each of these there was a Vuun. They rested, great leathern wings folded along the length of ghastly, mottled bodies; necks hunched back upon slate-gray, bone-slick shoulders; and head lying forward upon a breast that resembled nothing less than a giant kettledrum. The eyes were what I was drawn to. They were red with green pupils, saucer-sized, cold, completely detached. They were half lidded, with the leathern, membranous lids coming up from the bottom. And they seemed to slumber; to be unseeing, uncaring. I hesitated to stare briefly to right and left. Then I continued on. I passed, in the space of minutes—and indeed I seemingly walked for many a city block—a number of great niches, passageways, from which came the hellish orange-red-purple glow of far volcanic fires. The Vuuns had created these passageways, I knew, for even they were no friends of darkness. Then, in the distance, what had been but a blue-green glow came finally alive in definition. Nine great green and glowing pillows before a raised dais; equal to its height. And beyond them, for they were centered in the great cave, were the entrances to other passageways, each Vuun-sized, like subways of antiquity. Around the periphery of the dais, and in a perfect arc, was a small stream cut from the very rock. Its water was heated, green, and phosphorescent. I assumed it was of volcanic origin. The temperature within the cave had risen considerably, though it was not uncomfortable.

I continued on, vaulting upon the dais, for there were no steps. Of the nine pillows, but three were occupied. And, though the resting Vuuns seemed alike to those at the gates, still there was a difference. The great red eyes were not lidded, but rather they looked straight at me with a deathlike stare of monstrous, reptilian *Lazarae*. . . .

I placed my hands upon my hips and stared right back, from one to the other, albeit all were alike to me.

"And now"—the same voice probed my mind—"you are here. "And you will give us the simple reason why we should not kill you."

"That I will most certainly do. But first the two we spoke of. I would see them here and now."

"Then you are indeed but a mating animal."

I frowned, paused, then said mentally in tones sufficiently cold to match their own, "Keep those stupid thoughts inside your lizard heads and let us recognize and accept the fact that we are alien, one unto the other. We are alien, *but of the same galaxy*. I think that if we do this, we will soon see that we still have more in common with each other than with that blasphemous thing of Hish—before which *you* now scrape and bow."

The center Vuun—his eyes blazed briefly more scarlet—said bluntly, ignoring my gibes, "You speak of galaxies, Man. What know *you* of galaxies?"

"As much or more than you. And therefore am I here. Now where are the two?"

"They come."

And I waited. And apparently they had been already coming, for within minutes a metal-ribbed boat stretched with oiled and sewn skins appeared upon the artificial stream. In it were Murie and Caroween and two men, guards by their appearance. At sight of them I drew my sword. If the Vuuns had aught to say of this they let it pass. They simply glared with baleful eyes.

The stream passed to within but a hundred yards of the dais. The boat halted. The guards lashed it to a knobbed protuberance. Then they brought the two girls to the dais, lifted them, and placed them on it. It was a goodly hundred and fifty feet across, just right for Vuun hearing. For a man it was the width of a soccer field.

Murie looked beautiful, just beautiful! Her petite form was wrapped in a green velvet undersuit from which she had long since stripped her small link-armor. Her purple eyes sparkled with a glitter for me alone. . . . The vibes were great. Her surcoat, jupon, had been quite bloodied, as I remembered it.

It now, like her page-boy bob and beaming face, was well scrubbed. Caroween, other than her red hair and heather attire, was Murie's mirrored image—for both were of a similar size and shape.

Though the light in the cave was insufficient to spell me out, the very arrogance of my posture told them who I was, for they literally ran to me. They ran to me and I took the both of them; I could not have denied Caroween the presence of Rawl. And to her that's who I was. Murie would not have had it otherwise. So, with one hand still grasping my sword, my arms were filled with sweet-smelling, giggling—and half crying—female flesh; the best all Camelot had to offer. A redhead and a blond against either shoulder. Aye! That I should drop dead in just such a situation. . . . I stared beyond their heads to the red eyes of the three great Vuuns, daring them to think one stupid thought. They seemed impassive, not caring a Terran fig. Then I remembered the two guards who accompanied the girls. I gently pushed Murie and Caroween to one side.

They were two hulking brutes in leather harness and loincloths. They looked at me doltishly, though there was something of awe in their stare, too.

"Are you of Om?" I asked softly.

One of them answered gruffly, his eyes wavering: "What is Om?"

I simply stared and shook my head. I turned to look keenly at the three Vuuns and returned my sword to its sheath. *They knew nothing of Om,* and that was interesting.

If they had I would have killed them instantly, for I would not trust the Vuuns to maintain my presence secret, other than through themselves.

I said harshly, "Stand back. Move to the edge of this platform and do not come near us again until I say you can."

Then I kissed Murie, held her tight and held Caroween, too. When I drew away for breath she managed to choke out, "Hey now, m'lord! At first I thought you overlong in coming—and now it seems but seconds from that gray place of stone and ice." She buried her face again in the hollow of my shoulder.

"And did you ever doubt it—my coming?"

"Not for a breath, my lord." Her voice came muffled.

I tipped her face upward and kissed her again. When I let her go she asked pertly, "Now how will you deal with yon great buzzards—so as to free us?"

"I'll manage."

Then I turned to Caroween and kissed her, too, though on her comely cheek, and not with passion. "I have seen your knight," I told her. "And this but short hours ago. He is well. He goes to Reen in Ferlach, and from there to a great plain called Dunguring some miles from Corchoon, the capital of Kelb."

"Does my lord know of my circumstances?"

"Indeed, for I have told him."

"Then why, sir, is he not with you?"

"Because I could not let him come, my lady."

"Well now, indeed, m'lord," the girl began, almost angrily. But Murie spoke up sharply, saying, "Cari! Do not fault my lord, when he is here to take us from the taloned grasp of yon great pot-pies. Look to your reason."

Upon this my redhead burst into tears, kissed my cheek quickly again, and buried her face in the hollow of my remaining shoulder. At this last I detected a faintly raised eyebrow from my not-too-gentle Murie Nigaard, and I patted Caroween's shoulder for exactly three seconds, then let her go. I held Murie again, felt the length of her soft body since neither of us wore but simple clothes. I brushed her lips and eyes and pert nose with my lips. I even managed to nibble a pointy ear; all in defiance, I think, of those three great Vuuns —or at least in part.

I then said, "I ask now, Murie, that you give me your silence, your respect, and all your confidence. For I will converse with those Vuuns and you will not hear of what we say. And there is no time now to explain. With luck there will be forever, later."

She stared at me with those great purple eyes. Then she touched my chest with dainty lingering fingertips. "I do not know what you are, or who, or from where, my lord—except I know that you be here with me. Now say your say to those great monsters, and I am your true right arm."

Murie then stepped to Caroween and they stood with their arms around each other, as I deemed they had often done these three most fearful days and nights from Goolbie's keep. I advanced three paces toward the edge of the dais and faced the enemy. I placed my hands on my hips and sent an enlivening mental charge across that space that I knew was pure shock to them. . . . "And now," I said, "we will begin our parley. . . ."

"Indeed!" The icy thought came back to me. "Have you finally done with your obscene writhings and chucklings and sickening rubbings, which to our eyes are cause for reflex horror?"

"Have done," I answered softly. "There is no need."

"Have done, indeed! You miserable mating animal! Have done *completely*. And touch not again in our presence those ghastly, maggoty facsimiles of yourself. For if you do, we shall terminate this talk and you—and instantly! Now tell us of *galaxies* and delay no longer."

And I told them. I told them of Fomalhaut and of Fomalhaut II, and of the twin stars with their twin systems; and of those systems' total place in our total galaxy; and of the galaxies of our universe. And through it all a great and turgid silence reigned inside each monstrous horned head. And finally, when I was through, the middle Vuun—and somehow I gathered that he had a name and that the name was Ap—said bluntly, "So we have thought it to be, Man-thing. Across the centuries we have discussed it. And our conclusions, though not precise in fact, are in theory substantiated by all you say."

"You have arrived at this knowledge by pure reason?"

"We have had time for it, Man-thing."

"How long, then, is your life-span?"

"A thousand Fomalhaut years."

"Then how long has it been, exactly, since the arrival of the men from that far, other world—for *you* would know."

"Five thousand years and a score. And that is their brief history. There were twelve great ships, each with a thousand man-things; and some came here to this great world south of the river-sea. The others landed in the north. And they were all as children then, knowing nothing of their past or of the intricacies of their carriers. And we thought at first that all would die. But that was not to be. And in this short time —since their race memory has prevailed—they have created gods and cities in which to dwell and kings to rule and serfs to serve, so that now, though still few, they range the two great continents. And we who breed but slowly, and sometimes not at all, for we are not as you and have few such desires, have, with the coming of knowledge, little to do but watch and await our death in some far millennium. . . ."

"There were only man-things aboard those ships—no other life?"

"None but that which lies in Hish."

"Then all life here—?"

"Is as it was. We are the dominants; next come dottles, gerds, fixls and like ruminants, and the killer-things of Whist, and some others like them, and so on down the line to insects and the things of the sea."

"And great Yorns?"

"They are man-things, but different, for they are in some way diseased. They are from a single ship which landed in our median-tropic-upland zones."

"And Pug-Boos?"

"Tender leaf-eaters here in our southland. And if the trees do not leaf in proper time the Pug-Boos simply wait and stare, and stare and starve, and finally fall down to the ground."

"They are that stupid?"

"They *are* that stupid."

"What of ecological balance? Are there no carnivores?"

I knew the answer, in general, to that question, except for the Vuun's reference to "the killer-things of Whist—and others." But my desire was to place the Vuun; therefore the question.

"As stated, there are a sufficiency for the job. And they come in many kinds, those meat-eaters. They range both continents."

"And you," I dared ask the question, "are you meat-eaters?"

Again the icy calm of concentration, and then the words. "Think on it, Man. Were we carnivorous with our great size, life as you know it now would long since have vanished from this fecund world. We feed upon the flora of the sea from which we came. And we are at peace with all life."

"I have heard otherwise."

"In the beginning we did attack those from the ships, thinking them a great and perilous danger. When we found out differently, we let them be."

"And those of the guards who brought my companions here?"

"They are *our* men; from another, single ship of the twelve. They serve us."

"Indeed," I said.

"Indeed," Ap answered.

"Well now," I said bluntly, "let us get to our point. And in lieu of unnecessary prattle and dissimulation I will simply tell you that which *is*, for I think I know you now. And though we do be alien, one to the other, it remains as I said before—that there is more between us than there is between you and that *thing* that lies in rocky Hishian bowels—that which calls itself the Kaleen."

"Correction, Man-thing. It calls itself nothing. It is you and yours which have given it the name, Kaleen."

"Whatever. To what end, I ask, have you made pact with it, so that you go against the men of the north, and thereby, with their defeat, enhance its power?"

"This Kaleen, so we have believed, is not warlike. It lies quiescent, except when man-things go beyond their present status and seek to build; to *know;* to advance themselves to what they were when they first came. For us, too, this continued growth of man-things cannot be. For if it happens, then in all this world there will be no place for Vuuns. We are few now—less than five hundred. We have no great love of

173

life. But while we live, and while a spark of interest yet remains, we would be at peace and not be driven. We would think our thoughts and know our soil, our sky, and our great seas: we would not have our world change."

"I see."

"Do you?"

"Great Ap," I told him, "know this and know it well. In all our shared galaxy, nay, in all our great universe, there are ten thousand times ten thousand worlds like this one. Some are virgin, jungle and great forests, and they teem with life, while others do not. *And there are worlds where live those akin to you.* And finally, in some far future, this world will change and there is nothing you or any life-form can do about it. Certainly the thing of Hish will not prevent that change. Indeed, it fosters it even now—for its own ends."

And then I told them what the Pug-Boos had told me, leaving nothing out but that the information came from a source other than my Foundation. "And look," I said finally. "The control of this planet which the thing of Hish plans for itself—and this a control of *all* life here, including yours—this very act creates the circumstances for change. The thing has given the men of Om a magic power; though, as told to you, the power is derived of knowledge and not of magic. This power has extended beyond Om to all the lands of the two continents. In the northern world it is even taught in collegiums as a practical course. Think you not that each succeeding generation of men will not question further the real source of this power? And think you not that sooner or later they will find it? When that is done, well then indeed will men arise to the glory of their past—and all that is will change.

"So be it! Logic tells us that one of two things will happen then, The first: Om and the Kaleen will prevail—meaning that the force of Hish will dominate this planet, including you, to an end of which we know not. The second: That Om and the Kaleen will lose—meaning that if the force continues to be held in check, this planet will then come under the domination of a greater race of men; the difference being that unlike the Kaleen, they will not threaten *you.* Indeed, we of the Foundation now, and the ones who come later if you are still here, are prepared to offer you the stars and a companionship akin to yourselves which, without us, you could never know. Think well on that. And think well *now*, for the hours pass. I will give you time for council, and I will await your answer."

I stepped back my three paces to rejoin Murie and Caroween.

"Has there been converse, my lord?" Murie asked. "We have heard naught but a great silence."

"Aye, there has," I replied. "But 'twas a thing of the mind such as dreams are made of, though clearer pictured so all is understood. Now tell me, how was it with you these three long days?"

She moved toward me but I held up my hand. "Stay where you are, my true love. For we must not *disturb* yon sensitive horrors with our petty 'pats and rubbings.' They deem it unseemly."

Murie's mouth made a perfect "O" of absolute surprise and indignation. "Well do they, indeed, my lord," she began, her voice rising.

"Nay, nay!" I said again. "Softly, for they are conversing, and I have asked their aid. Now tell me of your travail."

She looked at me steadily then, until I smiled and blew her a masculine kiss from where I stood so that she sighed and finally said, "Well, m'lord, along that waterway and through those great cave halls there is a world of stone and people and houses and fields where strange vegetables are grown. At one point there is a great round valley open to the sky with a mountain on all sides. [I knew by this description that she meant the burned-out inner base of the cone of a volcano.] Upon this black soil more things are grown. And there is a lake in its center from which this very water comes. There we were kept, Caroween and I, in a great house not unlike those of our Glagmaron city. . . . The people of this Vuunland know nothing of the outside world. They are content here and go about their business with no complaint."

"But do they not resent their slavery to yon Vuuns?"

"In sooth, no! For they do not deem it slavery. They make the resting pillows you see which are of a strange material and hold the heated water from the lake so that the Vuuns rest warm. They bathe the Vuuns sometimes with great brush and giant scraper. Also they grow a certain pepper delicacy which the Vuuns do greatly love. Other than that, nothing. They look upon the Vuuns as their protectors from all the horror that is outside the mountain chain. And that is that."

"We sought to tell them of ourselves," Caroween put in. "But in sooth, they were hardly interested, so we let them be."

"What of the prince of Kelb?" I asked Murie. "You were slated, my dear, for his bed and board, and not for Vuunland."

Murie smiled. "We, too," she said, "were witness to this thing you speak of as 'dream pictures.' For after we left you our strength came back to us—though 'twas sore cold in the high air where that great monster flew us—and the pictures came. They were directed to that evil prince and his remaining warriors who clung here and there upon the net. The pictures said most clearly that only the prince and his men would be allowed to leave when we came to earth in Kelb. That black-browed prince did cry and moan then. But the Vuun said nothing more. And when the prince saw that Caroween and I were awake and to life again he threatened me and tried to mount the netting all around the great Vuun's body, so as to reach me with a fal-dirk. And I called him coward and base dubot, as did Caroween. But he came on. And it was then that the great Vuun's head, its saucer-eyes all ablaze, turned around on its long and ugly neck to dart toward the prince so that he retreated tailward, all white and sore afraid.

"We came aground in darkness and left the same way. And so it was. The next morn we were here, in Vuunland—ignored and waiting for my lord."

Great Gods! I thought. *The Vuun flew six thousand miles, and in only twelve hours. I have judged them right.*

"Do you fancy Vuun flight, my dearest honey-pot?" I asked, grinning.

"Were it not forced. And were I free, too, of the smell, it could be interesting."

"It may well be," I cautioned, "that you will return the way you came."

"And not with my lord?" Tears welled from Murie's eyes and I was hard put not to join her since she had the power, the singular ability, to evoke a like emotion in me.

"It may have to be that way," I continued. "But fear not, for you will land within your father's very camp, knowing naught of either the trip or its discomforts and danger. And mark you: *On that very day I will join you.* On that very day, too, will we fight a battle such as our world will talk about for all time. And then," I whispered softly, to Murie alone, "will you truly be my shield-maiden. And that, too—for all time."

They listened starry-eyed, an amalgam of wonder and tears. Murie opened her mouth to speak again but the Vuun's thought came strong, insistent. I raised my hand to Murie for her silence and took my three paces forward.

"Man-thing!" The voice rang icily, harshly, in my ears. "We have conferred. And other than our answer, I would inform you that there is one of us who knows you of the snow mountains in the north. He that brought those two mating creatures here. He says of you that you are a killer of life, a thing of nightmares. Yet despite this knowledge, we will trust you. For we have probed your mind and found you guileless. What you have said, though we know that there be things still hidden from us, is true. Therefore will we desist in all aid for the thing of Hish; rather will we await the outcome of the battle, and further contact with you."

I said courteously, "I welcome your decision. But know this, for you have lived too long in splendid isolation: *All* life remains what it is, a thing of struggle, a thing of change; the formula advanced a millennium ago that you are either a part of the solution or a part of the problem holds true today; here, now, on Camelot-Fregis. Therefore I caution you: There is *no* neutral ground. And if you do not do what you have agreed upon with the thing of Hish, it will someday do something to you."

"Over us it has no power," Ap said simply. "We have long known of magnetic fields and their simple cancellation—such as that which you use now. The thing knows we know and can do nothing. It is still too weak. We had allied ourselves with it for the reasons that we told you. And because we know that our ability to create null-magnetism may protect us now from the thing, this would not be true of the developing powers of Man."

"Well put," I said. "A question now: Other than your seizure of the princess of Marack—this facsimile of a man-thing, as you call her—how else would you have aided Om?"

"Ten of us were to appear over the field of the coming

177

battle, where we would terrorize your thousands with our presence."

"Om counts on this appearance?"

"Aye."

"When?"

"Since armies are gathered—and still gathering—we have been informed that the time will be soon."

"How are you so informed?"

"In the same manner whereby we converse with you now."

"There is danger, then, that the Kaleen will know of me through you?"

"None. For we ourselves control our thoughts and entry."

"Then, though I have said that there is no neutral ground, your participation could still be limited. I would ask but one thing: On the day of final battle, a single Vuun will land within the center of Marack's forces, and there deposit yon princess, Murie Nigaard, and her companion, the lady Caroween. . . . Then all upon that field will see and know that Vuuns are *not* allied with Om."

"And if we do *not* do as you ask, Man-thing?"

"Well then, nothing. I will simply take these two of ours with me now; the battle will be fought without your aid—and if it is lost, as well it may be, anyway—then you, in part, will share the blame. . . . For the thing of Hish will win the day and all that could have been will be as naught. Think on that and what it means for *you*. And remember, too, that which I ask is simple-small."

" 'Tis more than 'simple-small.' It is alliance."

"But you risk nothing. As you yourself have said, the Kaleen can bring no harm to you."

"But in the future, if you lose and the Kaleen grows stronger."

"By Great Ormon!" I mentally screamed at them. "Know you that on that blood-field one hundred times a thousand men will give their lives in battle against Om? And if we be in the right, those 'men-things' will have also died for *you!* Have you never heard of areas of agreement for mutual gain? Of positive unities of opposites? Think what you will, your future lies with *us* and not with the thing of Hish and that dark universe beyond the gateway. *So say you now! What will you do?* For, in all sooth, you try my patience sorely."

I stood proudly with folded arms and steely glare and held those six great blazing saucer-eyes as if in thrall. The silence mounted, bled off to every nook and passageway from that great dais. And somehow they communicated with each other; not just the three, but the whole five hundred.

Ap spoke to me. "Man-thing," he said. "Your logic does your courage justice, for you are right in what you say. I myself will go to that plain beyond the Kelbian city of Corchoon. But just how will you protect me against being feathered with ten thousand arrows?"

"Yon maid"—I mentally grinned, taking a certain license with the word—"will fly her father's colors from your back. And thus will you be safe."

"It will be done."

"Then, Great Ap, your flight accomplished, retire to here. And on some future date, if it be your desire, we will meet again and speak of galaxies and the others of your kind in this great universe which we share—agreed?"

"Agreed, Man-thing. You have our permission to leave."

"I will first say good-bye to my friends."

"Let it be done."

And then, as if the sight of my good-byes would be too much for them, the membranous lids of their great eyes flicked up and over so that only the faintest of red showed through.

I said softly to Murie, " 'Tis done. I leave you now. But first there is a thing I must do—for the both of you."

"And what is that, my lord?"

"I would that you did not suffer the long flight through the cold and the night. And I will, with your permissions, prepare you for it."

"How so, my lord?"

"Like this." I drew her slight figure to me and beckoned Caroween to join us. I put my cheek against Murie's for the space of seconds, then pulled back. "I want you both," I told

179

them, "to watch my eyes and nothing else, and to listen to my voice." They did so. And shortly, according to my powers, they were in deep hypnosis.

I told them what they were to do: that they would not fear the flight; that all they remembered of me in this hall would be swept from their minds, but that with Murie the faintest of memories would linger so that she would know that it was because of me that this had happened. One thought I implanted deeply. Murie was to tell her father, if she arrived at Dunguring before I did, and if he doubted that which he would hear from Draslich and Chitar, that I would arrive on the final day of battle—with all of Fon Tweel's thirty thousand. And then I freed them from my spell, and that was that.

We walked to the edge of the dais, my arms close around them. I even helped them enter the cockleshell boat. Before they left, of course, I held Murie tight once again and kissed her and told her that I would see her very soon.

And, as stated, that was that. . . .

The boat moved off into the passageway where it disappeared. I then turned to the three great Vuuns, saw that their eyes were open, and bowed respectfully in their direction. "Until that time, Great Ap," I said.

Great Ap said nothing, though he seemed to mentally nod his acquiescence.

I returned to the massive entrance with its Vuun guardians. I nodded to them, too, but they ignored me. It had begun to snow so that all was a swirl of white before my eyes. I advanced a few feet, gave the numbers aloud that phased in the starship, and continued cautiously, wary of the edge of the precipice, until I could feel its bulk with my hands.

Once inside, I shot straight up from the snow-blanketed ledge so that again the greater part of the southern continent of Camelot-Fregis lay below me. North then, and across the trackless jungle and the river-sea. I hovered thrice. The first time over Dunguring to watch the gathering hosts. The main body of the Omnian-Kerchian-Seligian armada had landed and the fields and roads from Corchoon were packed with hordes of marching soldiery. The Marackian army remained at twenty thousand. They had yet to be joined by Hoggle-Fitz. I would have stopped had I the time to make contact, to tell Caronne and the lord Per-Rondin that help was coming. But Fitz would be there shortly, anyway. Then to Glagmaron. All was as the previous day. No single tent struck, no charge of dottles to the west. . . .

On the great south road from Ferlach and Gheese there streamed a dottle horde such as few men have ever seen: three abreast for a full thirty miles. They were a flowing wash of color in the proudly displayed banners and pennons of Ferlach and Gheese. Forty thousand fighting men—three dottles per rider: one hundred and twenty thousand dottles. The very earth shuddered to their million pounding paws. The sight was as a flowing river of gray lava, mottled with white and black and buff—and it was beautiful.

Then to my last stop, the mountain road that crossed the southern sea-plain to the port city of Reen in Ferlach. I had directed Rawl to go to Reen because I had no desire to appear twice before the hordes of Chitar and Draslich. Now he traveled with but ten student warriors.

I followed the road down from the battlefield of the river bank to where I spotted their group some miles before the pass that led down to the sea. I settled to a shaded spot, damped the ship, and moved to the road and waited. Again I slept on a grassy hummock overlooking the path; for again I had time. It was high noon. It would take Rawl and his ten another hour to reach me, and I needed that hour. The road to the north from my hummock was straight for a good two miles. It crossed two small streams and a series of gog-meadows. I awoke with minutes to spare and lazed luxuriously. All around me were the strident voices of quarreling tuckle-birds, plus the sweet warbling of something in fluffy beige and purple feathers. I had been joined, too, by two small dubots. They sat on a log and nibbled ipy nuts and discussed me raucously.

And then, as predictable as Fomalhaut in orbit, there came Rawl. I slid down the fifteen feet of grassy knoll, stood in mid-road, and held up my hand.

They were eleven riders and thirty-three dottles. Rawl was shaking his head for the last one hundred yards. He knew full well who I was. "Sir Lenti, Sir Collin," he said lightly. "What now, Sir Sorcerer? I see that I shall meet you on every road on Fregis. Have you changed your plans?"

"Nay, Sir Fergis." I grinned. "I have simply come to change yours."

"My lord," he exploded. "Not again?"

"Gather around," I said to all of them.

And I explained what was to be; that their chief would go with me, while they would continue to Reen to help cement the needed unity among the ships of Marack, Ferlach, and Gheese. Our ten brave valiants groaned at this, but I never saw a man more happy to give up his command than Rawl. "Take your armor," I cautioned, for he was dressed as light as I, though all his men wore link mail.

Then we stood together in mid-road while our gallants, banished, as they saw it, to banal tasks while others rode to glory, nevertheless managed to shake our hands as they rode by us. . . .

"What now, oh mighty Collin?" Rawl asked when we were alone. "Here we stand with my gear beside me upon the ground, and neither dottle, gerd, nor gog-pet for our transport. . . . I await, sir," and he gave a most respectful bow, "your magic. . . ."

"First the magic of your strong back. Follow me and pick up that mess of pot-metal."

He did, and we struggled back up the hummock and down its far side and into the little clearing where I had left the ship. I phased it in, called on its port to open, and bade Rawl enter.

I sat him down in my contour's twin, ordered up food, and bade him eat of it. "Say not a word," I admonished, as we both munched hungrily from the trays of offered goodies. "Say not a word, my friend. For come tomorrow you will remember naught of this, save that by sorcery you traveled with me from Ferlach to far Glagmaron, and all in the space of minutes."

"Why not remember?" he asked blithely. " 'Twould be a pleasant tale for my old age."

"We'll see," I said. "But for the moment, believe me. 'Tis

a thing that no one should know. Someday," I said, "some-day. . . ."

"Someday indeed," he echoed me.

And now would be the last step before Glagmaron and the moving of Fon Tweel's host to the field of Dunguring. It was my definite intent to *zap* the lord Fon Tweel this very night, and to put Rawl, Griswall, and Charney in command of the thirty thousand for the six-hundred-mile dottle-dash to the aid of Marack and the north. I would not make that trip, or so I thought then; I would do one last flight of the starship and thereby arrive fresh for the denouement to this massive, alien web of plan and plot.

We chatted and spent some time. I told Rawl of the Vuuns and of Murie and Caroween, and that we would all meet on the plain of Dunguring. And then as it grew late I activated the ship and we rose straight up for a good two hundred miles. I bade Rawl—since he would lose all memory of it, anyway—to look his fill at "the fairest planet of them all." He did, then he said, "And I would fight even you, Collin, for the privilege of a memory."

"Nay!" I said. "Nay!" And I felt an utter bastard before the justice of his thoughts. "Someday, as stated. I *promise* you."

We cut back down then, through Fregis's atmosphere to Glagmaron. I asked Rawl to don his armor, stating that when next he blinked his eyes he would be at the spot where he first met me.

He looked at me strangely. "I should," he told me, "fight you, anyway. For it is not fitting that such as I should be played upon by you. It seems to me that I, we all, are as puppets to your hand. You say you will take my memory. You appear here and there, and always in battle—or the preparation thereof—so that all my world is now in perilous confrontation with the hell of Om and the dark Kaleen. Yet how know I really that this is not all a thing of yours, and yours alone?"

"You don't," I said gruffly. "But I think you have seen sufficient to know that it is not." And then I said a thing to him which, had the Boos or the Foundation overheard me, would no doubt have found me blasted—instantly. "Rawl," I said strongly, "I promise you—and this promise will not be

183

taken from your memory—two people will be informed of who I am and what I do when this is over. You will be one, Murie the other. Trust me until that time. You will not regret that trust."

He nodded slowly and looked away, which I knew was the only answer I would ever get.

Then he was in full armor and I caught his eyes and held them, and worked my little game so that shortly he was stretched out prone upon the starship's tiny deck.

I landed in the clearing, hauled the supine figure of Rawl —armor and all—through the door and out upon the greensward. And I trundled him beyond to the ring of sleepers, Charney, Griswall, Hargis, and the student, Tober. Then back to the ship where I arrayed myself in all my battle splendor— padded under-dress, link armor, helm, great shield with my colors of gold and violet, broadsword and sundry small weapons, and my surcoat, now cleaned and laundered by the ship's appointments. We would be a splendid crew indeed, I thought, when we rode forth to the great camp of Fon Tweel's thirty thousand. . . .

Dusk was fast approaching as I stepped from the ship to the green swale below. And as my foot touched the ground the ship faded without my calling. Simultaneously with this the node at the base of my skull signaled the Greenwich alarm. I switched on. "In," I said. "What are you doing with the ship?"

"You will use it now only if you promise to reenter and leave Camelot. You've had it, Sir Collin." The voice was Kriloy's. "You've broken every Foundation law in the book. We've been scanning. And if it were not for the fact that a case like this warrants a decision from H.Q., we'd cancel you out on our own. . . . For God's sake, Kyrie, you've got to be off your rocker."

"You're not restricting yourselves to the agreed two minutes," I said curtly. "Which means you're taking a helluva risk just to sink the shaft into me."

"*We* take risks? That did it, Buby." Ragan was talking now. "*You've* risked everything! We know there's a connection between the destruction of Alpha and the little game your Pug-Boos are playing with their opposite in 'goodness' in that pile of stones called Hish. We know, too, that the

Vuuns have a claw in the pie. But this is *their* planet, Buby!
You of all people should know that. You were sent to check
things out, to keep us informed as to what was happening,
and to insert what influence you could. And what have you
done? One: Your data on the tape wasn't. Two: Against
orders you've played games with the starship. Three: You've
done all this because—as we've psyched it—you've actually
begun to fancy yourself as the mythos-incarnate of these
people's folk hero, the Collin. Gods, what a ham! You were
supposed to just hint at it, you know, not jump into the role
with both feet. But there you are. The Great Collin, returned
in all his splendor. His armor glows in the dark. He is the
match of any ten Fregisians. And, he's already won and
bedded the fair princess of the threatened kingdom—and
thereby carved a niche for himself in this somewhat backward economy. And you just love it, don't you? You really
do. Our position, Buby, is that the moment you saw that
blond-furred, purple-eyed pixie in the scanners, you had a
case of instant brain-boggle. You've come a cropper, *Collin!*
You've had it! It's back to school for you, and now! So wave
good-bye to your five sleeping beauties, strip off that irides-
cent armor and get your whatnot into that ship and blast
off!"

I said softly, "You've got it wrong."

"Into the ship, Kyrie. No more talk."

"Un-unh!"

"There are penalties."

"I know. There are also a few things that I know that you
don't."

"Holding out, eh? All right, tell us."

"Can't."

"That's crap. The Foundation, Kyrie, is the heart of all
Galactic knowledge, the conglomerate of intelligent life. Decisions regarding the protection of that life are made by the
Collective: the computers. The knowledge of ten thousand
years and of tens of thousands of planets are in those computers: all at our beck and call—sufficient, Kyrie, to handle
any problem. And you're holding out!" Ragan drew a deep
breath and repeated: *"Get into the ship, Kyrie!"*

"Sorry," I said. "No deal. There's a battle shaping up. Contact me when it's over. Better yet—I'll call you after I've had

a chat with the Boos again, when we've won the battle. Right now, I'm going to ask that you get the hell out of this system until the battle's over. You can't help. You can only hinder. And, I might add, you're out of your league. From where I sit, I think we all are. . . ."

"That's your last word?"

"Right! And I'm not even going to wait for you to snap the proverbial umbilical cord . . . I'm snapping it! Me! Right now!" And I did. And because I'm essentially the sneaky type, I snapped it right back on again, in time to hear Ragan say to Kriloy, "He's flipped! Our Collin's flipped. Call forward. Get out as he requested. That's probably the least we can do now. But so help me . . . !" Then they cut me off.

I pressed the ship stud and said the phasing in numbers; nothing! They had most effectively loused it up for me. So be it! I would now have to go that six hundred miles with Glagmaron's finest: by dottle-back.

The idea made me physically ill.

One by one I awakened them, gathered them about me for a briefing. I pulled no punches. I told Griswall, Charney, Hargis, and Tober where I had been and what I had been doing. Rawl's presence, in part, underlined the truth of my words. They didn't question just how I had been to those places. About the Vuuns, I was deliberately vague, explaining only that I had convinced them to break their pact with Om, and to return the princess and Caroween to our armies on the field of Dunguring.

"And now, my lord," Griswall rasped, and after Rawl had thanked them all for their fight for his lady, "I take it that we will ride back to Fon Tweel, dispense with him, secure the army, and ride for Dunguring."

"You take it right."

Charney was laughing. He shook his head. "My lord," he confessed, "neither I nor my brothers, in our moldy keep and gog-pen above the village of Fuuz in Bist, have ever thought in our wildest dreams that someday we would ride the crest of the wave in Marack's greatest war. All of this is so new to me and mine."

The eyes of Tober and Hargis beamed a similar joy and gratitude.

Rawl stood up then to his full height. He looked first the others and then me straight in the eye. "Now listen, all," he said. "And you, too, Collin. For though I do love you, there is a thing that you must know. I say *you*. For though you *say* you are of Marack, and therefore Fregis, there are things of protocol that you do oft forget." He smiled slyly. "It is as if you never really knew them. Anyhow my words are these: My father, the lord Cagis Rawl, now dead, was brother to our queen, Tyndil. I am blood-cousin to our princess. There are no sons to the line of Caronne. And though the Collin here becomes prince-consort by marriage with our princess, still I and no one else, as of this moment—and since 'tis too early for an offspring of the Collin's joining—do represent the Royal House in Glagmaron. What I mean, Collin, is simple. I and not *you* will slay the traitor, Fon Tweel. It is my right—indeed, it is my duty!"

I looked to the others who had followed Rawl's words with rapt attention. They nodded "Aye" in unison.

"It is," I said lamely, "that I would bring you whole to your lady, Caroween."

"Hey, now, Collin? Do you think I am some mewling coward? Methinks you go too far, sir."

"Nay! Nay!" I held up a hand in mock fear. "I love you, too, sir. But you must admit that a redhead, Cari Hoggle-Fitz, is something to contend with. I want not her anger, should you not show up at Dunguring. Still, you are right in this argument. And none here, including myself, doubt that within the hour you will sweep Fon Tweel's lying head from his traitorous body. Now let's whistle up our dottles and be off."

Tober whistled, while Charney and Hargis and Griswall beamed at young Rawl Fergis.

And the dottles came, among them being Henery, and among them, too, a thing I had not counted on. *On the backs of half the ten were five Pug-Boos*. Hooli, Jindil, Pawbi—and, I reasoned instantly, the two lost Boos of Kelb and Great Ortmund. The eyes of my stalwarts lighted up like lasers in their welcoming joy. And they cast lots to see who would be the one to ride without a Boo, since Hooli sat on Henery's rump and no one questioned that.

Hargis, Charney's brother, lost. And he was Boo-less as we thundered up the great road in the direction of the camp of Fon Tweel's thirty thousand. . . .

To say that I felt somewhat oppressed and slightly skittish at this sudden weight of Pug-Boos would be the understatement of the Fregisian week. The little bastards were up to something. Was I glad that they had joined us? I had mixed emotions. A certain safety existed in the presence of Boos. But this, too, could be a chimera, wishful thinking. I tried opening my mind to Pug-Boo thoughts. Nothing happened. The little bastards—the double damned little bastards!

They were good for one thing. The very weight of their presence, plus my own, plus our students, plus Griswall, served to clear a path all the way to the entrance of Fon Tweel's command tent; served, too, to lend credence to Sir Rawl's challenge when he denounced Fon Tweel as a traitor to Marack, and to all the lands of the north, before that gathered chivalry of Glagmaron. It was Ferlach and Gheese all over again; with shouts of rage, support, cheers, and a half hundred contradictory exclamations. But I think the cheers favored our side, for they also had some faith in the old stalwart, Griswall—certainly in the Boos—even a little in me, though only my shield glowed now since I had put aside the trick of the ion-beam. Fon Tweel, therefore, and before all that mass of warriors, had no recourse but to comply with Rawl's challenge. For there were those present who had already questioned his lack of movement toward Ferlach and Gheese; especially since they had had word of the battles of Gortfin, and at the Veldian Pass.

A spot was chosen between four fires, at point. Additional torches—it was now quite dark—were brought to light this square of turf. Since Rawl was the challenger, Fon Tweel was given the choice of weapon. He chose that which he used best, the broadsword. He chose light armor, too, thinking his strength superior so that he could abide Rawl's blows, whereas Rawl could never abide his. He had five stalwarts to back him. For other than his treason, and his loud mouth, he was a personable fellow, capable of engendering friendships of a kind. From time to time I noted that Fon Tweel looked about him, and up and around, as if he were expecting something or someone, and was surprised that "it" had not made an appearance. I saw him muttering *words*, too. And the unhappy look on his face was most evident when he saw they had no effect.

'Twas then I realized that those five fat Boos—who never went to war—were at it again. Fon Tweel obviously enjoyed Kaleen support, otherwise he would never have played his perilous game. He expected it now, was waiting for it. But I knew it would never come. . . . "My boy," I said mentally, "my five fuzzy Boos have stirred the tea leaves with their hairy little pinkies, and you, sir, have had it!"

While it lasted, they were evenly matched. Fon Tweel's black-browed mass was offset by Rawl's lithe and wiry suppleness. Rawl was all around him, hacking and chopping. Once, when Rawl lifted his shield to protect his head, Fon Tweel cleaved that shield to the area—had there been one— of the bar sinister. Before he twisted free in rage, Rawl had sore wounded him with a smashing blow to midriff which cut through links to bite into the muscles of his rib cage. Then Fon Tweel struck back. And the two of them became a flashing, spark-flying, roaring duo of arms and armor, from which Rawl emerged with his helm struck from his shoulders. Luck, I thought, that it was not his head. He was truly at a disadvantage then. And, had not Fon Tweel made the mistake of slowly and confidently stalking him for the kill, he may have lost. But Fon Tweel's purpose was so evident, and his own disadvantage so clear, that Rawl threw all caution to the winds. He dropped shield to ground, seized upon his great sword with both hands—and charged! Some say he was exceeding foolish; others that he was mad! I would say simply that he had judged his man rightly, and knew his weakness.

There then happened a thing contrary to all held dear on Camelot—and a thing, in fact, which guaranteed Fon Tweel's death. Fon Tweel, weakened in part by Rawl's first hacking blow, was not prepared for this howling, maddened rush, and blued-steel arc of whirling sword. He held firm for brief seconds only. Then he turned and ran. *He ran!* But he was instantly tripped by a half dozen roaring warriors, so that he fell with a look of abject terror on his face. He knew he had committed the impermissible.

Without the slightest qualm they jerked the helm from his head, brought him to kneeling position, laced his hands behind his back with leathern thongs—and waited in a great and awesome silence while Rawl struck his head from his body. The whole fight had lasted, at best, but ten minutes. . . .

Rawl returned to our group in triumph and tossed his bloodied sword to those who had rallied to our side (if he had lost we would have been in grave danger), and received our earnest handclasps. He said bluntly to me, " 'Tis yours to do now, Collin." And I nodded and called for a table, had it mounted in the center of that grassy square where Fon Tweel's headless body lay, and climbed upon it. I bade Rawl and all our stalwarts to gather around me.

I waited dramatically until the shouting and the bedlam died and the mass of lords, knights, men-at-arms, archers, and camp provenders moved in. I waited still again until the ensuing silence became something more than that: a deadness, a vacuum, a breathlessness in which all waited for something they now instinctively knew would strike home to their very hearts and marrow.

Then I raised my arms. "Comrades of Marack!" I shouted. *"Friends!* All ye lords and men and warriors! There is a thing that I would tell you. There is a thing of your world, and that which comes against it from the foulest pits of Best. There is a thing that transcends all else in your lifetime. And there is a thing, therefore, that you must do."

Behind me there then began the faintest, the most delicate, and the most beautiful sound of music I have ever heard in my lifetime. And it seemed that to my words—but oh, ever so faintly, so as not to intrude—Hooli the Pug-Boo was playing his pipe. And so I told them. And the hypnotic, charismatic cadence of my voice, mixed with that subtle, insidious, and totally enthralling melody of Hooli, was such that I doubt will ever be heard again on Camelot-Fregis. And we had an audience of thirty thousand. And I think, when I look back upon it, that considering the affinity of dottles for Pug-Boos, and granting, too, their position within the culture, we had thirty thousand of these gentle creatures to ring us around, and to listen to the Pug-Boo's music. We were a great horde of *life*. In our hands lay the future of that world.

And so I talked and the Pug-Boo played. And one by one the great stars came out in our black saucered sky. And once, before I was through, small Ripple flew across the night: as a comet, an omen, a red portent of things to come—and soon.

We started out in the gray dawn of the morrow. The towns-people and the castle people lined the hills to see us go, for never had they seen anything quite like it. All that night we had mustered men and mounts for the journey. Scant sleep had been given anyone. The three lords of Marack's southern provinces who served under Fon Tweel pledged themselves fully to Rawl. And it was understood that the entire force—and we found that an additional ten thousand had been mustered and would be picked up along the way—was now under our joint command. We would ride this day, tonight, and all of tomorrow. They had accepted this new departure with well-received bravado. And on tomorrow's eve (we hoped) we would arrive on the plain of Dunguring. I frankly don't know which I dreaded more, the sight of a stricken field where all might be lost, or that damnable ride across six hundred miles of Fregisian terra firma.

I managed a bit of self-hypnosis to help me survive it. Our only rest was during the four-hour dottle browsing periods. And I would point out that this applied to the night as well. Recall that Camelot-Fregis had a twenty-six-hour rotation period. Two browsing breaks of four and four left us with eighteen hours of travel time, so that at twenty miles per hour we easily made our required mileage. Despite the rest periods, the ride was still pure blasphemy to mortal flesh. As stated, stamina was one thing, strength another. On the last stretch, at the end of our thirty-one-hour run, the Collin was collapsed over his saddle, to the amusement of my companions. I cared not a Terran fig whether school kept or not. I remember once during the sweating humidity of that last afternoon—the clouds were gathering again and great thunder

191

roared around the horizon—that a gentle paw was placed upon the small of my back. A resulting surge of power ran up the length of my spinal column. I mumbled something to the effect of: "All right! *All right!* So you've got the power. Quit showing off. The one thing you could do for me is to tell me what you and your fat-fannied friends are up to. You'll not ride with me into battle, you know. I'm not going to have you on Henery's rump when the whistle blows, hear?"

It was like talking to myself. I twisted in my saddle to stare at Hooli. Nothing had changed. He simply stared right back with his enigmatic, shoebutton eyes, and his nauseating grin. . . . He was beginning to reach me.

The clouds continued, but it didn't rain. At the last rest period—12:00 to 4:00 P.M.—we, the command group, departed one half hour before the main body: this, at my suggestion, so that upon our arrival we would have time to see the lay of the land and apportion our forty thousand warriors as they came up. In this way there would be no delay in decision, or confusion in the strengthening of this or that wing and whatever remained of the king's center. All this with the proviso that anything remained at all.

But it did. And it was a sight such as I will never forget; nor will anyone else who sees its reproduction in the great Ovarium at Glagmaron's new Art Center.

The plain of Dunguring was five miles in width and ten miles long. Its eastern border consisted of a high ridge sloping sharply down to the plain. At places this ridge was actually a cliff a hundred feet in height. As the slopes flattened to the plain a number of small hills still jutted to continue a domination of the plain by the ridge. Beyond these hills the ground was reasonably flat. A great part of the area had been planted to a form of maize, and it was trisected by two small streams. One of these rivers entered the plain from the southeast, circling a great volcanic cone; the second entered from the northwest. They joined in the center and then flowed northeast below the base of another volcano, and thence to the sea. The "Great Road," I noted, followed the path of this river.

Both the volcanoes were active. The far side of the plain rose gradually to another ridge, albeit a lower one than ours. Beyond it the ground swept farther down to rolling countryside and a final breakout to the seacoast and the port city of Corchoon some twenty miles distant.

Approaching this ridge from the east, we passed through great meadow-speckled forests. In every meadow, indeed under every tree, there were dottles. These were undoubtedly the spares of Caronne and Hoggle-Fitz—plus the great herds of Ferlach and Gheese. Altogether there must have been better than one hundred and fifty thousand dottles. When they greeted our arrival it was as a great wind soughing softly through the tall trees. I had never heard, nor ever will again, such a sound. Their presence, however, could mean but one thing. Beyond that ridge the valiant armies of Marack, Ferlach, and Gheese had not as yet gone down.

I came alive, concentrated on an adrenalin surge and got it. There remained but one hour until twilight. We literally raced the last mile to the ridge top. . . .

The plain of Dunguring was a three-dimensional stereophonic etching of Best, Hell, and any Galactic god's antithesis of Eden. It was inferno. . . . As far as the eye could see across that broad plain, there was bloody battle. Almost three hundred thousand men were killing and being killed. Directly below us and to the left at about two thousand yards was a small hill with a rectangular top. Upon it flew the tattered standards of Marack. The king was there. Far to the left, and perhaps a full quarter of a mile to the front, was another, larger, flat and rounded hill. And there, planted firmly, was the Dernim Tulip of Breen Hoggle-Fitz, the Black Swan of Chitar, and a half hundred other banners of Marack and Gheese. To our right, and again somewhat in advance of Marack's center, was still another hill upon which flew the Oak Tree banners of Draslich, king of Ferlach. The three strong points were cut off from each other and sore beset by hordes of mailed pikemen and swarms of Omnian-Kelbian kinghts in full armor.

The field for a full two miles to the front of our northern armies was strewn with the dead of the day's battle. And even now some still fought in that far distance, cut off, surrounded in their retreat from what had obviously been the area of the north's first stand. We gazed upon this great drama in silence. I held out both my arms as a sign that we should

193

keep it that way, so that all might evaluate the circumstances of the scene that lay before us.

I exacted the ultimate in magnitudes from my contacts. On the line of our north's first stand were the piled bodies of twice ten thousand Omnian heggles, lords, squires. Above these fallen flew the blazonry of their owners: pennons and banners attached to pikes, spears, and lances. One could follow the progress of the fighting by these great heaps of dead. There, to the right, and at a distance of two miles, was where Per-Rondin, the king's own commander, had gone down with all his troops and guards. And the banners of the great houses of Glagmaron itself waved like a forest over the bodies of a thousand of Caronne's picked young knights. To the south, like the dead of Per-Rondin, lay the flower of Ferlach. I could see the fallen banner of my erstwhile jolly and courageous lord, Gane of Reen, and of Her-Tils of the Gheesian city of Saks. Each pile of dead was surrounded by at least an acre of other bodies. Banners of Kelb mixed with those of the Omnian cities of Hish, Seligal, and Kerch. . . . Two square miles of the fallen, with here and there small groups of mounted knights still charging each other.

And over it all, from the three hills of Marack and the north, came the faint sound of skirling pipes and the rattling of kettledrums, like summer hail. Even as we watched a force of some four thousand picked Omnian knights, flanked by two thousand brass-mailed Yorns, flew up the slopes of Caronne's hill, to be met by a similar downward charge of Marackian knights. Om was again forced back and slaughtered on their flanks by Marack's archers. The same held true of the hills to the south and north. All were under attack by as many as fifty thousand Omnian and allied warriors. From these hordes would come ever and again the attacking force so that the north's defeat, in the long run, would be but a matter of time.

But I thought as I watched them that there still seemed to be some holding back on the part of Om—perhaps for some coordinated onslaught. As if to underscore this point my eyes lifted to the Omnian war headquarters situated at the joining of the two small rivers. The distance was two miles. But this second glance, at full focus, revealed what I had passed over before. There at their insolent ease was an additional fifty thousand fresh Omnian warriors. They had been held back for a reason—and it came to me that the reason was ourselves. They knew of our coming! They would therefore await our full strength before committing theirs. In that way, so they no doubt reasoned, they would destroy all the forces of the north. And I knew, too, that the Kaleen had so directed. . . .

Rawl grasped my arm to direct my attention to Draslich's redoubt on our right. There were massed foot soldiers with pike and spear. They ringed Draslich's remaining ten thousand; not only severing him from all contact with Caronne, but advancing, too, to cut the great road to the rear of our armies. . . .

While we watched the vanguard of our forty thousand had arrived. Rawl signaled the leading commanders to us. We had, perforce, in the meantime, sent pairs of couriers to break through to the three hills to advise them to hold; that help was coming. I had previously asked that the best trumpeters of our army accompany the vanguard group. And now, as Sir Rawl Fergis, together with the lords of Holt and Svoss in southern Marack, charged down that slope with a full five thousand of our best lances, I caused those trumpets to blast in unison.

Somehow, and I knew instantly *why*, the notes of those twenty trumpets were amplified. And zooming to the raging battles on the three hills, I saw that men had heard, and stood apart, and were looking back to us. And when Rawl's five thousand smashed into and through that mass of Kelbian-Omnian soldiery surrounding Draslich, there arose such a cheer as to be like a rolling thunder across that bloodied plain. The cheers were also amplified! I looked then to Hooli, who had been joined by Jindil, since Rawl had dashed off to battle. They both grinned back at me—and Hooli winked.

"Great Gods!" I exclaimed. "And will *that* be your total contribution?"

There was then no time for further nonsense. We, Sir Griswall and sundry lords of Marack, conferred briefly; decid-

ing which route to take to the three besieged hills, and how
many men should be sent to each, and how many held as
reserve so as to settle the battle in our favor for the night.
Lord Ginden of Klimpinge, a burly giant of a man, took the
next five thousand in the wake of Rawl. We followed with
the remaining warriors, ten thousand to join with Chitar and
twenty thousand to reinforce the center hill of King Caronne.
We left but two hundred dottle wardens to care for our
eighty thousand spares. These went to join their fellows in
the woods beyond the ridge. I looked to Hooli, Jindil, Pawbi,
and the rest to go off with the dottles. But such was not to
be. Pug-Boos were, apparently—and for the first time—going
to war! Hooli and Jindil clung to Henery's rump, and the
other three remained in their places behind Charney, Griswall, and Hargis.

As we rode down the slope of the ridge, trumpets blaring,
pipes skirling, and kettledrums thumping, the hosts of Om
withdrew slightly from contact with the defenders of the
hills. Then they withdrew still further; after which, couriers
having reached them, the whole mass of foot and cavalry—
numbering some one hundred and fifty thousand men—moved
back across the plain to a distance of a half mile.

Though we felt as rescuers, it gave us little pleasure to come
upon those stricken hilltops. We rode over the bodies of the
fallen, the slaughtered, and the wounded alike. I thought of
the night and of dead-alives. I conjured up a fantastic scene
of the mass of dead from this great abattoir, all converging
upon us in the small hours. Then I remembered the Pug-
Boos. And somehow I knew this could not happen.

Rawl returned victoriously from Draslich's hill to rejoin our
command. He had doffed his helm, and other than sweat
beading his face, he seemed none the worse for wear and
tear. He met us at the base of the ridge, as we turned left
toward Caronne's hilltop.

And now great Fomalhaut blazed a hellish red on the western horizon. And this coloration, tinting all the clouds a
scarlet hue, together with the belching flame from the two
volcanoes, lent an atmosphere to that place to exceed the
twisted imagery of anyone's dementia. From the king's hilltop
the great plain was as easily seen as from the ridge. And it
remained what it had been at first sight—an inferno!

As we rode along the hill's crest, the warriors of Marack who had fought so well that day cheered our coming. And we, to show our appreciation and respect for them, did likewise. Caronne and the sorcerer, Fairwyn, and the remaining lords of Glagmaron stood out to give us greeting. And we dismounted and shook hands and put our arms about each other. And when the banners of our forty thousand were enjoined with those on the three hills, swords and spears were brandished again against the enemy. The clamor of sword against shield, and pike butt against the hardened earth, was thunderous—and all false pomp and ceremony went by the board.

The aftermath of this great day-long hacking and hewing saw a fantastic hustle and bustle around us. Tents for the king and for his staff and entourage were produced and set up. Cooking pots had been hauled out. And what with dottle-briquettes, jerked gog-meat, and various bundles of dried vegetables and spices, a savory meal would be in the offing soon.

Both Rawl and I strained our eyes to popping for a first view of Murie and Caroween. They were not there, and Rawl looked at me, sore afraid. "Nay," I cautioned him. "The Vuun, Great Ap, is trustworthy. He will bring them, and on the morrow. And perhaps, friend, when you think on it, it may be best that he has delayed his coming."

Though dead-alives seemed no longer feared—what with the presence of the sorcerers of Marack, Ferlach, and Gheese, plus the great armies deployed by both sides—it seemed, still, that night fighting was unheard of on Camelot. Indeed, the night was such that an enemy didn't exist. And the space between the two armies was inviolate. . . .

And so we ate and held council, and Draslich came and Chitar, and Hoggle-Fitz, and all the remaining lords of the three countries. But, as Rawl said, "One would weep to see the banners of those no longer present." A full half of the northern chivalry were slain. And of the eighty thousand men of the three countries, fifty thousand remained alive. It was not enough that the enemy had lost twice again that amount, so that a full sixty thousand of theirs would never see their homeland—our coming had but made up, with a little over, for the day's losses.

And we told them of Rawl's slaying of Fon Tweel, and of the ride from Glagmaron; at which Draslich and Chitar shook their heads in commiseration. And I told them of the coming of Great Ap on the morrow, with Murie and Caroween, and that they were not to feather the Vuun's hide with arrows. This last knowledge—that we were not to be attacked by Vuuns, but rather would have one as an ally—cheered them considerably. Still, though our total report was accepted, I noted that sundry lords of the north now looked at me with a certain trepidation.

I did suggest in council that we dare the night for the simple task of collecting arrows; that on the morrow we would have great need of them. I also suggested that whole companies of our archers be kept in a state of mobility, and that at least a thousand of these be mounted on dottles so as to bring their weight to bear upon the most threatened point. We had, actually, ten thousand archers—without armor, easy prey to men-at-arms and knights. Because of this I further suggested that a number of squadrons of our lancers be set aside solely for our mobile archers' protection.

My thinking was looked upon as somewhat strange. But the tactic seemed reasonable to Chitar and Caronne, and the others acquiesced.

Before we slept I walked with Rawl to our hill's slope, and saw the unforgettable sight of the wounded who could still walk or crawl. All went toward the rear; to beyond the ridge where they could escape the morrow's charge of frenzied, blood-crazed warriors and swinging swords. They sought, I imagined, to die in peace—or perhaps, even now, to live. . . .

Dawn on Camelot, when the skies were cloudless, was a beauteous thing. Conversely—and so it was on our day of battle—when clouds were dark and lowering, there was a thing of ominous portent most active in the air. The volcanoes flamed to the north and south, joining with the blood-red orb of Fomalhaut to pearl the clouds for a full half of the eastern sky. I had hoped for clouds, however, since the rising sun on this sword-whetted day of Camelot's armageddon was to our enemies' backs and not in our favor.

Rawl, Griswall, and Charney, as well as our students, had chosen to stay with Marack's king as a part of his command council. We armed ourselves in that gray-red dawn, drank hot sviss, ate bread, and moved to our center position under King Caronne's standard of the Winged Castle.

Our front of the three hills extended a full mile and better. As many as twelve thousand mailed spearmen were before each redoubt now: a wall of shields and pikes for almost a full circle around each hill. Our archers were posted higher on the slopes. And between the hills ranging in squadrons and full companies, were our remaining lords, knights squires, and mounted men-at-arms. These numbered a full forty thousand. They were kept at the command of the center, under Marack.

Because of the clouds and the lack of sun, the plain seemed as a steel-point etching in its total clarity. Despite our losses the army of the north was a glittering array of steel and bright banners, for a full half mile to either side of our center's martial pomp.

This scene was duplicated across that half mile of intervening space. Om's center command, I noted, had moved up during the night.

If our array was both splendid and terrible to see, so, indeed, was theirs. On our left flank Hoggle-Fitz and Chitar were faced with no fewer than twenty thousand warriors of Great Ortmund, plus thirty thousand of Seligal and Kerch. Draslich, on our right, faced an equal number, inclusive of ten thousand Yorns and twenty thousand of the flower of Kelb; among these being Prince Keilweir himself and his father, Harlach. Their black banners and black and silvered armor, tinted now with red highlights from the southern volcano, gave to their entire line a most sinister quality.

But Om's center! That was a thing to see! They were one hundred thousand men and Yorns: all in squadrons, phalanxes, and spear squares. Though our front was but a half mile from theirs, their rear was a full mile beyond that—such was their strength. And in the core of that mass of steel and forest of banners was the red Hishian Towers, the standard of the greatest of lords, as pointed out to me—Gol-Bades, conqueror of Seligal and Kerch, overlord of Hish, "Voice of

Arthur H. Landis

the Kaleen"! He was circled by all the lords of Hish, and a picked, praetorian band of Omnian warriors. Each of these was the equal, if not the superior, of any Yorn—and the lord Gol-Bades was superior to them.

And also, to his back, I saw the black cowls of five wizards, and I knew that he had not come alone. . . .

To our front and theirs the kettledrums were already going. And, as was Fregisian custom, individual knights were dashing now between the lines to scream challenges and accept those given in return. As many as a dozen duels were already taking place before our eyes. A young Marackian squire—and he had no right to do this since he was no full knight—had ridden forth from a troop from Glagmaron. He seemed of an exceeding tender age, and my focused contacts told me that his armor was so ill-fitting that he was most likely rattling around inside it like a Farkelian jumping bean. The whole cast-iron ensemble was no doubt borrowed, as was the war lance which he just barely managed to raise above his head, while he screamed insults at the Omnian host in a high, falsetto voice.

This last, I must mention, prompted Sir Rawl to lean toward me from his high saddle and say, "And did I not know that my lady was safe on Vuun-back, m'lord, I would swear that there she was on yonder piebald dottle."

A wave of laughter ensued from all of us. But then a great knight of Seligal came out to face our challenger—except that he came out *backward,* blowing kisses to his comrades, and holding his shield over his shoulder in mock defense. Laughter swept all alike on both sides at this buffoonery. This caused our young squire to lose his head completely, so that he lowered his great lance and charged. The knight of Seligal, warned by his companions, turned quickly, advanced his shield, leveled his lance, and held his great dottle absolutely motionless. He avoided the wild charge of our neophyte at the moment of impact by twisting his massive body ever so slightly. Simultaneously with this his own lance tip dealt his adversary's helm a glancing blow so that it turned around on gorget and neckguard, rendering our Marackian hero as blind as a Terran bat. In this condition he continued straight on into the ranks of that Omnian armor. They, with great hoots of laughter, withdrew on all sides so that he rode in aimless circles. When he thought finally to achieve open ground again, and thus return to his own lines, albeit in a most erratic manner, those Omnian warriors stopped him, relieved him of his lance, sword, and fal-dirk, turned his helm around properly—and gave his dottle's rump a great whack to send her on her way back to us.

Though our "hero" was greeted with cheers, he seemed disconsolate withal. And I thought to ask later who he was.

The duels grew more intense. Coveys of threes and fours were already doing battle in the field. A point had been reached where, usually, the stronger of the two opponents moves to the attack. But such was not the case with Om. It seemed again that they were waiting for something. Ten great Vuuns perhaps? I wondered.

Then I had an idea. "My lord," I said suddenly to the king. "May I take these gentle Pug-Boos—if they will come—and ride down the front of our array? It strikes me that some good may come of it, withal—"

He looked at me curiously. "If you think it serves a purpose, do so," he answered. He gestured toward the Omnian hosts. "They do not move, sirrah. Therefore, perhaps there's time for everything."

The king's eyes also scanned the sky—as did all those who knew of the great Vuun's coming. I had time to wonder, as I called to Sir Griswall and Charney to accompany me, whether they, too, expected one Vuun—or *ten*. . . .

I rode with Hooli, Rawl with Pawbi, and Griswall with Jindil. Charney followed next with what we assumed was the Kelbian Boo, Dakhti, flying Kelb's royal colors from his lance tip. Tober had the Great Ortmundian Pug-Boo, Chuuk. Anyway, we rode down that mile-long front and there was a great thunder of cheers from our side, plus "ohs" and "ahs" at the very presence of the Boos. There were cheers, too, from the massed warriors of Kelb and Great Ortmund. These faded quickly, however, beneath the threats of their officers. But the fact that they cheered at all was indicative of a mood. My attempt at subversion had hit pay dirt, and I was pleased.

At the end of our ride I watched the Omnian warlords closely. Though they knew that Boos were court pets in the northland, I am sure they had no idea of the affection that was given them; they were therefore startled, even disturbed, at the cheering response to our flaunting of these small rodents. They were further confounded when we reached King Chitar's hill. For it was there that Breen Hoggle-Fitz of Durst in Great Ortmund rode forth to bounce Chuuk—or was it Dakhti?—in his arms. An absolute roar of approbation came from the Ortmundian warriors at this, for loudmouthed Fitz had been well loved in Ortmund. I noted that these same warriors, undaunted now by their officers, looked back to their center where sat the false king, Feglyn, surrounded by his cohorts. They were curious; puzzled that the Ortmundian Boo should be in Fitz's arms—and that Fitz, himself, should be in the ranks of Marack. This little show would make them think. And, I mused, if it helped to stay one hundred swords, the job was successful.

We returned to our positions on Caronne's hill. And still the great host of Om remained at ease. The dueling continued.

The sorcerers of Marack, Gheese, and Ferlach then got their skinny selves together. They were all—as per agreement with Chitar and Draslich—on Marack's hill. Their combined efforts finally sent a spate of whirlwinds romping over the waiting ranks of the enemy. This prompted Om's dark wizards to counter with a dozen whirlwinds of their own, plus the moving of a large cloud of pumice ash from one of the two volcanoes to a spot directly over our heads where, naturally, it fell. Within seconds Fairwyn, Gaazi, and Plati sprayed them with the ash from the second volcano. And so it went. . . .

In the midst of all this harmless folderol, a voice—Hooli's, my own—said loudly in my head, "So what are you waiting for, Buby? Your public would like to see more than just me sitting on old Henry's rump. Great Ap is on his way, *now!* Yonder is the lord Gol-Bades. I know your knees are shaking, because you just might be evenly matched for a change; but isn't that what you're here for?" "Hooli," I replied mentally, "Hooli, you little son-of-a-bitch, someday—*someday!*" And then I turned again to King Caronne. "Sire," I asked softly, "I would ask another boon of you."

Caronne smiled and looked at me slyly. I think he knew what I wanted, had been waiting for the question. "Hey, Collin?" he answered, and then, "Really? And what could *I* give *you?*"

I smiled, too. He was wiser indeed than I had given him

credit for. "I would," I said loudly, so that the others would hear, "exchange blows with a certain lord of Om. It is in my mind, sire, that those over there wait for *ten* Vuuns, whereas, we wait for *one*. I would not have them idle longer, and I *would* disturb their ordered program."

Caronne smiled again, nodded, and raised a hand. At that I signaled Rawl and Sir Griswall, told them what I was about to do, and up went the colors of the Collin. We rode forth to challenge Hish for Marack and the north.

We collected two young trumpeters on the way. At midfield we halted, pranced our mounts in a complete circle, and ended facing the great mailed horde of Om. The cheers when we rode out had been thunderous. They continued that way. For, in a sense, they had been waiting for me to do exactly what I was doing, and there wasn't a scarred warrior of all those northern lands who didn't know where my challenge would be placed. When the royal trumpets blasted out— amplified, of course—the cheers rose to crescendo.

Henery and I had positioned ourselves so that we had become a motionless frieze of man, dottle, and rigid banner: no wind could flatten it, for it had Pug-Boo starch. Then out rode Rawl and Griswall, their dottles doing a prancing, mincing, formal step, used whenever royal herald sought audience with his opposite or facsimile.

Then two black-armored Omnian warriors broke ranks and protocol to ride furiously toward us. They spun directly in front of my two advancing ambassadors. "What do you seek of our great lord of Om?" they screamed.

They were still but twenty yards to my front so that I could both see and hear the hoary Griswall when he answered icily, "We seek his life!"

"And just how do you propose getting it, you mewling cuuds of Marack?"

"We will take it with the arm of our champion, the Collin!"

"Well then! And first you must take *ours*," they shouted, and simultaneously drew their swords. Both had circled Rawl and Griswall while they yelled, so that at this last they plunged in from either side, each taking a man. The dust from the whirlwinds had settled. The air was clear, and the action easily seen. But clarity was still needed. For the new whirlwind of steel that then ensued was a thing that the eye could scarce follow.

Griswall, wily old gerd that he was, did a bit of shield-work that was a marvel to see. He parried every one of his adversary's blows. At a crucial point, when his man stood high in the stirrups for another sweeping blow, Griswall thrust out and up, sword penetrating the area of the *fald* between the two tassets of the man's armor. This was a deadly gut-blow, in which the spinal cord is severed below the stomach. The man fell away in instant paralysis, upon which Griswall made the sign of Ormon and trotted grimly back to my side.

Rawl, in the meantime, had simply beaten his man from the saddle with the edge of his shield; then he dismounted and ran his sword through the fellow's throat. At which point he, too, rejoined me where I continued motionless, flanked now by my two companions.

Then it was my turn.

I rode forward slowly. And Henery—who after all was a castle mount—lifted all six pads in measured cadence as he had been taught to do for such occasions. I wasn't glow-ing, but I had disrupted my magnetic field again. Though I, too, loved the Pug-Boos, I couldn't trust them completely. Also, the *thing* of Hish, the Kaleen . . . if it were watch-ing anything, it was watching *me!*

I halted one hundred yards from the steel ranks of Om. The silence over that great field was like the aftermath of a thunderclap. Then I stood high in my stirrups and shook my lance and shield mightily above my head. "I call the great lord of Gol-Bades, himself, to answer," I shouted. I used my own amplifying system in case the Pug-Boos failed me. My voice was truly stentorian—on the order of a gigantic brass gong; sufficient, I thought, to rattle the great Gol-Bades who, no doubt, at least until now, had thought he had seen and heard everything.

I continued: *"I shall prove upon thy carcass, Gol-Bades, that you be base to the world of Fregis: that you be false to the Gods of Fregis; To Ormon, Wimbily, Harris; yea, even unto the ones of Kerch and Seligal! I call you seneschal of evil: slave of the thing in Hish called the Kaleen. A thing yourself who would make all others slaves. . . . Come, great*

Gol-Bades! I am named the Collin, called for this moment 'The Champion of the Northlands.' I call you coward and traitor to all men of Fregis. And, foul thing of Hish, I will prove this on your body!"

Under ordinary circumstances I would never expect a great lord such as Gol-Bades to fall for such a crude provocation. But he did just that. I remember thinking at the moment that perhaps he thought me just another idiot. Or perhaps he felt it necessary to slay me then and there so as to dominate completely that horde of superstitious warriors. Whatever his reasons, he did come forth.

And it was a sight to see! A path was hurriedly cleared for him at the wave of a hand. And his great dottle cantered slowly along it to the measured beat of a hundred Hishian drums. No one accompanied him. At approximately twenty paces from me he halted in all his mighty, black-steel and yellow-bronzed splendor. He spoke in a voice that carried the twenty paces and no more. He asked in a peculiar, hollow voice, "Just who are you, Sir Knight?"

"Sir Harl Lenti," I answered calmly. "Called the Collin of Marack. Now have at me, great lord of Om, and we will settle this bickering."

"Not yet," he said, and I noted that there was a faint whistling sound to his words. "I would still know *who* you are."

"Would you indeed?" I rode forward easily so that only ten paces separated us, and leaned toward him from my high saddle. "I am," I whispered softly, mocking his secrecy, "your *executioner!* Now come, great slob, great butcher of men, and let us end this charade. For I would kill you now!"

It was my intent to upset him, to enrage him. Just watching him and hearing his last few words made me aware of one thing. Something was awry with the lord Gol-Bades. Indeed, I had the chilling sensation that I faced none other than the Kaleen himself, or his facsimile. . . .

All was silent then. Gol-Bades threw his lance to one side. I did the same. He moved his shield to the fore and drew his great sword. I did the same. Then he set spurs to dottle and charged. I did the same. . . .

I knew with his first great whistling blow that I had indeed met my match. Though his movements were sluggish, the strength of his blows, once in motion, were terrible. I successfully dodged the first two. He aimed a third. I moved to parry and he cleaved my shield to the vanbrace of my forearm. At which I—since I was strong also—hewed the very pauldron from his sword-arm shoulder! These two mighty blows evoked a soughing gasp from both armies that caused the dust to rise on all sides of that plain. We circled each other and fell to again. One smashing blow numbed my sword arm and caved in the right half of my breastplate. The pain was such that I knew some ribs were broken. I crushed his plates in like manner, though it slowed Lord Gol-Bades not one wit. Then we dodged, parried, and slashed, shield against shield, so that the sound alone was like to deafen me. Sweat streamed down my face beneath the heavy helm, the salt of it smarting my eyes so that I could scarce see. But I had to see! Whatever could be done, I had to do it. There were no Pug-Boos to help me now; no starship; no *Deneb*-3. Gol-Bades seemed never to tire, though. As stated, the strength behind his sluggish movements was fantastic—superior to mine!

The answer to all this came when I tried for the same blow dealt by Griswall to his man, and missed—Gol-Bades brought his sword from over his shoulder with such force as to dash the very shield from my arm. But I was still faster than he. I stood in my stirrups, grasped my sword in both hands, whirled it around my head, and smote his shield with such force that shield *and* arm flew from his body. A hoarse and breath-drawn cheer came to me from Marack's heights at this fantastic sight. And, indeed, I thought then that with his arm severed he surely could not last but seconds more. Such, however, was not the case. He came at me again, with great sword held at vance, prepared to sweep me from my saddle. I ducked beneath it, came up, whirled, and with one mighty blow struck both helm *and head* from his body.

Then I knew what I had sensed to be true all along—Gol-Bades was something else again. . . . That headless armor turned to fight me still. For there had been no head within that helm, nor arm within the severed rearbrace, cop, and gauntlet!

Over all the ranks of the northern armies there now arose a groan of fear and terror. And to exploit it still further, the black wizards of Om caused the skies to darken and the red of the volcanoes to give a hellish tint to all their massed and burnished armor. I did not flinch; indeed, I had no choice. I raised my sword on high, spurred Henery one last time, and struck deliberately with all my strength at the sword arm of the thing of Hish. His parry was such as to dash my great sword from my hand. And then, as if to mock me, he made as if to strike poor Henery's head from his body. Having developed an affinity for dottles, I could not let that happen. I brought Henery's head up short when I sensed the direction of the blow, so that only an ear was sacrificed to the Hishian horror's humor—and simultaneously I grabbed that sword and chain-link gauntlet with my metal-covered hands. Henery reared and screamed mightily for his lost ear; the saddle-girth burst, I fell to the ground, and Henery ran. But I still clung to the sword and arm of the thing of Hish—and I pulled all that remaining armor to the trampled greensward with me.

The mailed legs kicked, seeking purchase. But I had it now. I arose, still clinging to that sword arm. And I held the arm with both hands and began to whirl, turning faster and faster, until finally with a great screeching and clanging the armor literally flew apart in a burst of plates and broken rivets.

And I stood alone upon the field and held high the captured sword of Gol-Bades, lord of Hish—lord of Evil!

The roaring from both sides was deafening. But from the north it was for me alone. They yelled, "A Collin! A Collin! A Collin!"

And I, too, yelled. I faced the Omnian army and yelled for all to hear: "And so will it ever be for all who fight for Om and against true men!" My voice was amplified, of course.

At that very moment I was caught up beneath the armpits from either side by the strong arms of Griswall and Rawl. They whirled in a cloud of dust beneath a first flight of Omnian arrows, to carry me back across that broad expanse of bloodied field.

The cheering from our ranks was thunderous, and our lords were hard put to hold our stalwarts from charging Om head-on, so great was their enthusiasm.

And even as we rode into our lines—and though I was never one to believe in coincidence—there was a sunburst ray of yellow through those dark clouds to the south. And through that golden slot came Great Ap, Murie, and Caroween. And they flew the banners of Marack and the Dernim Tulip. . . . I hadn't the slightest doubt that Hooli and his friends had provided the "slot" in the clouds.

My head was spinning from both the battle and the pounding congratulations from all on Marack's hill. I still had time to think, *Great Gods! The deus ex machina has come to Camelot! In the sometimes ridiculous history of planets, there will be nothing to equal this!*

We arrived on the hill simultaneously, Great Ap and me. And Murie ran to me, and Caroween to Rawl. As Great Ap lidded his eyes while we "rubbed and clasped," from across the plain four thousand kettledrums began their martial beat. The massed armies of Om had no longer anything to wait for. Under the command of the five black-cowled wizards they were moving toward us. Their drums, I need hardly add, were answered instantly by our own great drums and trumpets, and by the skirling of a hundred pipes from every hill.

Murie had kissed me, holding my head in both her hands— and I did likewise. But time was short and I pulled her to me and glanced at Great Ap over her delectable shoulder. I threw out a thought to the Vuun who crouched prone upon our center hillcrest (all had withdrawn to give his leathery carcass purchase). "Great Ap," I said. "You have been true to our bargain. Now tell me, what says the thing of Hish at your withdrawal from his cause?"

"He is sore angry, Man. He threatens an end to life for all our creatures. But we do not fear him, for he is yet weak."

"There's no time for talk as you can plainly see," I told him. "But will you welcome me, and do I come again?"

"Indeed we shall, and come you not with your mating animal."

"Hey, now, Great Ap!" I began angrily, but shrugged and said instead, "So go you now with our friendship. For if you do not, and instantly, you soon will be in the midst of the blood which you abhor. And, too, we would save you from the danger of the flights of arrows."

"I will go then, and you will seek me out—if you conquer."

"I promise you—and we *will* conquer!"

"We shall see."

And upon that, Great Ap sprang into the now sulfurous air, and with six beats of his mighty wings he was again aloft and away.

"My lord," Murie said against my chest, "had you converse with him? You looked as if you were away."

"Yes," I said. I tightened my arm about her slender figure. "And do you not forget that, despite all, he was still your friend—well, almost so. Now help me to doff this armor. For I fear that I will not be much for the battle."

Murie examined me closely, saw my condition, grew big-eyed, determined. From her dainty lips orders rang out, and I was soon bereft of steel and padded shirt so that my right side, which was awash with blood, could be tended. I demanded that I be seated so as to watch all that would take place. They complied and I was padded about with cushions in the king's own chair. I held the captured great sword of Om across my knees. The king stood at my back. And Rawl and Charney and Tober, and Murie and Caroween (both in small armor now), and all the lords and knights of the king's own council and guard were gathered close to direct this battle, and to see to its end. I knew that the spot upon which I sat would be taken only if all this gallant company were slain. . . .

There then advanced against us all the chivalry of the Omnian allies, plus the Yorns—the janissaries of dark Om. They came as a great iron wave against the three hills. First their mounted knights and men-at-arms—of which they had only as many as we, since they had not dottles for the mounting. These charged to meet our lances; but our lances withdrew to either side of the hills. And our archers laid upon them such a rain of arrows as to darken the skies. A full quarter of their saddles were emptied before they ever reached the protection of their infantry.

And then our mounted warriors charged, coming out in six groupings from the slopes of the three hills, to smash the flanks of the three great infantry armies. They rode into them with lance and sword to slow their charge, to destroy, and then to retreat, suffering as little damage as possible.

There were fantastic feats of heroism upon that field. Whole squadrons of our men would be cut off in the flank charges; cut off, surrounded, and slain. And oftentimes the plumes of the young warriors—of Ferlach, Marack, and Gheese—would seem to float, as if upon a sea of armor, only to falter, drop, and disappear from sight.

Then, as per plan, our mounted knights withdrew to our left—since we had noted that theirs had withdrawn to the right. And once this was done the Omnian footmen and Yorns advanced upon our pikemen at the hill's base. Again they were met with a cloud of arrows. And again, to our left—where Chitar and Hoggle-Fitz fought—there did advance our thousand mounted archers. These poured flight after flight of arrows at close range into their mass of soldiery.

When the archers withdrew, and before this infantry had time to steady itself, they were hit hard by our twenty-five thousand remaining mounted armor. The effect was devastating. The entire Omnian right flank hesitated, crumbled, and fell back across that bloodied ground.

To our right, in the area of King Draslich's hill, all went not so well. There, other than the king's own squadrons of knights and lords, all was pike, sword, and arrow. And all were surrounded now by a full fifty thousand warriors of Kelb and Om. On the hill's slope nearest ours—and still too far for an arrow's flight—were the colors of Harlach, king of Kelb, and the black-browed Keilweir, his son. These advanced against Draslich's final line, cutting their way through the bodies of hundreds of Ferlach's finest. Draslich held. But it seemed that he wouldn't for long. And though each minute saw terrible losses to the attacking Omnians, so was it with Draslich also.

It was then that Sir Rawl, Sir Griswall, and the lord Krees of Klimpinge begged leave to take the king's two thousand knights, held in reserve, to cut a way to Draslich, and thus bring him and all who could be saved from that bloodsoaked hill. Permission granted, it took but seconds for those two thousand to stream to the aid of Draslich, so well trained were Fregisian warriors.

I watched the drama unfold. Murie stood at my back, small hands upon my neck and shoulders. Caroween, as she had sworn she would, had ridden to battle with Rawl. And the banners of the Dernim Tulip—so evident on our left where Hoggle-Fitz fought—were now with Rawl's three scarlet bars on Draslich's hill.

I think that Rawl had had other purpose than just to rescue Draslich. He had thought strongly on that battle in Goolbie's courtyard and the abduction of his lady; he had a score to settle. Both the king and the prince of Kelb did die that day. And Keilweir at Rawl's hands. Kelb did thereby gain her freedom.

Marack's two thousand seemed inspired. They never once stopped, but rather cleaved their way through the very heart of that weighty mass of metal, hewing and hacking so vigorously that none could stand before them. It was the lord Krees of Klimpinge who cut down the Kelbian king. The fight was bloody but short. And when Krees held Harlach's head above those bloodied slopes, Keilweir, maddened still further by the sight—if such could be possible—went berserk. He laid about him in such frenzy as to slay two of his own before Rawl's sword cut him down in turn, severing his head and sword arm before all that swarming host.

Then contact was achieved with Draslich's remnants, so that all together beat a fighting retreat to our hill, carving their way again through that mass of Om's warriors. Of Rawl's two thousand, he brought back but fifteen hundred. Of Draslich's fifteen thousand, but six thousand lived to join our redoubt.

The "conquering" enemy, however, were content to stay upon their captured hill, which was their great mistake. Had they rushed their remaining fifteen thousand to join with Seligal and Kerch before our hill, we might have been overrun. But such was not the case. Like the reluctant Ortmundian warriors on our left—who had contributed largely to the rout of that flank—they, too, were denying Om their strength at this critical moment.

Below our hill and to its front there raged a battle between our twenty thousand and a full thirty thousand warriors of Seligal and Kerch; amid these the banners of the great lords Roume-Fir and Fousten, of those allied countries, were most prominent. But they had yet to break our line. Indeed, they had hardly forced it.

But now, as if to bring things to a final denouement, there advanced across that plain the black-armored soldiery that I had seen yesterday, and today. The pride of Om, and the very flower of Hish. They had as yet to see battle. They were fresh, rested. They were also seasoned warriors who, among all that great host, believed most strongly in their cause. They were fifty thousand men. And in their front ranks rode their black-cowled wizards. I had time to wonder and to suggest to Murie that perhaps those cowls were akin to the armor of Gol-Bades—that there might be nothing beneath them.

On our left, the lord Breen Hoggle-Fitz, seeing his advantage, had ridden out to parley with the dissident Ortmundians. He told me later that he figured that even if he could not talk them into switching, he would at least hold them from battle. I worried at the time, however, that they would turn on *him*, and take his life. But even as Fitz parleyed, the burly leader had shifted his three thousand archers to join our own. Indeed, his twelve thousand pikemen and spearmen were poised to do exactly the same thing; still, and hovering on our left flank, was the entire strength of our mounted knights and lords. . . . Great Gods! I wondered. Did not Om see this? Was the Kaleen so blind to what could happen? Evidently he was! Either that or contact with alien life was so tenuous, really, that he was incapable of understanding its complexities —inclusive of its tactics in war and peace.

Unless the Omnian flanks joined quickly in the advance of the Hishian soldiery, there was an even chance that we could smash this onslaught. I noted that the distance between Chitar's force and ours was half again less than the distance from Chitar's hill to the warriors with whom Hoggle was talking. It was quite evident to me that Chitar was readying his men to come to our aid.

The commanders of Om threw out a heavy screen of riders to cut down our archers. But a few thousand of our lancers rode these down at full charge. The enemy continued to advance, however, slowly, inexorably. . . . In a way, Seligal and Kerch did Om no favors. For upon the approach of these fresh thousands, they fell back to either flank and left the center open. The Omnian mass had barely moved into this vacuum when they were met with great flights of arrows from our hill's base—aimed solely at *them*. None were wasted longer on Seligal or Kerch. Which, when you think about it, was excellent psychology, since the warriors of these two nations were instantly aware that a lessening of their own fervor in battle would guarantee that Om receive the greater punishment.

And then the Hishian warriors charged. And if there had been carnage before, the base of the hill now ran red with blood. Over it all were the constant drums and the mad skirling. Once the battle had been joined with Om's main force, Caronne ordered all archers to shift to the right to ward off the Kelbian-Omnian forces from that direction, should they stir off Draslich's hill; or to feather Omnian cavalry, should their remnants charge. In the meantime, Chitar, judging that those with whom Hoggle-Fitz parleyed would be delayed by their very distance in attacking him, came directly to the aid of Marack's hill. Chitar smashed into Om's flank with all his strength.

And suddenly, except for Murie who stood next to me, bared sword in hand—my shield maiden—I was alone upon that hill. The lords and knights of Caronne's council had all gone down to enter battle. And every lackey and cook went with them. It would never be said that Caronne, among all those kings, sat idle throughout the final battle of Dunguring plain. . . .

I followed their proud banners with my eyes. The king's great standard of a Winged Castle upon a purple field. The Oak Tree of Draslich, the Blue Birds of Fell-Holdt of Svoss, the Riven Shield of Al-Tils, son of Fel-Tils of Saks in Gheese; the gonfalons of Klimpinge, Bist, Fleege, Keeng, and of the provinces of Ferlach and Gheese—all the brave banners!

Did I say I was alone with Murie? Well, we were, but not quite. Fairwyn was there, and Plati and Gaazi. They were doing their best to see (from a distance) that no harm came to their kings, though it was doubtful that their spells would prevail in the midst of such carnage. I suggested to them, quite forcefully, that their powers could best be used against those black cowls of Hish, whose very presence was an abomination.

They joined forces for this purpose and had some degree of success—for one cowl at Om's center went up in flames of a strange and greenish hue. . . .

What can one say, really, of such a melee? Before me at the base of the hill, and stretching as far as the eye could see, was an ocean of swords, axes, spears, and shields, all rising and falling. The screaming of the wounded and the dying was as an incessant ululation, so predominant was the sound. And parallel with it were the usual shouts and cries of battle, and the pipes and the kettledrums.

From far to our right we heard the distant "*A*-la-la-la! *A*-la-la-la— *A*-la-la-la!" of a small, stouthearted band who had been cut off and were fighting to the death. And Murie turned to me with a shake of her golden-wreathed head to dash the tears from her purple eyes. The chant reminded her, no doubt, of our fight at Goolbie's keep. And I think her tears were in memory of skinny Ongus. . . .

And then a wave of yelling from far off to our left. It came as a shout for Hoggle-Fitz and for Great Ortmund! We were not to learn until later that Fitz had challenged and slain the false king, Feglyn, before the very eyes of the Ortmundian host. They then vowed to follow him to the rescue of Marack. But it was not to be. For in their forward movement they were in turn attacked by the remnants of Om's right flank, which had been with them from the beginning—a full thirty thousand warriors of Seligal and Kerch.

Until the end our good Breen Hoggle-Fitz had all he could do to hold his own.

Twice they drove us back so that it seemed to me that they would overrun our hill. But each time they were driven off. And through the two hours of noon they fought so that one wondered how any man could still lift sword and hold shield. One thing became quite obvious, though—if we had not lost, Om had certainly not won! And Om would not be given a second chance.

Two things happened then. And when I think back on it, both were expected; overdue, in fact. We would have been fools to think otherwise. The rationale, of course, is that one, is never quite sure before the fact. . . . The clouds, gray-black, grew blacker still. A roaring then seemed to fill the very heavens. It decreased to a thrumming such as I had heard twice before: on the south road two weeks before, and at Goolbie's keep.

Then the roaring returned. And all that I had heard before was as nothing compared to it. I arose in absolute horror, clutching Murie to me, throwing a null-magnetic field instantly around the both of us. "By Great Ormon!" I shouted to the three sorcerers. "If you would live, know, sirs, that the thing of Hish, the thing of Om, has come to us—*is with us now!* If there are spells or enchantments to counter this— use them! If there are not, then indeed are we doomed, and all our efforts lost. Now tell me! What will you do?"

"What would you have us do?" Fairwyn cried. He stood paralyzed, seemingly helpless, as were his two quite terrified cohorts. "We have no power against this."

"Tis as he says," Gaazi moaned, "and, we are indeed doomed."

"But you *know* of this magic," I shouted. "I, myself, have been its victim twice."

"Aye. We know of it. But not at such a level of strength," Fairwyn replied.

"Could you have bested that of the lady Elioseen?"

"Aye."

"Then the three of you together, you can *try!*"

"Yes," Plati whispered, looking at the others. "We can try."

"Try now then, damn it!" I literally screamed at them. "It gets worse. Do you understand? There is no time to lose!"

And so they tried. And I could tell by their very movements that the first twinges of paralysis were beginning to reach them. I, too, had not thought the thing of Hish to have such power as to match himself against the entire life-strength of the north. If he succeeded . . . in my mind's eye I could see these entire five square miles filled with the slaughtered. A complete generation of males would have disappeared from the northlands.

And around us now, on the hilltop, were groups of wounded who had escaped the battle below. They looked to me in terror. I watched them closely, steadily. So far the paralysis seemed not to have gained, though the sound around us—as of a thousand banshees—still prevailed. I looked to our three sorcerers where they stood in a row on the hill's crest. Their hands were clasped and they screamed their *words* against the banshee keening, and the first drops of rain fell from those lowering clouds. And they kept shouting them over and over and over again, so that their *words* became a sound beat, too, and the beat became a song—and the song was amplified! I lifted my eyes to those rainclouds and that terrible keening. And this time, because I faced to the rear, I

215

saw our hundred-foot ridge in the passing. And there on that ridge, perched lazily on the rumps of five dottles—including Henery with a bandaged ear-stump—were Hooli, Pawbi, Jindil, Chuuk, and Dakhti. And even as Murie and I shifted our gaze from the Pug-Boos to our three screaming sorcerers, and back to the Boos, and back to the sorcerers, the keening and the thrumming died. And the first tiny fingers of paralysis seemed to leave them.

And where the Pug-Boos sat their fat mounts, there appeared to either side of them more dottles. And more and more and *more*, until the entire ridge was covered with them, so that they were boiling over and coming down the slopes of the ridge. And that's when the second thing began.

There are those who fought on the field of Dunguring who say that the north would have won, anyway. I am not one of them. Some say this so strongly that I think they feel a need to hide the fact that for all their courage and their slaughtering and their heroism—and mind you, I'm not putting this down—it was really gentle dottles that won the battle of Dunguring.

That's right! It was dottles—dottles who loved Pug-Boos to distraction; sweet-smelling, fat-bellied, blue-eyed dottles—*who would do anything for Pug-Boos!*

Murie and I and our wounded and our three sorcerers, who still chanted their *words*, had a front-row seat to the strangest happening that Fregis-Camelot had ever witnessed. Earth had its fabled Pied Piper. Camelot did better than that. Camelot had Pug-Boos!

Streaming in a gray, black, and ocher wave from over the ridge, and from the twenty square miles of forest and meadow beyond, there came perhaps a quarter of a million dottles. They literally *boiled* down upon those armies and *through* them and *around* them, and *between* them, and *over* them; so that no warrior could swing a sword without hitting a dottle, which most simply would not do. And there was a *wheeeing* and a *wooohing* (amplified, you can bet, just as our sorcerers words had been amplified) that echoed throughout the very heavens, so that every warrior deemed it afterward a most religious experience. And more than one of them was *kissed* by a dottle to help substantiate this reasoning.

Of the warriors of Seligal and Kerch and Kelb, most just

surrendered. They weren't stupid. They could see that it was all over and that they had lost. This was doubly understood when certain great lords of Marack, Gheese, and Ferlach forced their way through that dottle horde waving the emptied cowls of the remaining four dark wizards of Om from their lance tips (I had been right there, too).

The warriors of Hish simply grabbed dottles and fled in the direction of Corchoon and the fleet; only to find themselves bottled up by the arrival of our ships, come down from Reen and Saks.

And I am convinced that the thing in Hish just gave up; sulked; retreated for the moment to whatever options it had prepared for itself; overwhelmed by what I am sure it thought was complete and utter alien nonsense. It had been nonsense, all right. Pug-Boo nonsense; the kind that works like magic. . . .

And it was all over. And it was that simple. Even while we were all congratulating each other in paroxysms of jubilation, bewhiskered kisses, back-slaps, and what-have-you when you have just won the greatest battle of all time, rain swept the field. When I look back on it, the cloudburst that hit Dunguring—and it was literally that—was the final Pug-Boo manifestation of what could be done, psychologically, with the proper gimmicks, and at the proper time.

True, the Foundation and I had helped. But in a sense a part of my efforts had simply been used to help set *their* stage. . . . Anyhow, if there had been any fight left in anyone, those torrents of rain wiped it out. Better yet, while we sat snug in our tents, we held parley on the terms of surrender of our erstwhile enemies. Most, led by the lords Roume-Fir and Fousten, of Seligal and Kerch respectively, were actually glad of Om's defeat. The Kaleen's work of a century had been undone.

I didn't attend—or rather I did, but only for a little while. I begged off and went to bed, my princess sharing a pillow with me, plus a jug of sviss that, until Rawl's ministrations, had been simple gog-milk. Hooli had come down off his high horse and joined us. He had returned to the princess, that is. He dared to curl up on a camp rug beside our bed. I winked at him. He looked stupidly back at me. That was my cue to kick him out, with some polite excuse to Murie for my action.

Then I turned to my own sweet-smelling, warm-tummied, purple-eyed vixen. . . . Beyond the walls and through the thin canvas of the tent next to ours we could hear the laughter of Rawl and Cari. And I thought then that I really liked him. For he, too, was not at council. Like myself, he had fled the field to fight another day.

Later in the night I removed Murie's head from my shoulder and reached for my belt. I tried for Greenwich just to see. . . . I tried and tried, and tried, and there they were!

"In! In! In!" I said. "Well, well! You're back, and without my permission."

"In!" Kriloy said. "And look who's talking!"

"You saw?"

"Everything! From the other side of Fomalhaut. We didn't make waves, Buby. So you're safe. By the way, all is forgiven."

"Is that a question or a statement?"

"Sheeeee!"

"So what did you think of the Third Act?"

"Better. What did *you* think of it?"

"The dottle finale was great," I said. "Anyway, it's all over, though there's still a big job ahead. The thing is Hish only lost the first skirmish, you know. For the moment, however, and on Camelot that may mean two hundred years, everything's cool! The war is over. The Vuuns are our friends. The north is safe. And everything is as it was—well, almost."

"We've got it on film, with a close-up of you popping Gol-Bades's rivets. They'll love it at the library. So what now? When do you want to return?"

"There are a few loose ends." I grunted cryptically. "A couple of problems."

"Yeah." Kriloy smirked. I know he did. "How's about the sixth hour after you're back at the castle?"

"No reason not to."

"You'll give us a tape, a good one this time?"

"No reason not to."

"You're repeating yourself."

"Well, yes. I've got this friend with me, you see. . . .

218

Friend, hell! I'm going to marry her—with pomp *and* circumstance. And right now she's waking up."

"Well, out then."

"Bless you."

And they were gone and I turned to Murie.

Among a lot of things there was one tidbit of knowledge that I really wanted out of all this conglomerate of complications. The next day, as Rawl and Cari, Murie and I, and an escort of fifty young warriors were resting during our dottle browsing period (we were on our way back to Glagmaron), I tried to get it. I lay back with my head in Murie's lap, and I closed my eyes and shot a thought to that miserable Hooli who sat on a large toadstool grinning and spreading goodness.

"Hooli," I said, "you once—or rather, *you* in the plural sense—suggested that you would tell me who and what you are. How about now?"

He came in on my wavelength. He actually came in!

"No big deal," he said with my voice. "What do you want to know?"

"I just asked, stupid."

"Well, what are *you*?"

"I'm an *Adjuster*. I've told you that."

"Well, that's what I am."

"What?"

"An Adjuster."

"Great Gods!"

"There is a difference."

"Tell me."

"Well, you're Galactic. I'm Universal. *I* adjust *you*!"

"Great Gods—"

"How about that?"

"Oh, no," I said. Then wearily, "All right. Again. Are you just one entity, or an entity for each Pug-Boo?"

"One for each," Hooli said. "But we come and go. Most of the time we don't occupy the host at all."

"I see," I said.

"Bye," Hooli said. . . .

Later, as we rode back through the thick forest toward far Glagmaron and I tried to contact him again, I just got that idiot smile. But after that, at dinnertime, I happened to glance over Murie's delectable shoulder, and there was Hooli. And Hooli winked at me. . . .

A GALAXY OF SCIENCE FICTION STARS!

- [ ] **JOHN BRUNNER Interstellar Empire**   UE1668—$2.50
- [ ] **JACK VANCE The Book of Dreams**   UE1587—$2.25
- [ ] **A.E. VAN VOGT The Silkie**   UE1695—$2.25
- [ ] **MICHAEL MOORCOCK Stormbringer**   UE1755—$2.50
- [ ] **JOHN NORMAN Savages of Gor**   UE1715—$3.50
- [ ] **ANDRE NORTON Horn Crown**   UE1635—$2.95
- [ ] **MARION ZIMMER BRADLEY Hawkmistress!**   UE1762—$2.95
- [ ] **LIN CARTER Kesrick**   UE1779—$2.25
- [ ] **M.A. FOSTER The Morphodite**   UE1669—$2.75
- [ ] **TANITH LEE The Silver Metal Lover**   UE1721—$2.75
- [ ] **C.J. CHERRYH The Pride of Chanur**   UE1694—$2.95
- [ ] **E.C. TUBB The Coming Event**   UE1725—$2.25
- [ ] **DRAY PRESCOT Mazes of Scorpio**   UE1739—$2.25
- [ ] **CLIFFORD D. SIMAK Destiny Doll**   UE1772—$2.50
- [ ] **DORIS PISERCHIA The Dimensioneers**   UE1738—$2.25
- [ ] **BRIAN M. STABLEFORD Journey to the Center**

  UE1756—$2.50
- [ ] **A. BERTRAM CHANDLER The Big Black Mark**

  UE1726—$2.50
- [ ] **PHILIP K. DICK Now Wait for Last Year**   UE1654—$2.50
- [ ] **GORDON R. DICKSON The Star Road**   UE1711—$2.25
- [ ] **PHILIP JOSÉ FARMER Hadon of Ancient Opar**

  UE1637—$2.50
- [ ] **RON GOULART Big Bang**   UE1748—$2.25

THE NEW AMERICAN LIBRARY, INC.
P.O. Box 999, Bergenfield, New Jersey 07621

Please send me the DAW BOOKS I have checked above. I am enclosing
$_____ (check or money order—no currency or C.O.D.'s).
Please include the list price plus $1.00 per order to cover handling
costs.

Name _____

Address _____

City _____ State _____ Zip Code _____
Please allow at least 4 weeks for delivery

TANITH LEE

"Princess Royal of Heroic Fantasy and Goddess-Empress of the Hot Read."

—**Village Voice** (N.Y.C.)

- ☐ DELUSION'S MASTER (#UE1652—$2.25)
- ☐ THE BIRTHGRAVE (#UE1672—$2.95)
- ☐ VAZKOR, SON OF VAZKOR (#UE1709—$2.50)
- ☐ QUEST FOR THE WHITE WITCH (#UJ1357—$1.95)
- ☐ DON'T BITE THE SUN (#UE1486—$1.75)
- ☐ DRINKING SAPPHIRE WINE (#UE1565—$1.75)
- ☐ VOLKHAVAAR (#UE1539—$1.75)
- ☐ THE STORM LORD (#UJ1361—$1.95)
- ☐ NIGHT'S MASTER (#UE1657—$2.25)
- ☐ ELECTRIC FOREST (#UE1482—$1.75)
- ☐ SABELLA (#UE1529—$1.75)
- ☐ KILL THE DEAD (#UE1562—$1.75)
- ☐ DAY BY NIGHT (#UE1576—$2.25)
- ☐ THE SILVER METAL LOVER (#UE1721—$2.75)
- ☐ CYRION (#UE1765—$2.95)
- ☐ DEATH'S MASTER (#UE1741—$2.95)

Attention:

DAW COLLECTORS

Many readers of DAW Books have written requesting information on early titles and book numbers to assist in the collection of DAW editions since the first of our titles appeared in April 1972.

We have prepared a several-pages-long list of all DAW titles, giving their sequence numbers, original and current order numbers, and ISBN numbers. And of course the authors and book titles, as well as reissues.

If you think that this list will be of help, you may have a copy by writing to the address below and enclosing one dollar in stamps or coins to cover the handling and postage costs.

DAW BOOKS, INC. Dept. C
1633 Broadway
New York, N.Y. 10019

Presenting C. J. CHERRYH